BLOOD SPORT

At dawn, Preacher gathered dry wood, built a tiny fire, and boiled water for coffee. He was so angry he had to struggle to keep his emotions in check. A bunch of damn foreigners was plannin' to hunt him down like some poor chased animal!

He had done nothing to any of those men. But damned if he was gonna run from a bunch of fancy-pants counts and barons and whoever else they thought they were. If it was war they wanted, he'd give them war. But it would be a war like none they had ever seen. It would be a war fought on his terms—and they would be harsh, count on that!

This was his country. The High Lonesome. The Big Empty.

And it was about to run red with blood.

BOOK YOUR PLACE ON OUR WEBSITE AND MAKE THE READING CONNECTION!

We've created a customized website just for our very special readers, where you can get the inside scoop on everything that's going on with Zebra, Pinnacle and Kensington books.

When you come online, you'll have the exciting opportunity to:

- View covers of upcoming books
- Read sample chapters
- Learn about our future publishing schedule (listed by publication month *and author*)
- Find out when your favorite authors will be visiting a city near you
- Search for and order backlist books from our online catalog
- Check out author bios and background information
- Send e-mail to your favorite authors
- Meet the Kensington staff online
- Join us in weekly chats with authors, readers and other guests
- Get writing guidelines
- AND MUCH MORE!

**Visit our website at
http://www.kensingtonbooks.com**

THE FIRST MOUNTAIN MAN

FORTY GUNS WEST

William W. Johnstone

PINNACLE BOOKS
Kensington Publishing Corp.
http://www.kensingtonbooks.com

This novel is a work of fiction. Names, characters, places, and incidents are either the product of the author's imagination or are used fictitiously. Any resemblance to actual persons (living or dead), events, or locales is entirely coincidental.

PINNACLE BOOKS are published by

Kensington Publishing Corp.
850 Third Avenue
New York, NY 10022

All Kensington Titles, Imprints, and Distributed Lines are available at special quantity discounts for bulk purchases for sales promotions, premiums, fund-raising, and educational or institutional use. Special book excerpts or customized printings can also be created to fit specific needs. For details, write or phone the office of the Kensington special sales manager: Kensington Publishing Corp., 850 Third Avenue, New York, NY 10022, attn: Special Sales Department, Phone: 1-800-221-2647.

Pinnacle and the P logo Reg. U.S. Pat. & TM Off.

First Printing: December 1993
10 9 8

Printed in the United States of America

Don't tread on me!

BOOK ONE

One

The townspeople of the long-settled eastern village never really grew easy with Preacher around. The mountain man walked like a big panther, silent and sure. A few of the town and the area's bully-boys felt compelled to call him out for a tussle. They very quickly learned that Preacher fought under no rules except his own. One bully-boy lost an eye, another was abed all winter with broken ribs, and the third—and final man to challenge Preacher—was buried one cold February morning.

"I reckon," Preacher said to his pa and ma one day, "I best be thinkin' of headin' back to the High Lonesome."

"It's been so good to see you, son," his mother said, placing her hand over his. "But I fear for you here."

"You don't need to be fearful for me, Ma," Preacher said. "That bully-boy pulled a blade on me. I had no choice in the matter."

"Your mother's right, son," Preacher's father said, stuffing his old pipe full of tobacco. He knelt by the fire and picked out a lighted twig and puffed. Back in his chair, he said, "You've left us money a-plenty to last for the rest of our years. I don't want to see grief come to you. And it will come if you stay around here."

Preacher knew his parents were right. He just didn't want to admit it. But he knew he'd out-stayed his welcome in town. He just didn't fit in. Preacher was all muscle and bone and gristle. He was tanned dark by the sun and the wind, he carried the scars of a dozen deadly battles, and he operated under no moral or legal code save that of his own. And nobody was going to make him conform to any standard except that which he considered fair. But in his own peculiar way, Preacher was a highly moral man for the time, this year of our Lord, eighteen hundred and forty. He had the utmost respect for womanhood. He loved the land and the critters on it. He could not abide injustice. He didn't like lawyers and thought the country in general was going to Hell in a handbasket.

Preacher nodded his head. "You're both right. My good brothers won't even come around whilst I'm here."

His mother smiled. "They're afraid of you, son. They belong to order and families and the clock. You belong to the wilderness. Their lives are routine. Your life is like the wind. They don't, can't, understand that."

Preacher cut his eyes to the west. "For a fact," he muttered, "I have missed the mountains."

His father's old eyes twinkled. "I see where you've packed your gear. You must have been thinking about leaving."

Preacher laughed and gently placed one strong hand on his father's stooped shoulders, bent from years of brutally hard work, clearing the land and wresting a living from the soil. "I reckon I'll pull out come the mornin'. Ma, if you'll make me a little poke of food, I'd be obliged." He stood up.

"Where are you going, son?" his mother asked.

"Oh, I think I'll take me a little stroll through the town. Give the good folks one last look 'fore they're shut of me." He looked at his parents. "You know when I leave this go-round, I prob'ly won't be back."

They nodded their heads.

Preacher stepped out of the house into the cold early

March air of Ohio. A thin covering of new snow the past night had laid a carpet of white over the land. Preacher checked on his horse, Thunder, and then decided to stretch his legs and walk the short distance into the village. A town, actually. Darn near five hundred people lived all crowded up like ants.

Preacher still drew stares from the citizens but he paid them no heed, just walked on to the combination coach stop, hotel, and tavern and opened the door. The buzz of conversation stopped when he padded silently up to the bar, the soles of his high-topped moccasins making no more than a whisper on the floor. He leaned on the bar and ordered a whiskey with a beer chaser.

Several ladies who had stopped there for the night and were waiting on the afternoon coach began whispering behind their fancy fans. Preacher paid them no mind. From the looks of them they was city women, all gussied up to beat the band. Preacher took a sip of whiskey and a sip of beer. He hid a smile as the few locals who were lined up at the bar backed away, clear down to the end, getting as far away from Preacher as they could. It had been in this very tavern, just two weeks past, that Preacher had killed that feller who shucked out his knife during what Preacher had thought was just a friendly fist-fight. Preacher had left him on the floor, cut from navel to neck.

The door opened and a frail boy of about nine or ten entered. The boy's clothing was ragged and the soles of his shoes were tied on with string. He carried a small bucket with a lid on it. The top of the boy's head just did reach the lip of the bar. He placed the bucket on the bar and said, "A bucket of beer for Mister Parks, please, sir."

The barkeep took the bucket to rinse it out and the boy looked at the free lunch on a table, hunger in his eyes. His pinched face was pale and his eyes held a strange brightness.

"You hungry, boy?" Preacher asked.

The boy's eyes were scared as they fixed on the mountain man. "Yes, sir. Some."

"Then fix you a sandwich or two."

"That food's for customers!" the barkeep hollered.

"The lad just bought a bucket of beer, didn't he?" Preacher asked. "So that entitles him to food. Fix you something to eat, boy."

"I'll slap you, boy!" the barkeep barked. "You stay away from that food, you . . . you woods' colt."

Preacher gave the barkeep a disgusted look as he walked to the table and fixed two huge meat and cheese sandwiches and gave them to the boy. "You sit over there by the stove and eat and get warm, boy." He turned to the barkeep. "You want to slap me?"

The man paled. "Ah, no, sir!"

"Fine. Now you pour that lad a big glass of milk and then go on about your business and leave the boy alone."

The boy fell into a hard fit of coughing that reddened his face. Bad lungs, Preacher thought. A wonder he lived through the winter.

Hard footsteps slammed on the boards outside the coach stop and the door was flung open. The hard and big bulk of Elam Parks filled the doorway, his face mottled with rage. He held a quirt in one hand. He pointed the quirt at the boy. "What the hell do you think you're doing, Eddie?" he shouted. "I didn't give you permission to eat."

"No. But I did," Preacher said.

In the time Preacher had been in town, he'd seen enough of Elam Parks to last him two lifetimes. Parks was an important man about the community. He owned several farms, a couple of businesses, and about fifty percent of the local bank. His brother was in tight with the governor, or senator, or some damn blow-heart politician. Parks thought himself the bull of the woods around these parts. He was a bully and a slave-driver to those who had the misfortune to work for him. He gave Preacher the same type of look he might give a roach. Then he turned to the boy.

"Get up and get back to work, you worthless whelp!"

"When he finishes his meal," Preacher said.

Parks turned to face Preacher. He was a big'un, all right. Preacher guessed him at about six feet, one inch, with the weight to go with it. A big man with hard packed muscle. "This is none of your affair, Mountain Man," Parks said, contempt dripping from each word. "So stay out of it. The boy is bound to me and does what I tell him to do."

"Bound, huh? I thought that practice stopped a long time ago. I never did hold with it. It's just a fancy word for slavery. I don't hold with that either. You eat your meal, Eddie. This big mouth can wait."

Elam started stuttering and sputtering, his face beet red. People just didn't talk to him in such a manner. He pointed the quirt at Preacher and shouted, "I'll have you run out of town, you, you ... *trash!*"

Preacher smiled and finished his whiskey. He sat the cup on the bar and said, "You figure on doin' that all by yourself, or you gonna call some boys to help you?"

Preacher cut his eyes to the little boy. Eddie was gobbling down his sandwiches as fast as he could. It was evident to Preacher that the sick little boy had not had sufficient food in a long time.

Elam dropped his quirt on a table. "Mountain Man, you have had your way in this town for long enough. You been strutting about like a peacock. You need to learn a hard lesson, and I am just the man to teach you."

"Is that a fact?" Preacher hesitated for a moment, not wanting to bring any further grief to his parents. "Well, mayhaps you're right. I brung mountain ways to this town and expected folks hereabouts to accept 'em. I do apologize for that. But I don't apologize for standing up for the lad yonder. He's a mighty sick little boy. And he's got

13

marks on his face that I just noticed under all that grime. Have you been beatin' on him, Parks?"

"The boy lacks discipline and motivation. Besides, he's bound to me and what I do is no concern of yours. But now that you have backed down from this issue, we'll call it even and forget it."

"Whoa!" Preacher said. "I ain't never backed down from no man. So don't you be puttin' the cart ahead of the horse." He looked at Eddie. "You want some pie or cake, boy?"

"Now, that's all!" Elam blurted. "I have had quite enough of this foolishness." He moved swift for a man his size. Elam slammed a heavy hand down on Eddie's shoulder and jerked him to his raggedy shoes. He flung the boy toward the door. Eddie struck the wall and cried out in pain.

Preacher took two steps forward and started his punch from down around his knees. The big hard right fist caught Elam on the side of the jaw and stretched the man out on the floor, blood leaking from his mouth.

"Oh, my God!" a local blurted. "Somebody run get Doctor Ellis."

Preacher knelt down beside Eddie. There was a bump on the boy's head and a slight cut oozing a tiny bit of blood. "Gimmie a wet cloth," Preacher said. When nobody moved, he added, "Now, damnit!"

One local ran out the door for the doctor while another handed Preacher a dampened cloth. Preacher gently bathed the frightened boy's face then picked him up and sat him in a chair. "You just take it easy 'til the doc gets here, boy."

"Mountain Man," a fancy dressed dude said, "you'd best haul your ashes out of here. Elam Parks is a big man in this state. You're prison bound when he wakes up."

Preacher ignored the warning. Obviously, Elam Parks

14

had the whole damn town buffaloed. He looked up as his older brother rushed into the tavern.

The older man looked at the prostrate Parks and blurted, "My God, Art! Have you taken leave of your senses? That's Elam Parks."

"No kiddin'? I'd a swore it was a brayin' jackass and nothin' more." He pointed to Eddie. "What's the story on this here boy, Brother?"

"He's a woods' colt. Elam bound him out of the orphanage to work for him. Nobody gives a hoot about that brat."

"Wrong, Brother. I give a hoot." The doctor ran in and started for the still unconscious Parks. Preacher grabbed his arm and halted him. "You check the boy first, Doc. Then you tell me about him."

Dr. Ellis hesitated, took a short look into Preacher's cold eyes, then shrugged his shoulders. He checked Eddie, put some antiseptic on the small cut and took Preacher's arm, leading him away from the boy.

"The boy is dying, Mister. Lung fever. It's a miracle he lived through the winter. The next winter will kill him for sure."

"All right. Now you can go check on stupid over yonder." He walked over to Eddie, past the out-of-town women who were vigorously fanning themselves, their faces flushed from all the excitement. "You got any belongin's, boy?"

"A few, sir."

"Go fetch them. You're shut of this town and its sorry people. You're comin' with me."

The boy's sad eyes brightened. "Really?"

"Really. Go on. Get back here as quick as you can." Preacher walked over to the bar and finished his beer. He watched through amused eyes as several men tried to get Parks up on his feet. "You best get you a hoist," he called. "It'll take it to get that moose up."

Parks finally managed to sit up on the floor, but his jaw

15

was swollen and his eyes were glazed. Dr. Ellis bathed his face and the man's eyes began to focus. Pure hate was shining through, all of it directed at Preacher.

"Was I you, Parks," Preacher said, "I'd be real careful what come out of my mouth right about now. As upsot as you are, you just might let your butt overload it."

Preacher's brother rushed over to help Elam get to an upright position. He brushed at Elam's coat, all the while apologizing for Preacher's actions.

"That's right, Brother," Preacher drawled. "Suck up to him."

Elam shoved the men away from him. "Mountain Man, if you're in town an hour from now, have a gun in your hand."

"I'll prob'ly be in town. And if I am, I'll have a gun to hand, Parks. But you best remember this, Parks: I ain't no poor sick little boy. You level a pistol at me and the undertaker will be givin' you your last tidenin' up."

Parks snorted his reply and stalked out of the tavern just as Eddie was returning. He drew back his hand to strike the boy and Preacher said, "I'll break your arm, Parks."

Elam lowered his hand and stomped off. Preacher looked at the rags Eddie had stuffed into a sack and tossed them into a corner. "We'll get you some new duds, Eddie. But first we get you a bath and a haircut. Then we'll dust this town."

"Where are we going, Mister Preacher?"

"Where the air is pure and clean. Where them lungs of yours can heal. West, boy. To the mountains."

Two

The barber was nervous as he cut Eddie's hair, but he managed to get the boy looking presentable without snipping off anything other than hair. Then it was into a hot tub with a bar of strong soap. While Eddie was washing off the grime, Preacher went to the general store and bought him new clothes, from underwear out.

Preacher checked his awesome four-barrel pistol and holstered it. He carried only the one pistol while in town; but even that made the local constable nervous. The county sheriff was half a day's ride away.

Preacher was under no illusions. He knew that Parks was no coward. If he said he'd come looking for Preacher, he'd come. Preacher returned to the barber shop and found a brand new boy waiting for him. Good lookin' kid, too. Preacher looked at the wall clock. He had about twenty minutes left 'fore Parks would start on the prowl. He walked the boy down to the livery and bought him a pony. The horse was small, but strong limbed and Preacher guessed it had plenty of staying power. He bought a saddle and saddle bags.

"You know where Elm Street is, Eddie?"

"Yes, sir, Mister Preacher."

"I'm Preacher, boy. Not mister. You go over to Elm. Second house on the right. Wait for me there. My ma and pa is there. You tell Ma I said to get that poke of food ready. I'll be along shortly."

"Mister Elam's a bad one. He's kilt men before, Preacher," Eddie warned.

"Not as many as I have. Go on."

Preacher made sure the boy was on his way, proudly riding his new pony, and then he stepped out into the street. The town lay silent under the cold sun. Preacher walked right up the center of the main street.

"You there!" the constable called to Preacher from under the awning of his office. "I order you in the name of the law to cease and desist."

"Go suck an egg," Preacher told him.

"I'm the law around here!" the man bellowed.

"Congratulations. Now go back into your office and drink coffee. Stay off the street."

"You can't talk to me like that!"

Preacher ignored him and kept on walking. A block ahead of him, Elam Parks stepped off the boardwalk and into the street, a pistol in each hand. The two men began closing the distance.

"This don't have to be, Elam!" Preacher called. "You abused the boy and got socked in the jaw for it. Now it's done and past. It ain't nothin' worth dyin' over."

But for Elam, time for talking was gone. He had been humiliated in his own town and had to redeem himself in the eyes of the citizens. He lifted a pistol and fired. The ball missed Preacher by several feet.

"You better make the next one count, Elam," Preacher called, his own pistol still holstered.

Elam fired his second pistol. Again he missed.

"Now it's over, Elam," Preacher called. "You took your shots and you missed. I ain't gonna fire. Go on home. You'll not see me nor the boy never again."

Elam was frantically reloading. "You son of a whore!" he yelled at Preacher.

Preacher's eyes hardened and he stopped in the street. "Insult me all you like. But don't never slur my mother's name. You hear me, Elam."

"You sorry, filthy trash!" Parks shouted. "Son of a whore!" He lifted a pistol and Preacher drew, cocked, and drilled him clean, the ball driving the third button of his shirt clear to his backbone. Parks stumbled and fell to the street, on his back.

The stores along the street and the houses behind them and on the side streets emptied of people, all gathering around the dead Elam Parks. Preacher reloaded the empty chamber and turned his back on the crowd. He walked to the house on Elm street. His parents had heard the shots and were waiting in the front yard, behind the picket fence.

Preacher's older brother came running up, all out of breath. He stood for a moment, panting, and then blurted, "My God, Mamma, Daddy. Art's done shot and killed Mister Elam Parks."

"He had it coming," the father said. "It's long overdue. I'm just sorry it had to be you who done it, Art."

"Had it coming!" the older brother said, horrified. "Daddy, how can you say things like that? Why, Mister Elam was a fine man. He . . ."

"Was a crook and a no-count," the father said. "Maybe with him dead and gone, now you can get that brown spot off your nose, boy."

Preacher laughed at the expression on his brother's face. The older brother turned toward him, his face red and his hands balled into fists.

"I'd think about it, brother of mine," Preacher said. "I'd give it real serious thought."

The brother stared at Preacher for a moment. "You're no brother of mine, Art. You've turned into a godless savage, just like the heathen Indians."

Preacher wanted real bad to hit him, but didn't want to

do so in front of his mother. However, he figured his pa would probably enjoy seeing it. But he contained the urge to deck his brother and instead turned his back to him. The brother snorted and walked off. Preacher kissed his mother and held her close, both of them knowing this would be their last goodbye. He shook hands with his pa.

"You take care, son."

"I'll do 'er, Pa."

"God bless, son," his mother said. "I put a sack of food on your saddle."

"Y'all take care." Preacher walked to the small barn, Eddie keeping up with him. Two minutes later, they were riding out, heading west. Preacher did not look back. He would not have been able to see his ma and pa through the mist in his eyes.

"I thought we were going to head west, Preacher," Eddie remarked.

"We are, boy. But we'll head south for a time. Tell me about yourself."

"There ain't much to tell, Preacher. My ma and pa died with the fever when I was little. I don't even remember them. I was passed from pillar to post for a time, then the orphanage took me in. I was sick a lot, and no one wanted a boy who couldn't work. Mister Parks got me last year. I reckon I'd a died working for him."

"Prob'ly. But you gonna get well with me." Preacher paused. "At least some better. I think what you need most of all is good vittles, clean air, and rest."

Eddie tired easily and Preacher was in no hurry. He stopped often and made evening camp much earlier than he normally would. He avoided towns as often as possible. But he was under no illusions about what lay behind him. If Parks was the big-shot people thought him to be, there would surely be arrest warrants out for him by now. But he wasn't worried too much about that, either. Worryin' caused a man to get lines in his face and gray in his hair.

Preacher skirted the town of Cincinnati and crossed the Ohio River by ferry and rode into Kentucky.

"That was some river, Preacher!" Eddie said, all excited.

"Wait 'til you see the Mississippi, boy. The Ohio runs into the Mississippi down in Southern Illinois."

"Will we see that?"

"We might. I was goin' to Saint Louie, but I think I'll skip that town this run. I'll take us down through Arkansas and then cut west from there."

"You're thinking that Mister Parks's friends might be after us, aren't you?"

The boy was very quick and very sharp. The lad didn't miss much at all. "Yeah," Preacher said. "That thought has crossed my mind a time or two."

"How old were you when you went west, Preacher?"

"Not much older than you, Eddie. My, but that was a time, back then. Back in the mountains. Why, you could go for months without seein' another white man. Now ever' time a body looks up, they's a damn cabin bein' built."

That was not exactly the truth, not even close to it. But people were moving west. It would be a few more years before the flood gates of humanity were thrown open and the real surge westward began. Many, if not most of the mountain men resented the pioneers' drive westward. They were, for the most part, solitary men—in some cases legitimately wanted by the law for various crimes—and they felt the vast West was theirs alone. But that was not to be. The mountain men were credited, however, with the carving out of much of the Far West. By 1840, the mountain man's way of life was very nearly a closed book, as beaver hats faded from vogue and the mountain men faded from view.

Many of the mountain men would drift back into a civilized way of life, opening stores or turning to farming or ranching on a small scale. But many others either could not or would not change. They elected to stay in the mountains and eke out a living. Others, like Preacher, became scouts and wagon masters. And, like Preacher, living legends.

As the days on the trail drifted into weeks, and the weather warmed, moving silently into spring, Eddie began losing his cough as his face and forearms first blistered, then tanned under the sun and the wind. The boy began putting on weight and his face lost the sickly pallor and his eyes lost their feverish tint. Then, as Preacher and Eddie were making camp one afternoon in Arkansas, Preacher realized that the boy had not coughed up phlegm even one time that day.

All he needed was a chance, Preacher thought. Someone to take an interest in him and show him the right paths to take.

The mountain man and the kid drifted down to Little Rock. Preacher had been this way back in the twenties. He'd run up on them two kids, Jamie and Kate MacCallister. They'd been headin' for the Big Thicket country of East Texas, running from Kate's pa and a bunch of bounty hunters. Jamie and Kate, Preacher had heard, had gone on to have a passel of kids and Jamie later made quite a name for himself during the Texas fight for independence.*

Preacher had heard that shortly after the fall of the Alamo, Jamie and Kate had pulled out for the Rockies in Colorado. Mayhaps he and Eddie would drift up that way and visit them.

Preacher provisioned up in Little Rock and didn't dally

*THE EYES OF EAGLES—Zebra Books

in doing it. Leaving Eddie with the horses, sitting in the shade and sucking on a piece of peppermint candy, Preacher stepped into a tavern for a drink and news. If there were warrants on his head, or bounty hunters after him and the boy, the tavern would be the place to hear it.

Preacher ordered whiskey and leaned against the plank bar, listening. It did not take long for him to learn the bad news.

"I'll not take up the trail of that mountain man," he heard a man say. "Not for five hundred dollars, not for five thousand dollars."

"I'd foller Ol' Nick hisself straight into the gates of hell for five thousand dollars," another said.

"Yeah, me too," another agreed. "Man, that's a lifetime's wages."

The first man said, "How you gonna spend it ifn you're dead? Man, this is Preacher we're talkin' about. He's nearabouts as famous as Carson and Bowie and Crockett and Boone."

"He's just one man traveling with a snot-nosed brat," the man who would traverse the gates of hell said.

Preacher was glad he had left the boy hidden in that little glen outside of town. He was suddenly conscious of eyes on him. He sipped his whiskey and then turned his head, meeting the direct gaze of the man who professed to have no fear of hell.

"Howdy, stranger," the man said. "Ain't seed you 'round here afore."

"Just passin' through," Preacher replied. "Come up from South Texas headin' north. Who you boys be talkin' 'bout that's so fearsome?"

"Some old mountain man called Preacher. He kilt an important gentleman back up in Ohio and taken a boy west with him. Big money on his head. Dead or alive."

Preacher nodded his head slowly. "I know a little something 'bout Preacher, boys. I trapped the High Lonesome for some years 'fore the fur price dropped. Preacher ain't old. I'd figure him for maybe thirty-five or so. And he's a ring-tailed tooter who was born with the bark on. I ain't never met him, but I know lots who has, and they'll all tell you the same thing . . . that you better let Preacher alone."

"See, I told you!" the first man said to his friends.

"He ain't but one man," the fellow with the desire to meet the devil persisted. "I'm supplyin' up and pullin' out in the mornin'. I am to get me a sack full of gold coins."

"Me, too," his two friends said in unison.

"Well, I wish you boys good luck," Preacher said, draining his cup. "Me, I'm headin' up toward Canada. Mighty pretty country up yonder."

Seated way in the back of the tavern, in the deep shadows, an old man wearing stained and worn buckskins sat, nursing a jug of Who Hit John. The old man smiled secretly and knowingly. He'd recognized Preacher the instant the mountain man had entered the saloon. Wolverine Pete had come to the high mountains back in the late 1790's, blazing a solitary trail and earning a reputation as being a man to ride the river with. He picked up his jug, corked it, and quietly slipped out the back of the tavern. He walked to the livery and saddled up, riding to the edge of town and reining up on a rise.

It was a good move on his part. About ten minutes later, Preacher came riding along, leading a packhorse. Pete rode down to the trail and intercepted Preacher.

"Wagh!" Preacher said. "Wolverine in the flesh. I heard you got kilt up on the Cheyenne last year."

"I took me an arry in my back for a fact. I'm a-headin' for Saint Louie—in a roundabout way—to get 'er cut out. It's botherin' me fierce. They's big money on your butt, Preacher. That shore must have been some important uppity-up feller you kilt."

Preacher told him what happened.

Pete grunted. "Sounds to me like you give him ever'

24

chance in the world to back off. But that don't mean you gonna get any slack cut you. I figure 'fore it's all said and done, they'll be forty or fifty men lookin' to collect that gold."

"They're welcome to try," Preacher replied.

"I wished I didn't hurt so bad, I'd go with you. Sounds like fun to me."

"I'll try to avoid 'em. I don't want the boy to get hurt."

"Sounds like you took a shine to this lad."

"He just needed a chance, and I aim to see that he gets it."

"You want me to lay up on a ridge and kill them fellers you was talkin' to in the bar?"

Preacher shook his head. "I'm obliged, but no. They didn't look like much to me. When they see how hard the trail is, I'm thinkin' they'll give it up."

"They might. You take care of yourself, ol' hoss."

"I'll do it, Pete."

Back at the shady glen, Preacher said, "We got man-hunters on our trail, boy. We got to shake them if we can. But we got to cross them damn plains 'fore we get to the mountains. Let's ride, son. We got hell nippin' at our heels."

Three

"Were you the first mountain man, Preacher?" Eddie asked.

"Oh, no, boy. There was lots of men in the High Lonesome long 'fore I come along. I got there right in the middle of it all, though. We had some high ol' times, we did."

Eddie loved to get Preacher going on some of his exploits. The boy wasn't that sure that Preacher was telling him the truth all the time, but the tales were lively and entertaining and they helped pass the hours between supper and bedtime.

Preacher was teaching Eddie the ways of the wilderness as they crossed the Arkansas line and headed into the Territories. "Wild country from here on in, Eddie. And it gets wilder the farther west we go."

"Will we see heathen Indians, Preacher?"

"I'd just as soon we didn't, but we prob'ly will. I best start your learnin' about Injuns, Eddie."

"They attack and scalp people," the boy said.

"Well, some do and some don't. Personally, I don't think Injuns started that scalpin' business. I think they learned that from the white man some years back. Your Sioux and Cree Injuns, to name a few, place a lot of value on scalps, but other tribes place much more value on countin' coup on an enemy or the stealin' of his horse.

And Injuns ain't bad folks, Eddie." He paused. "Well, maybe with the exception of the Pawnee. I ain't *never* been able to get along with them damn Pawnee. The Injun just ain't like us, that's all. Their values is different. You don't never want to show fear around an Injun. Remember that always. Courage is something an Injun respects more than anything else."

"Preacher?"

"Yeah, boy."

"You know there are men following us?"

"Oh, yeah. I been knowing that since yesterday afternoon. I wanted to see when you'd pick up on it. That's the way it is, Eddie. People look at lots of things, but very few actually *see* anything. I think it's them loudmouths I met back yonder in Little Rock. I don't want to have to hurt none of them, but I'll be damned ifn I'll let them hurt us."

Preacher had armed the boy and stopping often along the way, had taught him how to shoot both rifle and pistol. Preacher still carried his muskets, but back in Ohio, he'd picked up a couple of 1836 breech loading carbines, and one 1833 Hall North breech loader rifle. The breech loaders gave him a lot more firepower because they took a lot less time to load.

"What are you going to do about those men back there, Preacher?"

"I don't know, boy. Yet. But I got to discourage them and that's a fact."

"Is there a reward posted for you?"

"Yep. I don't know how much, but I 'spect it's a princely sum for the news of it to have traveled this far." Preacher pointed to a meandering creek, lined on both sides by cottonwoods. "We'll face them down over yonder."

Preacher took his time making camp, and making certain that Eddie was safe from any wandering bullets, then squatted down by the tiny fire he'd thrown together and boiled some coffee. He figured the men behind him would show up in about half an hour. He checked his guns and waited.

He didn't miss the time mark by more than a few minutes. Three mounted men reined up when they spotted Preacher, sittin' big as brass by the fire, drinking coffee right out in the open, making no attempt to hide himself.

At that distance, Preacher couldn't be certain, but the men looked like those who'd been braggin' back in Little Rock. They rode toward the camp, muskets at the ready.

"Hallo the camp!" one hollered.

"Come on in," Preacher returned the shout. "If you're friendly, that is. If you're not, you best make your peace with God, 'cause if you start trouble with me, you'll damn well be planted here."

The trio hesitated, then rode on. "You!" the man who wanted to shake hands with the devil blurted, as the men reined up close to the camp.

"In the flesh," Preacher said, standing up, his hands close to the butts of his terrible pistols. "What are you three doin' doggin' my back trail?"

"We're a-lookin' for a wanted desperado called Preacher."

"You found him, hombre. Now what are you goin' to do about it?"

The men exchanged glances. Preacher had the advantage, and the men, although unskilled in man-hunting, were fully aware of that fact.

The man who held a kinship with the devil cleared his throat and said, "In the name of the law, I command you to surrender."

Preacher laughed at him. "The Injuns call me Ghost Walker, White Wolf, and Killing Ghost. Now, before you push me to show you why I'm called that, you boys best turn them ponies around and head on back to Arkansas."

"Cain't do that," the second man said. "We done made

28

our brags back to home that we'uns was gonna bring you in—dead or alive."

"You boys is makin' a bad mistake," Preacher warned them. "That shootin' back in O-hi-o was a fair one. I give that Parks feller more'un a fair shake. Now back off and let me be."

The man who wanted to sit down with the devil got his wish. "I can feel that gold in my hands now," he said. Then jerked up his rifle and leveled it at Preacher.

Preacher snaked the big, heavy four-barreled monster from his leather holster and blew him out of the saddle. The double shot took him in the chest and face, making a mess out of the man's head.

The man's companions fought their spooked horses for a moment. One of them lost his musket in the process. When they got their horses calmed down, they sat staring at Preacher. The mountain man now stood with both hands filled with those terrible-looking pistols.

"You kilt Charlie Barnes!" one man said after finally finding his words.

"Shore looks that way," Preacher said. "Either that or he's mighty calm."

"Whut do we do now?" the remaining man asked.

"You boys dismount, careful like, and I'll tell you."

The two men carefully dismounted and stood before Preacher.

"Lay all your guns on the ground," Preacher ordered.

Guns on the ground, Preacher said, "Now bury your buddy."

"We ain't got any shovel!"

"Then use your hands and a stick! Move!"

While the men were struggling to gouge out a hole, Preacher stripped their horses of saddle and bridle. He kept their pack horse and supplies.

Charlie Barnes now planted in the earth, Preacher said, "Now strip down to the buff, boys."

"Do what?"

"Strip, boy! Are you deef?"

The men took one look at the eight barrels pointing at them and quickly peeled down to bare skin. "This is plumb humiliatin'!" one said.

"Now get on your horses and ride," Preacher ordered.

"Bareback? Like this?" the other one shrieked.

"Like that. Or I'll shoot you both and leave you for the buzzards. What's it gonna be?"

"But they's highwaymen back yonder. We ain't got no means of protectin' ourselves."

"One look at you two, nekked as a jaybird, and any outlaws will laugh themselves silly at the sight. You got ten seconds to get clear 'fore I start shootin'. If I ever see either of you followin' me again, I'll lay up and ambush you. And that's a promise."

Ten seconds later, the two would-be man-hunters were gone, moaning and complaining about their discomfort.

Preacher chuckled and stoked up the fire. "Come on out, Eddie. Let's fix us something to eat and see what we got new in supplies."

"Those men are gonna sure be rubbed raw and sore time they get back to town," the boy said.

"I 'spect so. Break out the fryin' pan, boy. I'm hungry."

While Eddie cut slices of bacon, Preacher inspected the newly acquired supplies. The men had provisioned well. The added supplies would take Preacher and the kid a long ways. Preacher stripped the saddle and bridle from the dead man's horse. It was a fine animal; too fine to be turned loose. Preacher could trade the horse for something later on up the trail. The men had brought along enough powder and shot to stand off an army. One had brought along a fowling piece, a fine double barreled shotgun that just might come in handy along the way. There was nothing like a shotgun all loaded up with nuts and bolts and the like to take all the fight out of a trouble-maker. Preacher had seen men cut literally in two with a shotgun.

"Those men might try to come back," Eddie said, laying strips of bacon in the pan.

"Yep. I 'spect they will, boy. Tonight. I 'spect Charlie Barnes will have company come the dawnin'."

"We could move on."

"We could. But we ain't. Learn this, boy: You start takin' water from one man, pretty soon you gonna take it from another. Then runnin' away becomes a habit. Eddie, out here, a man's word in his bond and a man's character, or lack of it, stays with him forever. I tried to warn them three back in town. They didn't pay no heed to my words. Barnes paid the price. Them others will too, I reckon. We'll see."

The boy smiled shyly. "If I was set loose in the wilderness bare-butt nekked, I figure I'd try to get my clothes back too. Wouldn't you?"

Preacher returned the smile. "I 'spect."

Preacher lay in his blankets and listened to the two Arkansas men as they made their return to the camp by the creek. He had to suppress a chuckle as the barefoot men stepped on rocks and thorns and oohhed and ouched and groaned along, trying their best to be quiet, but losing the game something awful. He figured it was right around midnight.

Preacher slipped from his blankets and picked up the club he'd chosen hours before. He really did not want to kill these two, just discourage them mightily. He glanced over at Eddie. The boy was sleeping soundly, a habit that he would soon break if he wanted to survive out here.

Preacher slipped like a ghost out of camp and away from the dying eye of the fire. By now he had the men spotted. It wasn't all that hard to do. Their lily white skin was shinin' in the faint light like a turd on top of a white-icin' birthday cake. Preacher slipped around and came up behind them, his moccasins making no sound as he moved from tree to tree. Preacher had to put a hand over his mouth to keep from laughing at the sight. The men had wrapped some sort of leafy vine around their waists. Looked to Preacher like it was poison ivy. The men must have tore the stuff down in the dark, not realizing what they were wrapping around their privates and over their buttocks.

They'd damn sure know come tomorrow, what with all the itchin' and scratchin' they'd be doin'.

Preacher whacked the one in the rear on the back of his noggin, and when the man in front turned around, Preacher laid the shillelagh across his forehead. Both men dropped like rocks.

Being careful to avoid the poison leaves, and it was poison ivy, Preacher tied them up, back to back, ankle and wrists, and left them on the ground. He returned to his blankets and went to sleep, a smile on his face.

The men probably realized it would only lead to more knots on their heads if they hollered during the night, so they remained silent until Preacher was up just before first light, coaxing some coals to fire and making coffee.

"Mister Preacher?" one called. "We is in some awful discomfort over here."

"I don't doubt it," Preacher called, setting the coffee pot on the rocks. "You got poison ivy wrapped all around you."

There was a long moment of silence. "Well, hell, Jonas!" the second man said. "No wonder I been itchin' all night."

"Mister Preacher?" Jonas called.

"What is it?"

"Ifn you'd give us back our clothes and saddles, we'd

git so far gone from here by noon we wouldn't even be a memory in your mind."

"You ain't gettin' your supplies back."

"You can have 'em, Mister Preacher. With our blessin's."

Preacher had already piled their clothes up and had them ready. He cut the men loose. "You boys head on down to the crick and pat mud all around your privates. It'll help take the itch out of that poison ivy."

"I know better than to wrap myself in poison ivy," Eddie said contemptuously, watching the men gingerly make their way to the creek. He looked at Preacher. "You could have killed them."

"Yeah. I could have. But they're followers, not leaders. That Charlie Barnes, he talked them into this. There's a time to kill and a time to talk, boy. I think it says something like that in the Good Book. I need to get me a Bible. It's right comfortin' to read them words. Had me a Bible. Lost it last year. I think I left it with Hammer."

"Hammer?"

"My old horse. Some scum kilt him. I tracked them and kilt them. Hammer was a good horse. I miss him. We rode a lot of trails together."

Jonas looked at his companion, both of them sitting in the creek, letting the water momentarily ease the itching and burning. He whispered, "That mountain man tracked down a bunch of men who kilt his horse and kilt them."

"I heard. I knowed we was makin' a mistake when we let that Charlie Barnes talk us into this. Jonas, you ain't never gonna say nothin' about this, is you?"

"No. Not a word."

"You promise?"

"Cross my heart and hope to die."

"Let's spit on it."

The men spat and their secret was sealed.

Both Eddie and Preacher noticed the men were a mighty

sorry lookin' pair as they climbed up the creek bank and joined them around the fire. They walked funny, too.

Preacher had cooked bacon and pan bread and he told the pair to sit and eat.

"We'll eat and be proud to do it," Jonas said. "But if you don't mind, we'll stand."

"I understand. You boys stop ever' now and then on your way back home and bathe the infected areas with mud if you can't find no goldenseal root to powder up and put on it. Apple cider vinegar is real good too."

"Much obliged, Mister Preacher."

"Think nothin' of it. But in the future, you boys best choose your company with a tad more care."

"You can bet on that," the younger of the two said. "Our days of man-huntin' just begun and ended with this trip."

"Wise decision, son," Preacher said drily.

Four

Preacher and the kid were gone within the hour. As they rode, Preacher pondered what Jonas had told him just before the two would-be man-hunters—now officially retired—rode out for home, both of them sitting in their saddles very carefully.

"The way I heard it, Mister Preacher, they's forty or fifty men huntin' you. Maybe more than that. Prob'ly more than that. For they's big money on your head. Several thousand dollars as of a couple of weeks ago. That must have been a real important man you kilt back east."

"Them men behind us know I'll be headin' to the mountains, Eddie," Preacher told the boy after only a few minutes on the trail. "If any of 'em has any smarts, and I 'spect some of them do, they've headed straight west and will be tryin' to get ahead of us, for an ambush."

The boy looked at Preacher. "So if they think we're going straight to the mountains, we don't go."

Preacher smiled. "You catch on real quick, lad. That's right. We don't go . . . leastways not right off."

"Where are we going, then?"

"North. Straight north. We got staple supplies to last us a long time. I'll kill us a deer or two and show you how to make jerky. We'll keep the skins and make you some proper clothing, or I'll have some fitted buckskins tossed

35

in when I trade that spare horse. We're gonna be skirtin' the edge of Pawnee country, and me and them damn Pawnees never has got on worth a damn. Once they know I'm in their territory, and they'll know, bet on that, we'll have us a fight on our hands. But I get along with the Sioux and the Crow and most others."

The mountain man and the boy turned their horses and rode toward the plains. When Eddie caught his first glimpse of the plains he was speechless. It seemed to stretch forever. Mile after mile of waving grass and an endless horizon that seemed impossible to ever reach.

Preacher smiled at the boy's expression. "Takes your breath away, don't it, lad?"

"Yes, sir."

"I've knowed people to go mad out here. Wind blows all the time. It's the vastness of it all. And the buffalo, boy, I can't describe 'em. I've seen thousands and thousands of them on the move. Maybe they was millions of them. The Good Lord alone knows. The earth beneath your feet trembles when they pass. The buffalo is life itself to the Plains Injuns. The buffalo and the horse. The Injun is a fine horseman. They worship the horse. Call him Spirit Dog, Holy Dog, Medicine Dog. The Injuns make their tipis from buffalo skins, they wrap up to keep warm in buffalo robes, they eat the buffalo, they use the soft skin of a buffalo calf to wrap newborn babies in, and the hide of a bull or cow will be used as a buryin' cloth. They use parts of the hide to make drums, moccasins, shirts, leggin's, and dresses for squaws. They use buffalo hair to make rope. The horns of a buffalo is used for drinkin' cups. The bones is used to make all sorts of Injun tools. The paunch of a buffalo is used as a cook pot. Without the buffalo, the Injun would prob'ly cease to be."

"You like the Indians, don't you, Preacher?"

"Most of 'em, yeah. I've lived with 'em and I've fought 'em. I've had me a squaw now and then. I been captured and tortured by 'em, and I've laughed and joked and ate with 'em." He reined up and swept a strong hand across the panorama that lay before himself and the boy. "Look at it, Eddie. The plains. Far as I know, they ain't another sight like it in the whole wide world. And there never will be again. For when the white man comes, and he's comin', they'll junk it all up and try to change it. They'll plow lines in the earth and change the flow of rivers and kill off all the buffalo herds. They'll kill off the wolves 'cause the settlers is ignorant of the ways of the wilderness. Each animal is dependant in some ways on other animals. The wolves kill off the old and the weak in a herd. Without them, the herds wouldn't be healthy. But the white man don't understand that. They *could* understand it, but they won't. I tell you, boy, there ain't nothin' prettier in the world than layin' in your blankets at night and listenin' to wolves sing and talk to one another."

"Won't they attack you?"

"Naw. Them's old wives-tales from scary people. There ain't never been no healthy, full growed wolf ever attacked no human person that I ever heard tell of. Hell, I've had 'em for pets. A body just has to understand the ways of the wolf and respect 'em, that's all. But they's do's and don't when it comes to wolves. Don't never corner one. You do that, you got big trouble on your hands. Don't never get between the he-wolf and his mate. They don't like that. A wolf pack is a real complicated type of society, Eddie. They have leaders and co-leaders. They real protective of their young. The male and the female take turns carin' for their pups." He smiled at the boy and lifted his reins. "Now you see why some Injuns call me White Wolf. I'm a brother to the wolf. I had one big ol' buffalo wolf stay with me for weeks one time. He must have weighed a hundred and fifty pounds. I'd toss him scraps of food and at night he'd sleep so close to me I could feel his breath. But

I never touched him and he never touched me. But we was brothers. I knew it, and he knew it."

"What happened to him?"

"I don't know. One day he just veered off and was gone. He sat on a rise and watched me ride off. He threw back his head and talked to me until I couldn't hear him no more."

"That's sad."

"Yeah, it was. I ain't never forgot it, neither."

"I think I would have liked to have been a mountain man," Eddie said wistfully.

"You'd have made a good'un, boy. I saw right off you got what it takes."

Eddie smiled the rest of the day.

Just a few miles from where someday the town of Wichita would stand, men had gathered. And what a strange collection of men it was. Some were eloquently dressed in the most up-to-date sporting clothes on the market. Others wore homespun, and some were dressed in buckskins. A few carried the most modern hunting rifles, made especially for them, while others carried long flintlock rifles and shotguns. Some carried short-barreled muskets. But despite their difference in dress and speech and weaponry and levels of education—or lack of it—they shared one thing in common: they were bounty hunters. Most were here for the money, but a few were here solely for the enjoyment of the blood sport of man-hunting—the most skilled and elusive game on earth. The ultimate sport. At last count, taken that morning, there were sixty-five gun-totin' men gathered, twelve servants, four cooks, one hundred and five horses and twenty pack mules. Oh, yes, and seven reporters.

There were two Englishmen, two Frenchmen, two Prussians, one Austrian, and one nobleman from Spain. The men had been communicating by letter, mapping out this expedition for two years. They had originally planned to travel Out West and shoot Indians. But after they had all gathered at a grand hotel in New York City, and heard of this Preacher person, why, this seemed like it would be so much more fun. One could always find a savage to kill. All the servants and cooks were in the employ of the "hoity-toity", fancy-dressed foreigners. They all beat it across the country just as fast as they could.

They called themselves professional adventurers, and to most men they were brave; they had traveled the world in their quest for the ultimate game animal. They had faced hardships and they were certainly not lacking in courage. Although it would be safe to say that they were all a tad shy on the common sense side. They were arrogant, aloof, and looked down on anyone who wasn't nobility. They all had some fancy title stuck in front of their names like sir, count, duke, baron, or prince.

On the other side of the coin, so to speak, were the bulk of those about to take out after Preacher and the boy. Most of them were the hard ones. Professionals in the art of man-hunting and tracking. There were about ten men who were along for the adventure of it all; or what they thought starting out would be adventure. They would all soon learn that trying to track down and kill Preacher was no grand adventure. Sixty-five men were riding deeper onto the plains that next morning. By the time they reached the Rockies, only about forty would be left. Forty guns against Preacher and the kid. One of the trackers leading the bounty-hunters was a renegade Pawnee called Dark Hand, so named because of a strange, large birthmark that covered nearly his entire right hand. Dark Hand despised Preacher. Hated him with a wild fury that was almost blinding in its intensity. Preacher had killed Dark Hand's older brother and Dark Hand had fought Preacher twice over the long years that followed, and twice Preacher had bested him, the last time leaving him for dead. But Dark Hand lived . . . and hated.

At that moment, Preacher and Eddie were no more than seventy-five miles away, west and slightly north of the location of the bounty hunters, camped along the Walnut.

A tiny band of wandering Cherokee, fleeing from the Big Ticket country of Texas after the death of their chief, Diwali, approached the camp of Preacher and Eddie and made the sign of peace.

"Come on in," Preacher called, knowing the Cherokee probably spoke English better than he did. Preacher had just killed a deer and told Eddie to start slicing it up.

"Ghost Walker!" one of the older Cherokees said, as he dismounted. "I saw you some years ago, when I was with a scouting party north of Bent's Fort."

Preacher shook hands all around and invited the Cherokee to sit, rest, and eat.

While the venison was cooking, the leader of the band said, "There are many men gathering only a few days ride from here, Ghost Walker."

Eddie and Preacher exchanged glances, Preacher knowing that the furtive exchange would be caught by the vigilant Cherokees.

"You know any of them?" Preacher asked.

"Bones Gibson."

Preacher grunted. Bones Gibson was a first class manhunter. He was first class in everything, including his ruthlessness. Some say, and Preacher didn't doubt it, that Bones had killed more than a thousand Indians and more than a hundred white men during his long career as an Indian fighter and man-hunter. It was also said, and Preacher didn't doubt this either, that Bones had never lost a man once he got on his trail. But Bones had never been west of the Mississippi and had no experience with the Plains Indians.

Preacher looked at Eddie. "I won't lie to you, son. We're in for it."

The boy nodded his head, a solemn expression on his face. Even he had heard of Bones Gibson.

"The men have with them a Pawnee tracker called Dark Hand."

Preacher cussed under his breath. Again, he looked at Eddie. "Dark Hand hates my guts, Eddie. I killed his brother and whupped him twice. The last time I thought I killed him. I should have made certain. Goddamnit! Bones is gonna have half a dozen hard-cases that have been with him for years. Andy Price, George Winters, Horace Haywood, Mack Cornay, Cal Johnson, and Van Eaton, I'm sure. Van Eaton is a bad one. Just as bad as Bones, and maybe a little worser."

"We are moving north to Canada," the spokesman for the Cherokee said. "Perhaps there we can find peace." He looked around and received nods of approval from the other men. "Why don't you and the boy ride with us? Your pursuers are looking for two sets of tracks, not many."

Preacher shook his head. "No. 'Cause when they find us, and they will, they'd kill you all for helpin' us. And don't think they wouldn't. But I do 'preciate the offer."

The Cherokee ate and socialized and then moved on, leaving Preacher and the boy alone by the small fire. "We got to move fast, Eddie. We got to reach the mountains. Once we's in the High Lonesome, them ol' boys will play hell takin' us. I know places there that even the Injuns don't know about." Preacher was thoughtful for a moment. "We can move a lot faster than that mob behind us. But we'll be riding right through Kiowa and then Southern Cheyenne country, after that it'll be mostly Utes. I get along all right with the Cheyenne. Kiowa and Utes can be right testy. You never can tell about them. Let's hit the blankets, boy. We ride steady tomorrow.

Bones Gibson sat on his horse off to one side of the gathering and watched with a sort of grim amusement on his hawk-like face as the many men tried to get packed and mounted up. The sun was just beginning to peek over the horizon. Horses were pitching and bucking as their riders were getting the kinks out of them, mules were braying and snorting, and men were cussing and hollering. All in all it was a scene of chaos and confusion.

Bones's right-hand man, Van Eaton, a heavily muscled, sour-faced man who was little more than a brute, said, "I don't see why you let them igits come along."

"Preacher will kill probably twenty or twenty-five of them long before we finally corner him. We can use their supplies and mounts as ours give out."

"I don't like them reporters along."

"We couldn't refuse them. Freedom of the press, and all that. But if they can't keep up, that's going to be their hard luck."

Van Eaton curved his thick lips into something vaguely resembling a smile. "Yeah. I see what you mean. Accidents do happen along the trail."

"Exactly."

"Bones?"

"Yeah?"

"Preacher ain't no pilgrim. And we all best keep this in mind: When we get up into them mountains, all of Preacher's friends is gonna be lined up solid agin us."

"That's true. But from what I've been told, there are few real mountain men left at this date. Certainly not enough of them to cause us any real worry. And I got that from a very reliable source."

But Van Eaton was far from convinced. He shook his

head. "When we hit them mountains, we best double the guard and sleep with one eye open."

Bones glanced at his long-time friend and ally. "I don't remember you ever being this worried before."

"Ain't none of us ever been this far west, Bones. We been all over the Smokies and the Blue Ridge and the Adirondacks and the Greens and so forth, but never out here. I ain't never seen no country like this. It's ... there ... well, there ain't nothin' out here, Bones. It's ... *empty.*"

"Except for thousands of Indians," Bone reminded him. "But you and I have fought Indians hundreds of times."

"We also knew the country, Bones. And we ain't never fought no plains Injuns. We're gonna lose men on this job. Lots of men. If it wasn't for all that money them silly foreigners offered to pay us, I'd say to hell with it."

"Van, those guns they's carrying is worth thousands of dollars, and they got thousands more in cash money with them. I seen some of it. The rings they's wearin' is worth a fortune. No, Van, them fancy pants, nose-up-in-the-air gentlemen ain't never gonna come out of the mountains alive. But we are. Rich enough to retire."

Van Eaton smiled. "You got it all worked out, don't you?"

"I always do, Van. I always do."

Five

Knowing that their chances for survival were nil if they were caught out in the open plains by sixty-five or so men, Preacher and Eddie packed up, saddled up, and rode out before dawn that morning, heading straight west. Seventy-five or so miles away, the gang of man-hunters finally pulled out, about two hours after.

Indians from several tribes saw Preacher and the boy as they crossed the great expanse of rolling hills and waving grass, but they made no hostile moves toward them. They all knew Preacher and most felt he was as one with them. If the boy rode with Preacher, then he too was one with them.

The Indians also saw the huge group of heavily armed and mounted men coming up behind Preacher. They watched the trackers study the ground and knew the men were after White Wolf and his pup.

But this was not their fight. And it would not be their fight unless the large group of men attacked them. For the Indian to mount an attack against such a large and well-armed army of men would be foolhardy. Nothing could possibly be gained by it.

"Preacher will not run long," one Indian remarked.

"No," another said. "There will be blood on the moon when Ghost Walker has his belly full of running."

"I think he runs because of the boy," yet another said. "When he finds a place where the boy will be safe, he will turn and make his move."

"It would be interesting to watch," the first one said.

The others smiled. "But dangerous, and would not serve us in any way."

That was true, the Indians agreed, then wheeled their horses and rode back to their village.

Preacher finally found what he was looking for. The country had turned higher and drier, the grass shorter, and the landscape dotted with buttes, cliffs, and mesas. Preacher stowed Eddie and told him to stay put. He tied sacking over the hooves of Thunder and Eddie's pony, and walked the horses back to where he'd found a blind canyon. There, he removed the sacking and rode the horses deep into the canyon. Then he replaced the sacking and walked them back out, staying close to the wall and carefully removing all signs of his departure.

He picketed the horses and then ran back to fetch Eddie and the other horses. He found a small creek and led them back along it. By the time Bones and his men reached the creek, the water would have cleared and the hoof marks would be long gone.

"Now, Eddie," Preacher told him, "we got about a day and a half, maybe two days, 'fore those men reach us. I know that Bones and Van Eaton don't know this country. What I don't know is whether Dark Hand does. I'm bettin' that he don't know this is a blind canyon. I got to shorten the odds some. And this is how you and me is gonna do it . . ."

"Preacher rides into the canyons to try to lose us," Dark Hand said to Bones. "But it is a clumsy attempt. I find his tracks going in. Nothing coming out."

"Is there a way around it?" Van Eaton asked.

"There is a way around everything," the Pawnee said, making no attempt to hide his contempt for the white man. "But we would lose much time. But time is what we have. I do not like this canyon country. I say we go around."

"Be lots of twists and turns in there," said Mack Cornay, a thug from Maryland. "Preacher could do 'most anything. Head in any direction, or circle around and come in behind us."

Horace Haywood and George Winters had dismounted and were studying the tracks that were plain before them. There was no doubt about it. Preacher and the kid and their pack horses had entered the pass and had not come out.

"I say we got no choice but to foller," George said. "If we don't, we run the risk of losin' them."

Bones looked up at the sun. Not yet noon. They had plenty of time. He made up his mind. "Let's go. We might trap him in there and end this show here and now."

High atop the mesa above the entrance to the blind canyon, Eddie and Preacher looked at each other and grinned.

"They took the bait," Preacher said. "I can't believe it, but they done it. All right, Eddie. You know what to do at my signal."

The boy nodded and then Preacher was gone.

The reporters from New York and Boston and Philadelphia did not like this canyon. It was hot and still and not one breath of breeze entered to fan them. John Miller, on assignment from a New York City paper, glanced at the Philadelphia journalist and saw that Raymond Simms was not happy about it either. William Bennett, writing for a magazine out of Boston was behind them, and one look at his face told Miller that he too was very unhappy about his present situation.

When their editors had handed them this assignment, all the men had been thrilled beyond words. They would be going into wild, savage, untamed, and unexplored country. They could all write books about their adventures, make a lot of money, and perhaps aid in bringing an outlaw to justice. But back in Missouri they had been told by a dozen well-placed gentlemen, that Preacher was no outlaw. He had worked for the government and was a highly respected scout and trail-blazer. And they had finally realized that Bones Gibson and his men were nothing more than common murderers, thugs, and hooligans, under the dubious disguise of bounty-hunters.

But it was too late to turn back. The reporters were depending on the bounty-hunters to guide them back to civilization. In other words, the eastern reporters were all lost as a dim-witted goose.

Dark Hand had fallen back to the middle of the column. He did not like these twisting canyon trails and he felt in his belly that Preacher had set up some sort of trap.

"I say," Sir Elmore Jerrold-Taylor said, twisting in his saddle and looking around him, "isn't this grand fun?"

Baron Wilhelm Zaunbelcher agreed, adding, "But I am so disappointed that we have not been able to kill any savages. Let's hope our luck will change."

Duke Sullivan said, "But what magnificent country we've seen. The vastness of it boggles the mind."

His mind hadn't been boggled just yet. But it was about to be.

All of a sudden, the trail ended against a sheer rock wall. For a moment, Bones was stumped. That confusion abruptly ended when the man next to him, Bill Front, toppled from his saddle, shot through the head. Cal Johnson screamed as Front's brains splattered all over the front of his shirt.

Dark Hand had leaped from his horse before the echo of the shot began reverberating around the canyon and jumped for the protection of a rock overhang.

Boots Baldwin was the next to go down, the front of his

shirt suddenly stained with fresh blood. He fell dying against another man and took him to the ground with him.

Preacher and Eddie had worked for most of a day and a half rigging another surprise for Bones and his party. At Preacher's yell, Eddie slapped Thunder on the rump and the animal jumped, stretching the rope taut. "Haww!" Eddie yelled, and the animal strained and a wooden platform gave way, spilling hundreds of pounds of rocks of various sizes down into the narrowest part of the canyon trail. The rocks took other rocks with them as they tumbled down the incline, some of them huge boulders, and within a matter of seconds, the trail was blocked by a pile of boulders twenty feet high and fifty feet deep.

Preacher had both hands filled with those terrible pistols of his and was wreaking havoc on those trapped inside the narrow walls of the dark trail.

Preacher had gathered up bushes to dry and he lit them and began throwing them onto the canyon floor. Then he started throwing small bags of black powder into the flames. The results were even better than he had hoped for. The concussion of the explosions brought down more rocks, hopelessly blocking the trail in a half dozen more locations. Horses were bucking and jumping and screaming in fright, throwing riders all over the place. Dead, dying and wounded men were lying on the sand, many of them calling out for help that no one was able to give.

A warrior's smile on his lips, Preacher ran around the lip of the blind canyon to where Eddie was, and together, they got the hell out of there.

None of the reporters had been hit by any of the rounds Preacher had fired, but they had experienced the sensation of having the crap scared out of them.

Bones squatted down after he realized that no more shots were coming their way and assessed the situation. It was terrible. It was going to take them a good day and a half, maybe longer, to dig their way out of the huge piles of rocks blocking the trail in half a dozen places. And they'd lose another four or five days tending to the wounded. Normally, Bones would have left the wounded to fend for themselves. But with the reporters along, he couldn't do that. They would write him up as a monster or worse.

"Damn you, Preacher," he softly offered the oath. "Damn your eyes."

Dark Hand squatted down beside him in the churned and bloody sand. "I tried to warn you about Preacher. Do not underestimate the man. Not ever."

Bones ignored that. "How many men down?"

"Eight dead. Nine others wounded. Two of them will not live through the night."

"One man and a snot-nosed kid and they take out nine-teen men and we never even got a glimpse of them."

Sir Elmore Jerrold-Taylor turned to one of Bones's regular gang and said, "Your Mister Preacher appears to have no fair play in him, whatsoever."

Andy Price looked at the Englishman for a long moment, then he shook his head, which had a big knot on it from a falling rock, muttered something under his breath and walked off to help move the tons of rock.

"Brutish lout!" Sir Elmore said.

"This here's Big Sandy Crick, boy," Preacher said, reining up and stepping down. "We'll make camp here."

They had been riding steady from before dawn to nearly dark for several days. Preacher figured they were at least a week ahead of the man-hunters and could finally afford to relax and rest the horses.

"How far to the big mountains, Preacher?" Eddie asked, as he gathered up dry wood for a smokeless fire without

49

having to be told. Preacher was as proud of the boy as if he were of his own blood.

"Five days easy ridin'."

"Preacher?" Eddie's tone was soft.

"Yeah, boy?"

"I know you been thinking I'm all better and such, but I know the truth. I ain't gonna make it, Preacher. There are too many scars on my lungs. And the sickness affected my heart, too. It's weak. Right now, with me all tanned and such, it's like the quiet before the storm. But I can't get no better."

"Boy . . ."

"No, Preacher." Eddie shook his head and smiled. "I know. Believe me, I do. But I'm not afraid of dying. Really, I'm not. I've been baptized. And I believe in heaven. So lets you and me just have a real good time for as long as it lasts, all right?"

Preacher looked long into the boy's eyes and saw the truth there. He sighed and said, "All right, Eddie. We'll have a high ol' time until who flung the chunk. I got cold mountain lakes for you to see and catch big trout out of. I got waterfalls and wild rushin' streams for you to witness. And meadows bustin' with flowers of all colors. We'll have us a summer of fun, you and me. But mayhaps you be wrong about yourself, boy."

But Eddie only smiled sadly.

Bones and company buried their dead and tended to their wounded and the reporters noted it all in their journals. They carefully coded their words in case Bones or some of his men who could read might get their hands on the journals, for they were not being kind to Bones or any of the other men with him. The reporters now realized, after listening to some of the men talk, that Preacher was no desperado, and the shooting back in Ohio had been a fair one.

The thousands of dollars now on Preacher's head was not an officially sanctioned reward, but money put up by friends and family of Elam Parks. And the reporters now were having doubts that any of them would live to tell of this terrible travesty of justice. For, to a man, they believed Bones and his men intended to kill them, and the so-called noblemen who were on this blood sport.

The reporters began to make friends with one of the men who had come along for the adventure of it, a man from St. Louis who was having a lot of second thoughts about this trip. His name was Jim Slattery.

On the evening before they were to resume the hunt, Jim came to the reporters' fire and squatted down, pouring himself a cup of coffee. In a soft voice, he said, "I figure in about a week, we gonna be about sixty-seventy miles north and some east of Bent's Fort. I'm fixin' to leave this den of thieves and murderers and head there. Y'all want to come with me?"

"I've heard of that place," the Boston reporter said. "We could perhaps hire an escort back east from there."

"I'm sure you could," Jim agreed. "They's supply wagons rollin' in and out all the time, so I was told. Boys, I got me a real bad feelin' about the company we're in. I think them foreigners are in for a rude surprise. If Bones and his bunch has their way, I don't believe none of them hoity-toity barons and dukes and counts and the like is gonna come out of this alive. But they're a nasty lot themselves, so I don't hold out a lot of sympathy for them."

"Nor do we," another reporter said.

"All right, then. That's settled. When I'm ready to make the jump, I'll give you boys the high sign. Stay loose."

"Mr. Slattery, what do you think is going to happen to this Preacher person?"

Jim grinned. "Preacher is a war hoss, boys. That little deal back in the canyon should have warned off any reasonable-thinkin' man. Damn shore did me. What do I think is gonna happen? Well, I think these ol' boys is gonna chase Preacher and the sick little boy until they catch up with them. And when they do, they're gonna be the sorriest bunch of people east or west of the Mississippi River. That's what I think."

"We are all in agreement with that. Tell us, Mister Slattery, why we have not seen any savages."

"They've seen us. You can bet on that. We're too big a bunch for them to attack. Now, I ain't gonna lie to you, when we leave the main body, we're gonna be in considerable risk. We're gonna have to ride light, fast, and cautious. But if we have any kind of luck at all, we'll make it. We're all armed, and from what I've been told, it'll take a big bunch of savages to attack us. Dyin' young ain't real attractive to an Injun." He stood up. "Stay ready, boys. Night."

Across the way, Van Eaton had been watching the Missouri man and the reporters through very suspicious eyes. "I think them reporters is plannin' on pullin' out when they get a good chance," he said to Bones.

"Good," the leader of the group said. "I hope they do. They'll be fair game for any band of hostiles who spot them. None of those reporters can shoot worth a damn. The reason we haven't been attacked is because of our size. Wherever those nitwits are thinking of heading, odds are they'll never make it. With them gone, it'll be a whole lot easier for us to kill Preacher and the kid."

"Bent's Fort," Van Eaton said. "That's the only place they could be heading."

Bones was thoughtful for a moment. "Let them go. Even if they do make it through and tell their story to the Army, and the Army decides to do something about it, this hunt will be long over before patrols can find us. I say good riddance."

"That kid had something to do with that ambush back yonder," Van Eaton said, his eyes shining hard and cruel.

"I want that little puke alive. I'll skin him and listen to him holler."

"You can sure have him. Might be fun listenin' to him squall. Say, cut me off a hunk of that venison, Van. Talk like that makes me hungry."

Six

While Eddie and the horses rested, Preacher prowled around and found what was left of three wagons. He looked at the shaft and head of an arrow still embedded in the charred wood of a wagon bed. Kiowa. They had probably been on a raiding party and come up on these poor folks, he mused. But he could find neither graves nor bones. He rambled through the burned wreckage looking for anything that might be salvageable. He found a saw and laid it to one side. He had a use for that. He found a good sized piece of lead and a bullet mold, which he took. He also found a small Bible. He opened the cover and tried to make out the writing, but the weather had blotted the words. He saved the Bible; most of it was still readable and Preacher did find comfort in the words of the Good Book. Besides, he felt that Eddie might like to have it. The boy had said he liked to read the Bible.

That got Preacher to feelin' maudlin, and with an effort, he shook off the depression. When the boy's time came, it would just have to be. Eddie seemed resigned to it.

Back at camp, he hauled out the shotgun and went to work cutting off most of the barrel. He cut it down and hefted it. Now it was one of the most dangerous weapons man ever devised. A sawed-off shotgun at close range could stop just about anything that moved.

Eddie carried two smaller caliber pistols hooked onto his saddle, with two more in the saddlebags. Whether he would use them against a human being was something that Preacher did not know, but he had a hunch that Eddie would not hesitate to cock and fire if it came right down to the nut-cuttin.'

Preacher stowed the now short-barreled shotgun and gave Eddie the battered Bible he'd found. "Figured you might like to have this, boy. I found it in what was left of some wagons over yonder."

"I wonder who they were?"

"No way of knowin', boy. There ain't a sign of a grave nowheres." He shrugged his shoulders. "But that really don't mean nothin'. Even if they was buried, it was prob'ly in a shallow grave and the critters dug 'em up and et 'em then scattered the bones." He watched the boy shudder at that prospect and said in a softer tone, "That'll not happen to you, Eddie. I give you my word on that."

"That makes me feel better," the boy replied, a somber expression on his thin, tanned face. "Preacher? Are there any towns out here?"

Preacher chuckled. "No, boy. Nothin' like a town. Some south of us is Bent's Fort and it's sorta like a town. Further on west they's a big adobe buildin' with log walls around it where some mountain men live with Mexican and Injun wives. I understand they taken to farmin' now. Don't know how long that will last.* But towns?" He shook his head. "There ain't no towns 'til you hit the West Coast. And that's a far piece."

"I'd like to see the ocean," Eddie said, a wistful note to his words.

"Mayhaps you will, boy."

---

*Not long. Fremont visited there in 1842 and reported all was well. The next year when mountain men came through, the place was deserted. The town of Pueblo was started around 1860.

Eddie smiled. "No," he said softly. "I won't. But you have. Will you tell me about it?"

Preacher leaned back against a fallen log and stuffed and lit his pipe. He pondered that question. "The Pacific Ocean. First time I seen it I couldn't believe my eyes. The water was blue. And when it come crashin' up aginst the rocks along the shore it made a thunderous noise and spray and foam went to flyin' ever'where. Liked to have scared my horse to death, and my heart beat some faster too. I rode down there and took me a swaller of that water. Spit it out fast. Salty water. Ain't fit for man nor beast. I can't see how a fish could live in it, but they do. And they's monsters in the ocean that eat folks. Now, I ain't never seen none of them monsters, I won't lie about that, but I was told about 'em by some sea-farin' men. They tell me they's somethin' called an octo-pussy that's got about twelve arms that's twenty-five feet long each and the arms has got suckers on it; that's what holds you whilst the thing eats you." Preacher and Eddie both shuddered at that thought.

"It was a whale in the sea that ate Jonah," Eddie offered.

"Say! You're right, it was. Tell you what, why don't you read some aloud from the Bible whilst I rustle up some vittles?"

"Any passage you favor, Preacher?"

"Naw. I'll leave that up to you."

The boy turned to Psalms and read aloud the 23rd. Preacher soon realized that the boy had that one memorized, but said nothing about it. Must be plumb awful to be so young and knowin' that any day could be your last, Preacher thought. That there is a mighty brave little boy. He's got more courage in his big toe than a lot of men have in their entire body.

Eddie had stopped reading and Preacher saw that the boy had read himself to sleep. He covered Eddie with a blanket and set about making supper as quietly as he could. He thought to himself, "Another day of rest and then we head for the mountains. I got a lot to show the boy, and prob'ly not a lot of time to get it done."

Shortly after crossing into what would someday be Colorado, the reporters, led by Jim Slattery, slipped away from Bones and his men and simply vanished into history. Somewhere between the White Woman and Bent's Fort, the small party of men met their fate. But no one knows what that fate was. Not one trace of them, their horses, or their equipment has ever been found. Their newspapers and magazines hired scouts to try to find out what happened, but to no avail. It is doubtful they became lost, for historians have noted that Jim Slattery was an experienced woodsman and a fine warrior. Over the years that followed their disappearance, several hundred Indians from numerous tribes were asked about the party of men. If any of the Indians had any knowledge about the eight men, they went to their graves carrying the secret.

The West holds many such mysteries, and it yields its secrets reluctantly. Only one man is reported to have known what happened to the reporters and to Jim Slattery, and he did not solve the mystery until almost a quarter of a century after their disappearance. He died an old, old man, near the turn of the century. It is said that the old mountain man told only one person, the legendary gunfighter that he helped raise: Smoke Jensen.

But that is quite another story.

"Well?" Bones demanded impatiently.

Dark Hand and two other trackers stood up and shook their heads. "Lost it," the Pawnee admitted. "These are not their hoof prints."

Bones threw his hat on the ground in frustration. Three weeks had passed since the ambush in the blind canyon and Preacher and the kid seemed to have vanished into the air.

Only the noblemen seemed unperturbed by the delay in finding their prey. It didn't make any difference to them if the hunt took five weeks, five months, or five years. They all had more money than they could spend in ten lifetimes. Besides, this was good fun. The air was clean and fresh and quite invigorating, the scenery magnificent, the food tasty. The company was lousy and the conversations lacking in grammatical correctness and substance, but one couldn't have everything.

"I say, old boy," Sir Elmore Jerrold-Taylor called to Van Eaton. "Do calm yourself and try some of this wonderful pâté, won't you?"

Van Eaton told the Englishman where to put his pâté, and stalked off. He walked to Bones and said, "Let's give this up and head on back, Bones. We ain't never gonna find them two in all this wilderness."

That idea was becoming more and more appealing to Bones. They were camped on the eastern side of the Rockies and Bones had to admit he had never even dreamed of country such as this. Mountains two miles high, in country that looked so rough it seemed incredible that any human being could possibly live there.

Bones was beginning to understand why that breed of men called mountain men were held in such awe and respect. He just thought he'd seen mountains and rough country in the Smokies.

"All right," Bones said. "Let's talk to the fancy-pants crowd and see what they say."

"Why, heaven's no!" Jon Louviere said. "The hunt must continue. We're paying you to guide us, so guide on."

Bones put it to his men.

"Arapaho and Cheyenne behind us, Ute in front of us and all around us," Dark Hand pointed out. "Is not good."

"I figure we been real lucky to get this far without havin' trouble with the savages," Jimmie Cook said. "I think we're pushin' our luck to go any deeper. But if them lords and the like want to go on payin' us . . . I'm for it."

"Exactly where the hell are we?" Sam Provost asked.

"Just east of Ute Pass," Dark Hand said. "None of you have seen rough country yet. The Rockies are just beginning here. Preacher does not know it, but I left my tribe and spent two years in these mountains. I do not know them as well as he does, but I am not lost."

"You really think we can find them?" Bones asked.

The Pawnee was honest in his reply. "We will be lucky if we do. Or unlucky," he added.

Bones nodded his agreement with both remarks. He did not know whether to go north, south, or west. But he did feel strongly that Preacher had not doubled back to the east. Bones had forty-eight men left, six of them still suffering from wounds that had left them just able to sit in a saddle and not much more.

"In your opinion, Dark Hand," Bones asked, "where do you feel in your heart Preacher went?"

"Deep in the mountains," the Pawnee answered quickly. "West and slightly north of here."

"You've been there?"

"One time only. It is wild country. And do not allow yourselves to be trapped in there when the winter comes. You will surely die."

"Do mountain men live there in the winter?" Willy Steinwinder asked from the group of noblemen.

"Some of them. But they are used to hardships. It does not bother them."

"Bah!" the Austrian scoffed. "This is nothing compared to my Alps. Let us push on."

"Yes. Quite right," Burton Sullivan said. "And if we see

painted hostiles, we shall engage them. I feel the need for some blood-letting."

The Pawnee looked at the Englishman. "You are a fool!" he said bluntly. "The Ute, the Arapaho, and the Cheyenne have all been watching us since we approached the shadows of the mountains. You think that pack horse broke loose the other night? Bah! A warrior slipped into camp and took it. That is sport with my people. You all sleep like the dead. If you continue to sleep in such a manner you will all *be* dead." He walked off.

"The guard is doubled from here on," Bones said. "Dark Hand knows what he's talking about. We push on at first light."

As the crow flies, Preacher and Eddie were only about seventy miles from where Bones and his man-hunters were camped. But traveling through that country is not counted in miles, rather in days and even weeks. They were camped along a tiny rushing stream in a camp so cleverly disguised that Bones and party could ride to within twenty-five feet of it and not know it was there. The Utes knew it was there, but they did not bother Preacher and the boy. They knew some sort of deadly hunt was taking place, and they were curious about that. They were both amazed and appalled that such a large band of white men would want so desperately to kill so frail-looking a boy. The Utes shook their heads and again thought how silly white men were.

Preacher had been their enemy and he had been their friend, as he would be again. For that was the way of things. But for now, the Ute and Cheyenne chiefs passed the word: Leave Ghost Walker and the boy alone. And leave the stupid white men alone. Steal their horses if you like, but let them play out this game to its end.

"The Indians know we're here, don't they, Preacher?"

Eddie asked. He wasn't feeling well and Preacher had made him a soft bed of boughs and was letting him rest.

"Oh, yeah. I see sign of them near'bouts ever' day. They're curious and puzzled 'bout what's goin' on. Injuns is naturally curious folks. And the ways of the white man is real strange to them. It's puzzlin' to 'em why all them men is chasin' us. They can't figure out what harm we is to them." Preacher looked over at Eddie and saw the boy was asleep. He walked over to him and put a hand on Eddie's forehead. Hot. Real hot.

Preacher had found some catnip plants and he crushed some and made a tea. While he was letting it steep, Eddie moaned and opened his eyes. Preacher was at his side. "Ain't feelin' so good, right?"

"I'm hot, Preacher."

"I can fix that." He poured some of the vile smelling liquid in a cup. "It don't smell very good, but it's good for you. Sip it, Eddie. Trust me."

Eddie wrinkled his nose at the smell. "Smells like old dirty socks."

Preacher laughed. "Yeah, it do, don't it. Wait 'til you taste it. It tastes even worser. But it'll knock that fever right out. My mamma used to have us drink this ever' day, and we never was sick. I want you to drink three cups a day, Eddie. Ever' day. You start sippin'."

Preacher found him some wild onions and Indian potatoes and started up a venison stew. The broth would be real good for Eddie. "A body don't have to starve in the wilderness, Eddie," Preacher talked as he worked. "But to survive in the wilderness, you got to work with nature, not aginst it. You drink your tea and sleep. Sleep is good for a body. When you wake up, this here stew will be ready to eat and it'll be larrepin' good. If you wake up and I ain't here, don't worry. I'll be prowlin' around."

Preacher sat the kettle to one side so it would simmer slow, and rifle in hand, he worked his way up the mountain until he found him a vantage spot. He took his spy glass from his pouch and extended it, then slowly looked the country over. He saw a few plumes of smoke, but they had been there for several days, and he knew that it was a small camp of Utes about fifteen miles off. He saw no other signs of life.

He wondered for a moment if Bones had given up the hunt? But he shook that off. Bones wasn't known for givin' up. He had to take a prisoner from the group and find out what the hell was going on. The only problem was, he couldn't leave the boy alone.

Well, there was one thing he could do: He could take the boy down into the Ute camp and see if they'd take care of him. He'd rather go into a Cheyenne camp, for he'd always gotten along well with the Cheyenne—except for a few minor skirmishes over the years—and the Cheyenne revered children. But he didn't know of any Cheyenne village close by. So it was the Utes or nothing.

Preacher worried about that all the way down the mountain. But when he reached his camp, he stopped worrying about getting into and out of a Ute village alive.

About a dozen Ute warriors were waiting for him, and one of them had a hand on Eddie.

Seven

The man with a hand on Eddie lifted his other hand, palm out, in a gesture of peace. Preacher lifted his hand as recognition flooded him. The Ute was a tribal chief called Wind Chaser.

"Ghost Walker," Wind Chaser acknowledged. He patted Eddie's shoulder. "Boy sick."

Preacher deliberately laid his rifle aside and walked away from it, a move that did not go unnoticed by the other Utes. "Yes, he is, Wind Chaser. But I'm gettin' him well."

"No get well running all over the mountains," Wind Chaser said.

"I was gonna bring him to your village and see if you'd take care of him whilst I checked my back trail."

That pleased the Ute. He solemnly bowed his head. "My woman take good care of him. How is he called?"

"Eddie."

"Ed-de," Wind Chaser repeated. "Means what?"

This was always difficult to explain to an Indian. Indian names mean something, or stand for an event or happening. "He's named after his father."

"Ummm. Confusing. But I have never understood the white man's ways. Why men chase you and boy?"

This, too, was chancy and Preacher chose his words

carefully. "The boy was a slave. His master was cruel. You can see what condition he left the boy in. I took the boy and the man came after me with a gun. I kilt him. The man's friends put a bounty on my head."

"Ummm," Wind Chaser said. "Yes. This is true. My warriors have been close to their camp and heard them talk. But there is more."

"More?"

"Yes. But my warriors did not understand it, and I do not understand it. There are men of great importance among those who hunt you and Ed-de. Men who have slaves who see to their needs. Cook for them, wash their clothes, and saddle their horses. It is all very strange."

Damn sure was. Preacher sat down by the fire and poured a cup of strong coffee. He took a sip and passed the cup around. It was returned empty and he poured more until the pot was empty. He stirred the stew. He shook his head. "I don't understand it, Wind Chaser. It's confusing to me, too. But it's noble of you to offer to care for the boy whilst I scout the camp of my enemies."

Wind Chaser shook his head. "It is nothing. I remember a winter when Ghost Walker provided meat for my old father and my family while we were away at war. A debt is something that must be repaid."

Preacher had forgotten all about that. That had been a good fifteen years back. Preacher went and fetched the horse that Charlie Barnes had ridden. He handed the reins to Wind Chaser and spoke to the chief in his own tongue, using sign language when the Ute words did not come to him. "The boy is very sick and knows he is going to die." Wind Chaser's eyes widened at that. "Eddie wishes to have a set of buckskins like mine before he passes from this world to the next. Please accept this horse from me to you in exchange for the buckskins."

Wind Chaser rose and carefully inspected the horse, his eyes shining at the sight of the animal. "One small set of coverings is not enough for such a fine animal. I will have my woman make you a fine set of buckskins. Is that fair?"

"That's fair."

"Ed-de is a brave boy," Wind Chaser said, kneeling down and stroking the boy's hair. "He faces death like a Ute, without whimpering and whining. He will be warm and safe in my own lodge. When you return from your scouting, you will be welcomed in my village like my brother. We go!"

"See you, boy," Preacher said to Eddie with a wink. "I'll be back in a couple of weeks. You mind your manners, now, you hear?"

Eddie smiled and nodded his head. This was a grand adventure for the boy, and he showed no signs of fear.

Wind Chaser slashed down with a hand and a big brave picked up Eddie and gently carried him to Eddie's paint pony, already saddled. That told Preacher that the Utes had watched every move he and Eddie had made since coming into the mountains.

"I will not lead those men to your village, Wind Chaser," Preacher said.

Wind Chaser shook his head. "You come when and how you like, Ghost Walker. If those men hunting Ed-de come to my village, they will be fed a good meal and then we shall see how well they die. Do not worry yourself about Ed-de. He will be cared for."

The Utes left like wisps of smoke, flitting silently through the timber.

Preacher sat for a time, eating the stew and drinking coffee. The Utes would take care of Eddie and defend his life to the last man. If an Indian gave his word on something, chisel it in stone. Preacher rose and began construction of a crude corral for the pack horses and a cache for his supplies. The animals had access to water and forage and if food ran out, or a puma or bear threatened them, they could easily break out of the brush enclosure. Preacher erased all signs of the camp, packed a few things, saddled up Thunder, and was gone that afternoon.

Dark Hand looked nervously around the camp. He had just returned from his afternoon's prowling and did not like what he had seen, or rather, what he had *not* seen.

"What's wrong with you?" Van Eaton snarled at the Pawnee. "You're makin' me nervous."

"We are alone," Dark Hand said.

"What do you mean, alone?"

"No Ute. No Cheyenne. No Arapaho. We are alone."

"Why . . . you ninny! That's good."

"That's bad," Dark Hand contradicted. "That means the chiefs have met and agreed to stay out of the fight. That means that Preacher is on the hunt. For us. He is probably out there now, looking at us. Waiting. Watching."

"Now, just how did you come to that?"

"It is the only thing that makes any sense."

"Well, it don't make no sense to me," Van Eaton said sourly.

"Yes. That makes sense to me, too," Dark Hand said haughtily.

Van Eaton watched the Pawnee walk off. He figured he'd been insulted but he didn't quite know how. He looked all around him. Birds were singing and feeding, squirrels were hopping around, all having grown used to the presence of the large body of men. Van Eaton snorted. "Preacher out there," he muttered. "Hell, he ain't within fifteen miles of this camp."

Preacher was about two hundred yards away, lying on his belly in some brush. Part of him was clearly visible to the naked eye, if anyone would just make a very careful visual inspection of their surroundings. But he knew none of the men would. What Preacher was doing was one of the oldest of Indian tricks—hide where your enemy would least suspect.

Preacher was puzzled by what he saw and the few words that he could hear. He couldn't figure out who those fancy-dressed men were, and what they were doing with the likes of Bones Gibson. Nothing about this made any sense to Preacher. Those duded up men had servants and cooks waitin' on them hand and foot. So why were a bunch of rich folks like them tied in with Bones, and why were they hunting him?

Preacher saw Dark Hand looking carefully all around him. He immediately averted his eyes so he would not be staring directly at the Pawnee. Dark Hand spoke with Van Eaton for a moment, and then walked away.

Preacher watched the Pawnee until he disappeared and then backed away from the scant cover and into the thicker brush and timber. He didn't think Dark Hand had spotted him, but he wasn't going to take any chances. He made a slow half circle of the camp until he found a good spot to lay under cover until dark and he could make his move, or until one of them in the camp came out alone to answer a call of nature.

A half a dozen came out to the area together and Preacher could do nothing except listen to them swear, grunt and make other disgusting sounds. Then his ears perked up when he heard one say, "Them royal folks has upped the ante on Ol' Preacher and the kid."

"Yeah, I heared," another said. "But what they want is foolish to me. They want us to take Preacher alive, and then turn him a-loose unarmed and on foot so's they can hunt him down for sport."

Preacher blinked at that. *Sport?* What the hell kind of people were these fancy-pants men? Royal folks? What in the world did that mean?

"But Van Eaton wants the kid," a third voice was added. "What did the kid do to get on Van Eaton's bad side?"

"I don't know," yet another voice said. "But Van Eaton ain't got but one side, and it's all bad. He's even worser than Bones, and that's sayin' a lot. He says he's gonna skin him alive slow-like just to listen to him holler."

Preacher felt a coldness wash over him with those words. A dark and deadly hand touched his heart. Any man that would torture a kid, of any color, was too low to let live. And if Preacher had his way, Van Eaton would not be counted among the living for very much longer.

Skin Eddie? What matter of men were these people? How low-life could man be? Preacher figured he was right close to just about the lowest of the low.

Preacher fought back with some effort an urge to rise up and blast these men into eternity. But doing that would only wound the tip of the snake's tail. He wanted Bones, Van Eaton, and those fancy-dressed men. And he wanted just one man from this bunch to question. And if he didn't want to talk to Preacher, Preacher knew a way to loosen his tongue—he'd just turn him over to the Utes.

Preacher lay under cover until dusk. Then he got his chance to grab one of Bones's men. A man he'd heard call John Pray wandered over to the area, alone, and started to drop his trousers. Preacher coshed him with a leather pouch filled with dirt and the man hit the ground unconscious. Preacher tossed the man over one shoulder and quickly took off.

When John Pray awoke he fully expected to get whacked on the head, like had happened three times already that night during the ride from camp. His head hurt something fierce. But no blow came. He tried to move his hands, but they were tied behind his back and his back was hard up against a tree. He looked across a hat-sized fire into the hard and cold eyes of a man dressed all in buckskins.

"You be Preacher?" John croaked out the question.

"I be Preacher."

"Are you gonna torture me?"

"If I have to. And believe me, John Pray, I will."

John believed him. Oh, how he believed him. "What do you want to know."

"Everything. Front to bottom and side to side. You tell me ever'thing you know about this gang that's chasin' me and the boy, and I'll cut you loose. And that's a promise. You can either hook up again with Bones, or clear out. It's up to you. Start talkin', John Pray."

John Pray was a brigand and a scalawag, but he was no fool. He opened up and talked for a full ten minutes, nonstop. So complete was his confession, Preacher didn't have to ask him a thing.

When John Pray fell silent, Preacher hauled out his Bowie and cut him free. Preacher gestured toward the coffee pot. "Help yourself."

"Mighty nice of you," John said sarcastically. "Considerin' that you're sendin' me to my death."

"I ain't sendin' you nowheres, John Pray."

John sipped and smiled. "You know damn well I can't go back to Bones. They'd know I talked and kill me for sure. I ain't got no hoss and no guns. The savages will kill me 'fore I get ten miles from here."

Preacher picked up John Pray's brace of pistols, shot and powder, and knife. He tossed them to him. "I took the liberty of unloadin' them pistols. You got ample shot and powder. 'Bout ten miles from here, anglin' south, they's a crick. Follow it down to Ute Pass. Stay southeast 'til you come to another crick. That's Rock Crick. Follow that and you'll come to a settlement. Mex and Injun women and mountain men that's done takin' up plowin' and plantin'. You got money in your purse 'cause I seen it. They'll sell you a horse. Bent's Fort is due east of there. Keep ridin' and don't never come back to these mountains. If I ever see you again, I'll kill you, John Pray. Now, git gone!"

John Pray was gone in a heartbeat, not even looking

back. Preacher immediately doused his fire and took up Thunder's reins and was gone in the other direction, putting miles between the man-hunter and himself before he settled down for the remainder of the night in a cold camp.

At dawn, Preacher gathered dry wood and built a tiny fire under the overhang of branches and boiled water for coffee. He was so angry he had to struggle to keep his emotions in check. A bunch of goddamn foreigners were planning to use him like some wild animal to hunt down ... for sport. Preacher had a dirty opinion of people who hunted animals for sport and trophy and not for food. And Indians took an even sourer view of folks like that. Indians hunted animals for survival. They never killed what they couldn't use.

Preacher calmed down some and drank his coffee and chewed his jerky. He mulled over his situation. Counting the cooks and servants, he was outnumbered about fifty-some-odd to one. He knew that common sense told him to get Eddie and head deep into the mountains. Bones and them goddamn foreigners would never find them. Preacher knew that. But Preacher didn't much cotton to runnin' away. That cut against the grain. It wasn't that he hadn't run from trouble before, because he had. There was a time to fight and a time for a feller to haul his ashes. Said that plain in the Bible—sort of. But damned if Preacher was gonna run from the likes of Bones Gibson and a bunch of fancy-pants counts and barons and dukes and princes and so forth.

Now, about the boy. Eddie was safe in the Ute village. Bones would never attack an Indian village, even if he could get close enough without bein' seen, which he couldn't. Bones was arrogant, but he wasn't stupid.

Preacher drank the last of his coffee and made up his mind as the fire began dying down to coals. All around him lay the magnificence and majesty of the Rockies.

Birds were singing and squirrels were playing and chattering.

He had done nothing to any of those men huntin' him. They wanted to do harm to him and Eddie. They wanted to use Preacher like some poor chased animal. But that would never happen. They wanted a war. Well, all right. That could happen. Preacher could damn sure give them a war. But this war would be on Preacher's terms—Preacher would lay down the rules of warfare. And they would be harsh. This would be a war like none they had ever seen. Count on that.

Preacher doused his fire and covered all signs of the camp. He saddled up Thunder and packed his few supplies and stepped into the saddle.

He rode for about fifteen miles before topping a rise and there, staying in the timber, he surveyed his surroundings. This was his country. The High Lonesome. The Big Empty.

And it was about to run red with blood.

Eight

Bones had shifted his camp.

It only took Preacher about one minute to determine which direction they'd gone. He did not immediately follow the tracks. Instead, Preacher threw together a small fire, made some coffee, and then sat for a time, ruminating.

Bones and Van Eaton had assumed rightly that John Pray would blab, telling Preacher everything that he knew. Dark Hand would point out that he'd been right all along in saying that Preacher was close-by, watching. So the smart move would be to shift locations. But this time it would be a much more secure camp, one that could be easily guarded and defended while the man-hunters made new plans.

The men had made no attempt to hide their tracks, so to Preacher's mind, that meant they wanted him to follow. "They think they gonna ambush you, Ol' Hoss," he muttered. "They got some boys layin' in wait for you to come amblin' along so's they can put a ball in your noggin. So you just sit right here and figure out where the main bunch is headin' and then circle around and do some dirty work of your own."

John Pray had told him that the Pawnee, Dark Hand, had spent a couple or three years in this area. That was news to Preacher, but he didn't doubt the man's words. It made sense to him. Without someone who knew this country, Bones and his men would have been wanderin' about like a lost calf a-bellerin' for its mamma. So where would Dark Hand lead the men now that they knew Preacher was on the prowl?

That was a question that Preacher could not answer. Putting himself in Dark Hand's moccasins, he could come up with several dozen places where he'd go. But what he could do was pretty much determine the direction. Preacher carefully extinguished his fire and swung into the saddle.

"Let's go see what misery we can cause, Thunder. Then we'll go check on Eddie."

"We lost the mountain man!" Van Eaton said, an evil smile curving his lips.

"We will never lose Preacher," Dark Hand said sourly. "And he will not fall into your stupid and clumsy attempt to ambush him."

The men had taken a break and were watering their horses and resting after several hours of riding over rough country. Tatman, a Rogue out of Indiana, looked at the Pawnee, disgust in his eyes.

" 'pears to me, Injun, that you're 'bout half skirred of this Preacher."

Dark Hand smiled, sort of. "I fear no man. But I have much respect for many. Preacher has been in this country ever since he was a boy. He is respected, if not liked, by all. Songs are sung about him around the night fires, and stories are told and retold about his courage and cunning and fierceness in battle. Do not take your enemies lightly. To do so is to die. If you would but open your eyes and your brain, you would know that the Utes in this area have made a pact with Preacher. If you would have but looked at the signs back at our old camp, you would have seen one horse only. That means the boy is safe somewhere. Preacher would not have left him alone in the wilderness. This is grizzly and puma country. And this is also Wind Chaser country."

By now, the camp was silent, the men standing or sitting, all listening to the Pawnee speak.

"Wind Chaser is a war chief of the Utes. Very brave and very cunning in battle. I think the boy is in Wind Chaser's village. I know that we have been watched, and I think the watchers are warriors from Wind Chaser's village. For the time being, they are going to leave us alone. This fight is between us and Preacher. Any attempt to take the boy would mean instant death for us all." His eyes touched the eyes of every man in the camp. "Or a very long and slow and painful death by torture. Chances are slim that any of you will see one of Wind Chaser's warriors, but if by accident you do, do not shoot. Make no hostile moves toward any Indian you might glimpse. We must concentrate our efforts on finding and destroying Preacher. No one else."

Tatman snorted. "I still say you're skirred of Preacher."

Dark Hand cut his eyes. "You are a fool. I do not think you will die well."

"Injun," Tatman said. "You don't call me no fool!"

"He just did," Bones said. "And I would suggest we all pay heed to his words. Now mount up. Let's get out of here."

Bates and Hunter, the two men Bones had assigned to spring the ambush on Preacher were growing restless. And more than a bit edgy. It was getting late in the afternoon. They both felt that Preacher should have been along hours before. And they both felt that Preacher had figured out Bones's plan and that the ambushers were now the hunted.

It was a feeling that neither of them liked.

Suddenly to their right and in the dark timber, came the unmistakable sounds of a mountain lion on the prowl. The cough and huff and angry snarl. Hunter and Bates both turned to face the chilling noise.

But they could see nothing. No movement of brush or low branches. The mountain wind died down to no more than a whisper and the men waited, their hearts thudding heavily in their chests. They were both uneducated men, neither able to read or write, and both very superstitious.

Preacher, crouched no more than fifteen feet away, suddenly split the high mountain air with the scream of a panther. Bates fired his rifle and hit nothing and Hunter peed his dirty underwear. Preacher screamed again and the horses of the men broke loose from their picket pins and went racing off, eyes wild with fear.

"Shoot your damn gun, Bates!" Hunter yelled, frantically reloading.

"At what?" Bates hollered.

Two young Ute braves, in their late teens, hiding and watching on the other side of the animal trail, had to shove their fingers in their mouths to keep from laughing at the antics of the two frightened white men. They knew it was Preacher on the other side of the trail, and not a panther. This was going to be a good story to tell around the night fires. They would entertain the whole village with its telling. They might even make up a dance, showing how frightened the silly white men were. Yes, they would definitely do that.

Hunter got his rifle charged and brought it to his shoulder just as Preacher picked up a rock and flung it. The fist-sized rock caught Hunter in the center of his forehead and knocked him down and goofy. His rifle went off and the ball missed Bates by about an inch, slamming into a tree. Bates yelled as blown-off bark bloodied one side of his face.

"You've shot me, you goose!" Bates hollered, dropping his rifle and putting both hands to his bloody face. Bates suddenly stepped on a loose rock, lost his footing, and began flailing his arms in a futile attempt to maintain his balance. He lost and went rolling down the side of the rise, yelling and hollering for help. He banged his head on about a half dozen rocks on his way down and came to rest against a tree, totally addled.

The two young Utes were rolling on the ground, clutching their sides in silent hysterics at the sight unfolding before their eyes. This story and dance would be remembered and retold and danced for years to come. This was the funniest thing they had seen since Lame Wolf's fat and grumpy and ill-tempered wife, Slow Woman, sat down on a porcupine's tail while picking berries one day. Even Lame Wolf thought that was funny. Until she hit him in the head with a club and knocked him silly. Slow Woman never did have much of a sense of humor.

Preacher knew the young Utes were on the other side of the trail. They were good in the woods, but not as good as Preacher. And by now he could see them rolling on the ground in silent laughter. That was good. They would tell Wind Chaser and he would have them dance it out and the entire village would be amused.

Preacher stepped out of hiding and jerked the shot, powder, and pistols from the near-unconscious Hunter. He picked up both rifles and vanished into the timber. He caught up with their horses and led them off. Bates and Hunter were going to have some tall explaining to do when they caught up with Bones and party. If they caught up with Bones.

The two young Utes left in a run, back to their village. They could not wait to tell this story.

* * *

Wind Chaser was clutching his sides, his face contorted with laughter long before the young braves had finished telling their story. When they had finished, he wiped his eyes and said, "Our hunters have brought in much meat this day. We will feast and dance this evening. Ed-de will be entertained and be happy with this news." He pointed at the two young Utes. "You two go now and bathe and prepare your dance for this evening. You have both done well." He rose and entered his tipi to tell Eddie of the feasting and dancing and story-telling that evening. Good food, rest, and the attentions of the women had done the boy good. His fever was gone and he was able to walk about for short periods of time. Wind Chaser had talked it over with his wife and they had both agreed to ask Preacher if they could have the boy, for as long as Man Above allowed him to live. If Preacher did not agree, well, that was the way it had to be. But Wind Chaser felt he could prevail upon the mountain man. He had known Preacher for a time, and known of Preacher for a longer time. And Preacher possessed uncommon good sense for a white man. Not as much sense as an Indian, of course, but one could not expect too much of a white man.

Preacher had found him a snug little hidey-hole for the evening. He had trapped a big, fat rabbit and it was on a spit. He was smiling about his day's work as he drank the strong black coffee and savored the good smells of food cooking.

Hunter and Bates had staggered into the camp of Bones and company just about dark. Both of them were footsore and weary, and both had knots on their heads.

Bones took one look at the pair and said, "I don't even want to hear about it." He turned and walked away.

Van Eaton took his plate of food and joined Bones, sitting down on the ground. "We got to talk, Bones."

"So talk."

"If Dark Hand is right, and I 'spect he is, and the Utes has taken a likin' to the kid, we can scratch him off the list. We won't be able to get within five miles of that Ute camp."

"Agreed."

"Preacher is playin' with us. He could have kilt both them men but didn't."

Bones nodded his head in sour agreement.

"I just don't like it, Bones. It's a black mood that's layin' on me. I get the feelin' that Preacher is tryin' to tell us that if we'll leave now, we can leave alive. But if we stay, he's gonna turn this game bloody."

"After seeing Hunter and Bates, I tend to agree with you. But them crazy foreigners has upped the ante, Van." He stated the amount and Van Eaton almost choked on his food. He swallowed hard and stared at Bones. Bones nodded his head. "You heard me right. We don't even have to think about robbing them. They're offering us enough money to retire on, Van. Think about it. With that much money we could both buy them farms and horse breeding stables and the like we've always talked about. We could live like gentry."

Van Eaton thought about that for a moment, his eyes shining with greed and cruelty and cunning. "Yeah. And oncest we got shut of the foreigners, we could kill ever'body 'ceptin' our own men and we'd have twicest the money."

"That's right. And them crazy lords and dukes and such has agreed to divvy up money right now if we'll stay. And they's this to think about: We might not even have to kill the men to get the money. You know damn well if we stay, Preacher is gonna kill fifteen or twenty, at least, 'fore we get him. Maybe more than that. Probably more than that. We could just take the money off their bodies and nobody would be the wiser."

"Is them lords and such carryin' that much money on them, Bones?"

"No. Of course not. But they are carrying bank drafts that's legitimate. All they got to do is fill them out and they're good. I know that for a fact. They're kill-crazy, Van. All of them. I ain't never heard tell of some of the things they claim to have killed. Rinossoruses and wild crazy-sounded animals all over the world."

Van Eaton blinked at that. "What kind of ossorusses? What the hell kind of animal is that?"

Bones shook his head. "I don't know. I never heard nothing like it. They may be tellin' great big whackers for all I know. What do you say, Van? Do we take the deal?"

Van Eaton slowly nodded his head. "Yeah, Bones. We take the deal."

"I got a plan," Bones said. "And it's a good one. The way I got it figured, it shouldn't take no more than a week to push Preacher into a pocket and let them fancy-pants foreigners kill him."

"And then we can get gone from this damn wilderness." Van Eaton looked around him at the night. The mountains were shrouded in darkness and it was cold for this time of the year. "I really hate this damn place, Bones. You can't get warm at night. Can you imagine what it's like out here in the *winter?*"

"No. And I don't want to find out, neither. I just can't imagine anybody in their right mind who would want to live in this Godforsaken place."

At the Ute village, Eddie was having the time of his life watching the two young Indians act out what they had witnessed earlier that day. The boy was laughing and clapping his hands, his belly full of meat from the feast. Wind Chaser gently put his arm around the boy's shoulders and patted him.

Deep in the wilderness, Preacher snuggled deeper into his blankets and slept to the sound of wolves talking back and forth to each other. It was a comforting sound to the mountain man, for many people, both Indian and white, believed him to be a brother to the wolf. Some even went so far as to say Preacher was part wolf himself.

They were not that far from the truth.

Nine

Preacher rose from his blankets and squatted for a moment in the grayness of pre-dawn. In the brush and timber surrounding the little pocket of clearing where Preacher had made his camp, he could see gray and black shapes moving silently about, slowly circling him but making no attempt to enter the clearing.

"My brothers," Preacher said softly, his eyes on the big ever-moving wolves "You've come to warn me."

Low snarls greeted his softly-spoken words.

"So today it really starts," Preacher whispered. "They're really gonna come after me."

As one, their mission accomplished, the wolves vanished, running deeper into the timber.

Kit Carson once said that Preacher was the "gawd-damnest feller" he'd ever seen. He had a way with animals like no man he'd ever known. Ol' Bill Williams said Preacher was spooky. He felt that Preacher could actually talk to animals, most especially with wolves. Jim Beckwouth once told a writer that of all the mountain men he'd ever known, the man called Preacher was the most fascinating. John Fremont confided in friends that the mountain man called Preacher was almost mystical in his dealings with animals. He swore that he actually witnessed a pack of wolves playing with Preacher one day, in a small meadow deep in the Rockies. He said that when they all tired of playing, they fell down on the grass and flowers and rested in a bunch, Preacher right in the middle of the huge wolves. Jim Bridger said that Preacher could be as rough as a cob, mean as a grizzly bear, and as gentle and compassionate as a mother with a baby.

Smoke Jensen, the West's most talked about, written about and feared gunfighter, whom Preacher took under his wing as a boy to raise after Smoke's pa died, wrote later in his biography, that the man called Preacher was a highly complex man, who lived under only one set of rules, his own. He said that Preacher was an inordinately fair man, but once his mind was made up, and his moccasins set on the path of his choosing, would brook no interference, from any man.

If those who made up the party who were now hunting Preacher for sport had known anything at all about the inner workings of the man, they would have immediately packed up and left the mountains as quickly as possible.

But they did not really know the matter or manner of man they sought. And by the time they finally found out, it would be too late for most of them. It wasn't just that Preacher was a mountain man. For there were mountain men, albeit not many of them, who were as skittish as an old maid in a men's bath house. It was the individual himself that should have been studied closely. Bones had never had any experience with Preacher, or with men like him. His reputation as a successful man-hunter had come about by chasing down escaped convicts, weakened by physical abuse, poor food, and brutally hard work. He had chased down embezzlers who by the very nature of their work were not physically imposing people. Bones had chased down and captured—or shot dead—men who had killed their wives and wives who had killed their husbands. He had killed or captured ignorant farm boys who broke jail after some minor infraction. True, Bones had tackled some mean and vicious men and emerged victorious. But he had never taken on anyone who came even close to being in Preacher's league.

As for the royalty who were members of this party of man-hunters, to them this escapade in the wilderness was still nothing more than good sport and fun. Quite entertaining, really, don't you know? It was irritating to them that Bones had forbidden them to kill a savage or two, but perhaps when this Preacher matter was concluded, then they could hunt some Indians. They'd never taken a scalp, and that would be quite a novel thing to take back to show their friends. They were all looking forward to scalping some savages.

It just never entered their minds that they might be the ones to get killed and scalped.

Preacher struck first, three days after he'd waylaid Hunter and Bates. He still had it in his mind that he could maybe harass them into leaving the mountains. There was no way he could have known that the blood-hungry royalty had upped the ante on his head. He had checked on Eddie and found the boy was happier than he had ever seen him.

Wind Chaser was uncommonly blunt with Preacher. "My woman and I wish to keep Ed-de as our own, Preacher."

Preacher nodded his head. "And what does Eddie think about that?"

"He is a child. He does not know what is best for him. As adults, we do."

Preacher had to hide his smile. The Indian and the white man were so much alike, in so many ways, and yet, so far apart that their two cultures could probably never co-exist side by side.

"Well, when the time comes, I'll talk to Eddie. If it's all right with him, it's all right with me, Wind Chaser." He

83

smiled and to soften his words added, "And I'm purty sure it'll be just fine with Eddie."

Wind Chaser smiled. "The boy will want to stay with us. You will see."

"I 'spect you're right. I've cached supplies all over these mountains, Wind Chaser. So I'm gonna leave my horses with you and go this on foot."

Wind Chaser had noticed the huge pack and had suspected as much. He nodded his head. "This is no longer a game, White Wolf. Why don't you take some of my warriors and end this foolishness once and for all?"

Preacher shook his head. "This is personal, Wind Chaser. I talked to the wolves the other mornin'. They told me."

Wind Chaser felt the hair on the back of his neck hackle and he resisted the temptation to step back, away from Preacher. He had heard about Preacher and his relationship with the great gray wolves that roamed the countryside. It was just that sort of thing that made many people, Indian and white alike, believe the story that Preacher had been found as a baby and raised by wolves, suckled on their milk. Preacher had, of course, heard the story, and, naturally, being Preacher, he had never done anything to dispel the myth. Indeed, whenever he got the chance, he added a few words to strengthen the myth. The more Indians were spooked by him, the safer he was.

"Your brothers, the wolves, they were close to you?" Wind Chaser asked.

"'Bout as clost as me and you is right now."

"Ummm!" Wind Chaser said softly.

Smiling, knowing Wind Chaser would repeat the story and the legends about him would grow all over the Indian nation, Preacher walked out of the Ute village and made his way toward the timber. His pack would have bowed the back of a normal man. Preacher walked like he was carrying a pack full of feathers.

"Not a sign of him," the teams of men reported back to Bones after an all day search in an ever-widening circle around the base camp of the man-hunters.

"We seen savages," Mack Cornay said. "Plenty of them. But all they done was look at us. They didn't make no move, no gesture, nothin'."

"No tracks of that big rump-spotted horse he rides?" Van Eaton asked.

"No. Nothin'."

"He is on foot," Dark Hand spoke from where he sat on the ground. "He has hidden supplies all around and is now living with some wolf pack."

"Aw, hell!" George Winters said. "No human man lives with wolves. They'd tear him to pieces. All that talk is nothin' but poppycock and balderdash."

Dark Hand shrugged his shoulders in total indifference to what these foolish white men believed. Dark Hand and Preacher were about the same age, and Dark Hand had heard many things about the mountain man called Preacher over the years. Much of what was said about him was indeed nonsense. But some of the talk was true. Dark Hand knew that Preacher was not unique in his ability to get along with wolves. He knew of Indians who possessed the same talent. He also knew that Preacher did not sit with the spirits for guidance. Preacher was just a very highly skilled woodsman—as good as any Indian—and he had honed those skills to a knife blade sharpness.

Dark Hand also knew that Preacher had not killed the man called John Pray. He had scouted for miles the day after Pray had vanished and found where Preacher had taken him, tied him, questioned him, and then turned him loose.

And most importantly, he knew he would be much better off if he would leave the company of these foolish white men and strike out on his own. But the white men fascinated him. They were so ignorant about so many things. Dark Hand never tired of listening to them babble. They praddled on and on about the most unimportant of subjects.

Tatman said sarcastically, "All right, Injun. You seem to think you know more'un the rest of us. So what is Preacher gonna do now?"

"Start killing you," the Pawnee said matter-of-factly.

"Oh, yeah?" a big, ugly unwashed lout called Vic said, standing up. "I reckon you think this here Preacher is just gonna walk right in this camp and start blastin' away, huh?"

Dark Hand smiled knowingly. None of the white men had taken note that when he sat, he sat with his back to a boulder, or log, or tree. No one seemed to notice that Dark Hand utilized every available bit of cover even when in camp. How these men had lived this long was amazing to Dark Hand.

"No," the Pawnee said. "He will not come into camp firing his guns."

"Well, then," Vic said, his voice dripping with ugly sarcasm, "I reckon you think he'll call down lightnin' or something to strike us all dead? You seem to think this feller is some sort of god."

Dark Hand sighed. An instant later, Vic cried out and looked down at the arrow that was embedded deeply in his belly. Vic screamed as the pain hit him hard. His legs seemed to lose strength and he stumbled and sat down heavily on the ground. "Oh, mother!" he hollered. "Oh, my dear sweet mother!"

Dark Hand had bellied down on the ground before the first yell had passed Vic's lips, presenting no target at all for Preacher, and he was certain it was Preacher lurking in the dark brush and timber around the camp. The men started shooting wildly, hitting nothing and accomplishing only the wasting of lead and powder. Dark Hand suspected that Preacher had turned and slipped away as soon as he saw the arrow strike its mark. That was what he would have done, and Preacher could be as much Indian as he was white when he had to be.

When no more arrows came silently and deadly out of the brush, the men slowly began crawling to their knees and reloading. The cooks and the servants of the gentry remained where they were, belly down on the ground, eyes wide with fear.

"Halp me!" Vic bellered. "Oh, sweet baby Jesus, halp me."

There was nothing anyone could do for the man. The arrow had torn through his stomach and when they laid Vic out on the ground and cut away the back of his jacket and shirt, they could see that the point was very nearly all the way through his back.

"Go ahead and shoot him," Jimmie Cook said. "I don't want to have to listen to all that hollerin' for days and nights."

Sir Elmore Jerrold-Taylor waved to one of his men. "Franklin here has received some medical training. See what you can do for this unfortunate wretch, Franklin."

Franklin knelt down and inspected the puncture wound. "I will have to push the arrow out the back, remove the barbed point, and then pull the arrow out from the front. But I fear the lining of the stomach has been penetrated front and back so all that would accomplish is a great deal of agony for the man. He will die no matter what I do."

"Oh, very well," Elmore said. "Wilson," he called to one of the cooks. "Be a good fellow and fix some tea, will you? I feel the need for something warm and soothing. Something to calm the nerves, don't you know?"

Preacher's big rifle boomed and Elmore's plumed hat went sailing about twenty feet away. His Lordship yelped and unceremoniously hit the ground, belly down in the mud.

The Frenchmen, Louviere and Tassin, jumped behind a fallen log and landed right on top of the Prussian, Rudi Kuhlmann, knocking the wind out of him. Preacher's rifle boomed again and the Austrian, Willy Steinwinder, got a faceful of bark splinters as the heavy ball smacked into the tree he was trying to hide behind. One of Bones's men, Cal Johnson, sprinted for cover just as Preacher fired one of his pistols. Cal turned a flip in the air as the ball slammed into his right leg and sent him sprawling and hollering. Preacher fired again and the ball whined off the big iron cook pot and went ricocheting wildly and wickedly around the camp. One of the servants ran into a tree and knocked himself silly. Van Eaton jumped for cover and landed squarely in a big pile of horse crap. He was so afraid to move that he lay in the dung and suffered the indignity, cussing Preacher loud and quite emotionally. Bones had jumped behind a boulder as the rest of the camp sought cover wherever they could find it. Dark Hand lay safe behind a fallen tree and took silent satisfaction in watching the panic of the white men.

Just before Preacher took off for safer territory, figuring he had done enough damage for one day, he turned and unloaded his pistols into the panicked camp. The sound was enormous and the double-shotted barrels spewed lead in all directions.

Baron Wilhelm Zaunbelcher was just getting to his fancy, hand-made boots when Preacher cut loose and Horace Haywood jumped into the slight ground depression and landed right on top of the Baron. The Baron did not appreciate that at all and began roaring in German. Horace figured rightly that Wilhelm was giving him a sound cussing and rared back and slugged the Baron right on his royal snoot. Horace and Wilhelm, ignoring the whining lead balls, began rolling around on the ground, cussing and punching and kicking and biting and gouging, the blood and the mud and the snot flying in all directions.

Bones rose to his knees and looked at the fist-swinging, bleeding, cussing men, rolling around in the dirt. He shook his head in disbelief.

Horace tried to knee Wilhelm in the groin and then gouge him in the eye with a thumb.

"Oh, I say now!" Burton Sullivan called. "That's a foul. Unfair. Unfair. Fisticuffs is one thing, but ungentlemanly behavior simply won't be tolerated here. I must protest this. Why . . ."

Jack Cornell busted the Duke in the chops and Burton went down, his mouth bloody. He jumped to his boots and assumed what was then considered a proper stance for bare-knuckle fighting—the left arm stretched out, left fist knuckles to the ground; the right first held close to the face. "I'll thrash you proper!" Burton said.

"That'll be the damn day!" Jack replied and bored in. Much to his surprise, Burton Sullivan knocked him flat on his butt.

Dark Hand lay behind cover and smiled at the antics of the white men. With danger all around them, the fools were making war against each other. To Dark Hand's way of thinking, it had to be some sort of a miracle from Man Above that the white race had survived this long.

"Break them up!" Bones yelled to his men. "Right now. We can't afford this. Preacher might be back at any moment. Do it, damnit!"

The cussing and fighting men were hauled apart and led off, to be widely separated from each other until they cooled down. Cal Johnson's leg was bathed and bandaged by Franklin; but Cal was going to be out of action for a time.

Vic was moaning and carrying on something awful. Van Eaton walked over to the man. He stood looking down at him for a moment, then cocked and lifted his pistol.

Vic yelled, "No, Van! Don't do it, man. Please, no. For God's sake!"

Van Eaton coldly shot him in the head, abruptly silencing the moans. "Gettin' on my nerves," Van Eaton said, recharging his pistol.

The camp was silent for a moment. "Oh, well. What the hell? He wouldn't have lasted the night noway," Mack Cornay said. "I'll get a shovel."

"No!" Bones called. "We don't have the time. Just roll him over the side of that ravine yonder and let the buzzards have him. We're breaking camp."

"Where to this time?" Van Eaton asked.

"The scouts found a much better place. It'll be harder for Preacher to slip up on us." He looked around him. "I sure don't want a repeat of this day."

Ten

By the time the man-hunters ended the confusion in their camp and stopped fighting among themselves, Preacher was long gone. When Bones asked Dark Hand if he was going to attempt to pick up Preacher's trail, the Pawnee looked at the man as if he had taken leave of his senses.

"That's what Ghost Walker would like some of us to do," he told Bones. "I tell you, those who pursue Preacher now will not return."

"By God, I'll pursue him!" Tatman said, picking up his rifle and moving toward his horse. "That Injun's yeller. I knowed it all along."

Dark Hand shrugged that off and turned his back to the ignorant loudmouth.

"Take Brown with you," Van Eaton told him.

"I shall accompany the men," the Frenchman, Jon Louviere said.

"Suit yourself," Bones told him.

"I'll go with them," Burton Sullivan said. "I just don't believe this man is the will 'o' the wisp you people claim him to be.'

"Good show, Burton!" Sir Elmore shouted.

"Hip, hip, hooray!" Robert Tassin yelled.

Dark Hand grimaced at the very premature congratulatory shouts and poured himself a cup of coffee. The Pawnee watched the four men ride out and thought: Some of you will not return.

"Hell, he's a-foot!" Tatman said, reining up about a thousand yards out of camp, leaning out of the saddle and studying the ground. "We got him now, boys. He's ourn for shore."

"Splendid!" Louviere said.

"Do push on," Burton urged.

About a mile from camp, a rattlesnake, as thick as a man's forearm and mad as a hornet, came sailing out of the brush and struck Brown's shoulder and landed stretched out from saddle horn to Brown's thigh. Brown, terrified out of his wits, let out a wild whoop and left the saddle just as the snake bit him on the leg. The snake left the saddle with the frightened and yelling man, biting him several more times before Brown hit the rocky ground. Preacher screamed like a panther and the horses went into a panic and began pitching and bucking, doing their best to throw off their riders.

Burton Sullivan's butt left the saddle an he went rolling and squalling down the steep grade to the left of the trail. Jon Louviere dropped his rifle and grabbed onto the saddle horn as his horse became more panicked and started bucking more fiercely. His rifle discharged when it struck the ground and the ball struck Tatman in the shoulder, knocking him out of the saddle. He hit the ground, screaming and cussing the Frenchman. Brown was dying beside the trail, the rattler having bitten him a dozen or more times, the last few times on the neck and face. The bounty-hunter was already beginning to swell grotesquely.

Tatman landed about two feet from the horrible scene and clawed at his pistol. The snake shifted its attention from the dying man to Tatman and opened its mouth to strike. Tatman finally pulled the gun from behind his belt and shot the rattlesnake, blowing its head off.

Preacher picked up a rock and flung it, the heavy stone impacting against the side of Louviere's jaw and slamming him from the saddle. The Frenchman, out cold, landed on top of Tatman, knocking the wind from Tatman, and bringing a scream of pain from the frightened and wounded man.

Burton Sullivan, several hundred feet below, had no idea what was taking place above him. He was frantically attempting to claw his way up the rocky incline. He had lost his fancy rifle and one of his pistols and was thoroughly disgusted. He had busted his head on a rock and it was bleeding. His safari clothing was ripped and torn and he had lost one boot. All things taken into consideration, this day was not going well at all.

And it was about to get worse.

By the trail, Preacher had taken all the guns and powder and shot from the dead and wounded men. He was waiting for Burton Sullivan when the man finally, panting and grunting, hauled himself over the side.

"You lookin' for me, Fancy-Britches?" Preacher asked.

Burton gazed upward and into the coldest eyes the Englishman had ever seen.

"I say now, my good fellow," Burton gasped. "Can't we discuss this like civilized men?"

"Nope," Preacher said, and busted the man on the side of his jaw with one big fist.

The nobleman's feet, minus one boot, left the incline and down he went, rolling butt over elbows. He went back down the grade a lot quicker than he came up. He rolled over rocks, smashed into small sturdy trees, and uprooted bushes in a frantic attempt to halt his descent. He finally came to rest all tangled up in a pile of thorny bushes. He was so addled he thought he was a child back in England.

"Oh, mummy," he muttered. "I'm afraid I've poo-pooed in my nightie."

"I'll kill you for this," Tatman told Preacher, pushing the words past the pain in his shoulder.

"I doubt it," Preacher told him, settling one moccasin against Tatman's big butt. Preacher shoved and Tatman began his journey down to join Burton Sullivan at the bottom of the incline.

After two trips, Burton had pretty much cleared the way, so Tatman didn't really encounter much in the way of obstacles on his way down. He must have been covering about fifty feet a second when he slammed into Burton Sullivan, who was just getting to his shaky boots, his back to the incline. Burton, his butt filled with thorns from the bramble bush, and his mind foggy, was staring dreamily down at a lovely little creek about twenty feet below when Tatman slammed into him. Both of them sailed over the edge and landed in the creek.

Preacher looked down at the pair and laughed at them, wallowin' around in the creek. Preacher knew that creek was snow-fed year round and that the water was icy cold. Them two down yonder was liable to come down with pneumonia.

Preacher hoped they did.

Van Eaton recovered the money the noblemen had paid to Brown, stuck it in his pocket, and then shoved the body over the side for the buzzards to eat. Van Eaton didn't give a damn about Brown, or anybody else for that matter, but this meant that Preacher was slowly whittling away at their strength. And the man was still playing with them. He just didn't seem to be taking this hunt seriously. It seemed to Van Eaton that to Preacher, this manhunt was . . . well *fun!*

At that thought, the hired killer looked nervously around him. Van Eaton didn't like these Rocky Mountains. He didn't like them at all. He quickly walked over to his horse, swung into the saddle and took off.

I should have killed him, Preacher thought, on his belly about two hundred yards from where he'd waylaid the four men. That Van Eaton is one cold hombre. He sure wouldn't give a second thought to killin' me.

But Preacher still clung to the rapidly fading hope that the men would give up this foolishness and let him be. Deep within him, however, he knew they would not. That sooner or later, he was going to have to start killing them on sight. The problem was, he didn't want to kill these men. Well . . . maybe Bones and Van Eaton. The world wouldn't miss them at all. These noblemen, now, that was something else. Preacher figured them to be nothin' more than just spoiled rich boys who'd suddenly got all growed up without the maturity that came with bein' an adult man. And he hadn't meant to hit that man with the rattlesnake. Problem was, when you start flingin' rattlesnakes about, you got to be careful, 'cause they can whip that head around and give you a fearsome bite. That knowledge sort of threw Preacher's aim off some. It wasn't that he was feelin' bad about Brown, 'cause he wasn't. After all, the man had been out lookin' to kill him.

Preacher looked carefully around him, then rose up and began trailing Van Eaton. Which wasn't a big deal. Any ten-year-old Injun boy could have done that with one eye closed. Van Eaton did not know this country and that would have been evident to anyone with any knowledge of the land. From all the smoke from cook fires he'd seen plumin' up into the air, Preacher had a pretty good idea where Bones had chose to camp. He'd try one more time to warn these men off, to stop this foolishness. If they didn't heed his warnings, then Preacher reckoned, he'd just have to get nasty about this thing.

* * *

Jon Louviere's jaw was swollen up something frightful. He could just barely speak. Which came as a great relief to most of Bones's gang. Burton Sullivan sat gingerly on a pillow in front of a roaring fire, a blanket wrapped around him. The long and numerous thorns had been plucked from Sullivan's butt, his skin had lost its blue color from the icy waters, and he had stopped shaking. Both Louviere and Sullivan had been thoroughly humiliated by what had taken place. But their eyes shone wildly and silently spoke volumes of revenge.

Tatman was not badly injured, the ball punching a hole in the fleshy part of his left shoulder and passing through without doing any major damage, except to his pride. All during the cleaning out of the wound, he had cussed and spoke of dire consequences should he and Preacher ever meet again. Bones sat with his back to a large rock and listened to it all with a disgusted look on his face. It wasn't that any of the men lacked courage, for he knew that those who'd stuck with him thus far had more than their share of that. He was just sick of Preacher making fools of them all. Playing with them like this was some sort of kid's game.

Problem was, Bones didn't have a clue as to how to bring the hunt to a conclusion. He was going to use the boy, somehow get him away from Preacher and use the brat as leverage. But with the boy in the protective hands of the Utes, that was out. No one in their right mind would attack an entire Ute village; not with as few men as Bones had, anyway.

And to make matters even worse, Dark Hand had told the gang, with no small amount of satisfaction in his voice and smugness on his face, that the Indians were watching it all, spying on them, Ute and Cheyenne for sure, and probably Arapaho, too, and were making up dances and telling stories about how foolishly this large band of white men were behaving. Now Preacher was out-foxing them all and making them look stupid. That really rankled both Bones and Van Eaton. A bunch of filthy ignorant savages making light of them all.

Bones watched as Van Eaton rode back in and stripped the saddle off his horse and rubbed the animal down. No matter how evil the men were, they knew to take good care of their horses. Horses were life in this country.

"Any sign of Preacher?" Bones asked, after Van Eaton had poured coffee and walked over to squat beside him.

"No. But I shore felt his eyes on me. I 'spect he followed me here."

"Well, if that's the case, we best get ready for more fun and games from him. Make sure the guard is doubled and changed ever' two hours so's they'll stay fresh."

"Will do."

"Did you get the money from Brown?"

"Shore did. I stashed it in my gear."

"What'd he look like?"

"Turrible sight. All swole up like nothin' I ever seen afore." He shuddered. "I seen that big rattler, too. Damned if I'd pick that big ugly thing up alive and fling it at anybody. Personal, I think Preacher's 'bout half crazy. I was tole a lot of these mountain men is off the bean somewhat."

"I can believe it. This country would drive a body loony. What are you grinnin' about?"

"Thinkin' 'bout his majesty over yonder rollin' butt over boots down that hill and landin' in them briars. I'd give a pretty penny to seen that."

He and Bones started snickering at the thought and had to cover their mouths so the others would not hear. Van Eaton sobered after a moment and said, "I'll tell you the truth, Bones. I ain't lookin' forward to the night."

"Neither am I," Bones whispered. "But just maybe Preacher feels he done enough for one day."

"I hope so. I ain't had a good nights' sleep in I cain't 'member when."

He wasn't going to get much sleep that night, either, for Preacher had found the camp and was planning his mischief with a grin on his face.

Eleven

"Eight guards," Preacher muttered under his breath. "I got them scared, for a fact."

He had slowly circled the camp then made himself comfortable and waited for the guards to change. Every two hours, he noted. These folks are learnin'. Man stays on guard more'un two hours, he tends to get careless.

Preacher waited until the shift changed at midnight, and then waited for another thirty minutes or so before he made his move. With all the supplies he'd taken from Bones's men, Preacher had gunpowder to burn ... in a manner of speaking. Preacher slipped around to where the horses were picketed and went to work for a few minutes. Then, having to really struggle to keep from giggling, he took aim and chucked a bag of powder into what was left of a dying campfire. Coals aplenty to do the job. Preacher had already found a good spot to watch the show, and he almost made it. He had tossed a second bag of powder into another fire but he thought he'd missed the dying coals. Obviously he hadn't. The big bag of powder blew and the quiet camp turned into a scene of mass confusion.

The horses pulled their pins and jerked free of the picket line and stampeded right through the camp. Ever seen what fifty or so wild-eyed horses and twenty odd big runnin' mules can do to a camp? Preacher jumped behind a rock when the action started and the outcome went way beyond his wildest expectations. The explosions blew hot coals all over the place and set a dozen or so blankets on fire and that only added to the chaos. The horses ran right over the fancy tents of the gentry and Preacher had never seen such a sight as that. In the light from the fires, the gentlemen were exposed in their nightshirts. Several of them had what looked to Preacher like little bitty fish nets tied around their heads. Damnest sight he'd ever seen, for sure.

Sir Elmore Jerrold-Taylor got in the way of a big Missouri and that mule knocked him about twenty feet from point of impact. Sir Elmore landed right smack dab on his butt on that rocky ground and commenced to squallin'.

Bones got himself run down by a spooked horse and before the dust and smoke got so bad that Preacher couldn't see, Bones was on all fours, scurryin' away like a big ugly bug. Van Eaton had climbed a tree, so Preacher just hauled out one of his pistols and let 'er bang.

But the smoke and dust threw his aim off and the ball took a chunk of meat out of Van Eaton's butt. Van Eaton started screamin' and turned loose of the branch he was holding onto and fell about fifteen feet, landin' hard on the ground.

Preacher took aim at a running man and squeezed off another shot; the ball flew true and the man stumbled and fell, pitching face-first onto the ground.

Preacher changed locations, flitting soundlessly through the timber, staying low, working his way around the scene of wild confusion. The only one in the camp he was really worried about was Dark Hand, but his worry was needless. Dark Hand had left his blankets before the echo of the first explosion had faded and jumped into the narrow space between two boulders. And there he sat. Dark Hand would choose his own time and place to confront Ghost Walker.

And this night definitely was not the time nor the place. All the advantage was Preacher's.

Mack Cornay jumped onto the back of a galloping horse and grabbed a double handful of mane, trying to halt the frightened animal. But the animal was not to be stopped. The horse raced into the timber and Mack was knocked from the horse when his face impacted with a low limb. Mack hit the ground, his nose busted and his front teeth missing.

A man-hunter known only as Spanish made the mistake of taking to the timber after Preacher. Not a wise thing to do. Preacher noticed the movement behind him and to his left and waited, crouched in the brush. When Spanish drew up even with Preacher, he caught the butt of Preacher's rifle in his gut and doubled over, all his breath gone. Spanish lay on the cold ground, gasping for breath and unable to move. Just to be on the safe side, Preacher quickly tied the man's hands behind his back with a length of rawhide. Preacher tossed the man's weapons into the night and took off.

Preacher continued his circling of the camp, which by now was beginning to settle down somewhat. But the dust and smoke were still thick.

"He shot me in the butt!" Van Eaton hollered. "Feels like it's on fire!"

"My buttocks are on fire!" Willy Steinwinder yelled, frantically slapping at his rear end. A running horse had knocked him into some burning blankets and ignited his nightgown. Prince Rudi Kuhlmann tossed a bucket of water on him.

Preacher underwent a mental wrestling match for a moment, and better judgment won. He left the camp and headed for his hidey hole and safety. He needed a few hours sleep. He figured the bounty-hunters would spend the rest of the night trying to round up their horses and mules, picking up their scattered supplies, and seeing to the needs of the wounded. They'd be after him with vengeance come daylight, but by then, Preacher would have once more shifted locations.

Bones Gibson sat up on the ground and looked at the confusion that still reigned all around him. He began cussing Preacher soundly.

At daylight, the man-hunters began assessing the damage done to their camp, and it was extensive. The tents of the royalty had been burned beyond repair. A lot of their supplies were either missing or destroyed. Two men were wounded and a half a dozen more were injured.

"Indians watched this," Dark Hand announced, returning from a scouting of the timber around the camp. "I don't know what tribe, but several were in the woods. They left heading north. That might mean nothing, or it might mean they were Arapaho."

"Preacher?" Bones asked.

"I lost his trail. He was heading east when I could no longer track him. He took to the rocks."

Dark Hand went to the fire for coffee, leaving Bones again doing some fancy cussing.

Van Eaton and Willy Steinwinder were laying on their bellies, Van Eaton due to the bullet from Preacher's pistol, Willy because of burned buttocks. Van Eaton's rear end was bandaged and Willy's spread all over with lard. Neither man was terribly pleased with their present situation but Willy did express his discomfort much more eloquently than Van Eaton.

Preacher was up at dawn and took a quick wash in a little creek . . . a very quick wash, for the water was ice cold. He boiled coffee, ate some berries for breakfast, and then packed up and moved out.

About a mile from his old camp, Preacher ran into some Arapaho. They grinned at him and the leader said, "You gave us much enjoyment last night, White Wolf. The behavior of the white men was funny. We will have a fine time retelling the story. We thank you. Go in peace."

The Arapaho rode off without another word.

"I ought to start chargin' admission," Preacher muttered, then shouldered his pack and moved on.

"How far back to Bent's Fort?" Bones asked wearily, his eyes sweeping the devastated camp.

"As the crow flies, 'bout two hundred or so miles, I figure," Andy Price said.

"Soon as we get the mules rounded up, take ten men and head there. We got to have supplies. His Lordship, Sir Jerrold-Taylor done made up a list and he'll give you the money. You ought to be safe with that many men. You 'member that valley we rode through southeast of here? We'll be there. We'll do nothin' 'til you boys get back. Last night's affair done scattered and ruint near'bouts ever'thing we got. Head on out."

"You want me to see about pickin' up some more men?"

"Yeah. If you can. But don't tell nobody who it is we're chasin'. Preacher is bound to have friends there." Bones gave the man some gold coins. "Just tell them we're after a murderer and they's big money in it. This here gold ought to get their attention."

The men were gone by midday. It was to be a long, hard trip, and no one in the camp expected their return in under a month. Three weeks at best.

"Pack it up," Bones ordered. "This time, by God, we'll secure our camp and do it right."

Preacher watched the men through his spy glass. He knew immediately they'd sent a party back for supplies. And he saw right off he'd have little chance of slipping into this new camp. The men were working steadily, clearing away brush, cutting down and hauling in logs, and laying out fields of fire. This was going to be a regular little fort.

"Somebody down yonder's had some military experience," Preacher said, collapsing his spy glass and standing up. "They're buildin' a stockade. This is a good time for me to check on Eddie."

Eddie was all decked out in a brand new set of fancy buckskins. He grinned when Preacher walked into the village. But the boy was not well, and there was sadness in Wind Chaser's eyes.

"He dies slowly before our eyes," the Ute said. "And there is nothing that anyone can do."

"Except make him happy," Preacher spoke in low tones.

"That we are doing. My woman, and the whole village. Come, Ghost Walker. Sit, eat. Let us talk about ridding ourselves of these silly white men who hunt you . . ." He smiled. "Or try to hunt you."

Over a thick, rich stew, Preacher said, "It's time for you and your people to be moving to the hunt, Wind Chaser. Past time, actually."

Wind Chaser smiled. "You are wrong if you think we stay because of Ed-de. We stay because the buffalo are late in coming this year. We are leaving soon, though. Ed-de wants to go with us."

Preacher nodded his head. "It'll be an adventure for him. Prob'ly his last one."

Wind Chaser's face tightened at that, but he said nothing. Privately, he agreed with Preacher's assessment. Neither man had any idea that it would be the last adventure for most of Wind Chaser's band.

The sounds of a horse ridden hard reached the men and they stood up. The young brave jumped off at Wind Chaser's lodge. "Crooked Arm says the buffalo are moving."

Wind Chaser gripped Preacher's shoulder. "You should come with us, Ghost Walker. The hunt will be fun and we shall all feast until our bellies swell."

"I got business to tend to, Wind Chaser. I'll speak to the boy and then be gone. I know you got packin' up to do."

Preacher kept his goodbye brief. He didn't want to get all emotional, besides, Eddie was all flustered with excitement and rarin' to get gone huntin' buffalo. The boy was trembling with anticipation. Preacher suddenly had a bad feeling about this trip. But seeing that the boy was all set up to go, Preacher kept his feelings to himself.

"You mind your manners, now, boy," Preacher said, placing a hand on Eddie's frail shoulder.

"Yes, sir, Preacher. I will."

"I know you will, Eddie. You're a good boy. Might be a while 'til you and me hook up again. But we will. That's a promise. So you take 'er easy, you hear? You mind what Wind Chaser says, too. You hear?"

Eddie laughed. "I hear. I'll see you, Preacher."

Wind Chaser's band was not a large one to begin with, and many of the men had gone on ahead to scout for the buffalo. What was left was mainly women and kids and a few warriors. Preacher stood and watched them break camp and head out. He waved his farewells and then saddled up and rode out, in the opposite direction.

He made camp early that afternoon, high up and protected by huge boulders. That night, he woke up with a stir and listened. Seemed to him like he could hear the faint sounds of gunshots. But they faded away or were lost in the sighing winds and Preacher snuggled warm into his blankets and drifted back off to sleep.

Over bacon and pan bread and coffee, something in the far distance caught Preacher's eyes. He dug out his spy glass and extended it. He could just make out the circling of buzzards. A lot of buzzards, and they were already making their slow glide down to the ground to feast on the dead . . . whatever it might be, human or animal, and Preacher had a hunch it was human.

Preacher suddenly lost his appetite as a feeling of terri-

105

ble dread settled over him, hanging on his shoulders like a stinking shroud. He knew that many buzzards didn't congregate over a lone dead animal. It would have to be a whole herd dead, and that just wasn't likely.

With an effort, Preacher forced himself to eat what he had cooked, 'cause in the wilderness, it was good practice to eat when you can, drink when you can, and rest when you can, 'cause you never knew when the chance might come again.

He drank his pot of coffee and then rinsed the pot and scrubbed out his frying pan and cached it with the bulk of his supplies. He made sure his stock had plenty of grass and water, and then slowly saddled Thunder.

"I know what's down there, Thunder. I know in my heart and it makes me sick to think about it. I don't wanna go down yonder, but I gotta. I gotta," he repeated, and then swung into the saddle and started for the valley far below and to the north.

He could smell the scene long before he reached it. The buzzards had torn open the bodies, exposing the innards to the air.

The first thing he came up on was Eddie's little paint pony, lyin' dead. The sorry man-hunting trash had cut its throat and let it bleed to death. Preacher looked at the pony for a moment.

"You was a good horse to a good boy when he needed some good in his life, pony. I won't let the buzzards have you."

He rode on, reading the signs as he went. They were easy. Wind Chaser and his band had made camp along the banks of a stream. That night, when they were settled in, Bones and his bunch had hit them, and hit them hard. He knew it was Bones's bunch 'cause the lone white man he found dead he'd seen several times before.

"I'll not bury you, you sorry son!" Preacher said, considerable heat in his voice.

He found Wind Chaser beside his woman. The chief had died protecting his woman and their children. It didn't take an experienced eye to see that the women had been raped, and used badly. Preacher felt a chill run over him when he saw that Bones and his men had even raped the little girls.

"Sorry white-trash," he muttered.

But he couldn't find Eddie. He didn't want to fire a shot and bring Bones and his people back, so he rode amongst the dead, using a Ute lance to knock the buzzards away. He really didn't have anything against the carrion-eatin' critters; they were just doing what God had put them on the earth to do, but damned if they were gonna do it in front of him. Least not with people he had known and liked.

Preacher rode around the circle of death twice, looking for the boy. He had steeled himself for the worst. But it was worse than even he had thought.

He found Eddie and almost lost his breakfast.

Twelve

The boy had been dragged to death.

The boy's new buckskins were bloody and torn. Preacher just could not bear to look at him any longer. He dismounted and gently laid a blanket over what was left of Eddie. Preacher squatted down for a moment and tried to piece together what had happened.

He figured that Wind Chaser and his small band had been spotted by scouts from Bones's camp. John Pray told him that the foreigners had expressed a desire to kill some Indians. Bones and his party had waited until the Ute camp had settled down and then had slipped up on them under cover of darkness. This was Ute country and Wind Chaser had felt no great need for a lot of security. How Bones and his men had managed to pull this off was a mystery to Preacher, and probably always would be. The important thing was that they had done it. And Eddie was dead.

With a sigh, Preacher stood up and began the task of burying the dead. And he had to do this right, for more than one reason. If Wind Chaser's scouts returned and found this massacre, the entire Ute nation would go on the warpath, and no white man would be safe for months or even years to come. Preacher couldn't allow that to happen.

Preacher built him a travois and began toting the bodies to a dry off-shoot of the creek. He placed Wind Chaser and his family together and carefully caved in part of the bank over them. He did that with all the Utes, choosing his spots with care. Then he took bushes and small saplings and transplanted them in the soil that covered the Indians. It took him most of the morning to get it done, stopping often to look around him for trouble and every fifteen minutes or so taking up his club to knock buzzards away from the remaining bodies.

He searched the area, gathering up everything that had belonged to the tribe and scattered it throughout the timber: clothing, utensils, tipi poles; everything he could find. Then he carefully cut squares of sod out of the earth, worked throughout the afternoon greatly enlarging the hole, dragged and sometimes having to muscle the pony into the hole, and then burying Eddie beside his little paint pony. Preacher carefully replaced the squares of sod and toted water from the creek to dampen the disturbed earth, making certain the grass would stay fertile and grow, insuring Eddie a proper grave.

As the sun was setting, Preacher stood over the grave of the boy and took off his hat. It was rare for Preacher to be at a loss for words, but for a long time late that afternoon, words failed him.

"This here was a good boy, Lord," he finally said, the waning rays of the sun casting shadows about him. "He never done a harm to nobody. I reckon he was about ten years old and in all them ten years, he never knew much comfort. Shore didn't know no love and affection 'til he come to the Utes. They give him a home, and it was a good one."

Suddenly, Preacher realized he was crying, tears streaming from his eyes and rolling down his tanned cheeks. He remembered the last time he shed a tear it was over Hammer's body. He sure had liked this little boy.

He waited for a few moments, wiped his face, and said, "Eddie liked this little paint pony, Lord. So I'd consider it a debt owed if You'd let this here horse into heaven with him. I think You'll find they'll serve You well.

"Now them Utes I buried this day, well, they didn't have no fancy church buildin' like them so-called civilized Christians back East. But what they did have was a belief in Man Above, and that's You, and their church was the whole wide country around them. I think that's a fittin' thing, since it was You who created it all. Includin' the Utes.

"I reckon Eddie and his pony is standin' beside You now. Or maybe beside Jesus, or one of them appissles, or somebody up yonder. Leastwises I shore hope so. I'd hate to think I done all this for nothin'."

Preacher held up the Bible he'd given to Eddie after finding it amongst the ruins of the burned out wagons back on the Big Sandy. "This here is the Good Book, which I'm shore You can plainly see. I ruminated some about plantin' this with Eddie and his little pony. Then I decided I'd keep it and read it from time to time. I ain't no Christian man, but I do find the words to be right comfortin'. I'm a-fixin' to read it now, 'cause what I'm gonna read is one of Eddie favorite verses. I ain't no real good reader, so You excuse my stumblin' around on any big words I might run acrost."

Preacher read the 23rd Psalm, then closed the Bible and tucked it away in his parfleche. "I reckon that about does it, Lord. I don't know what else there is to say. I'm gonna miss this boy. I liked him. That's all. Good evenin'."

Preacher turned to go, hesitated, then once more stood over the grave. "Well, there is somethin' else. Them no-count, trashy heathens over yonder behind them log walls in that valley done a turrible thing last night. They's rich men over yonder that's had fancy education and all the trimmin's that most of us don't get. They knew better. As a matter of fact, all them men over yonder knew better. Now, Lord, there ain't no law out here in the wilderness. But they is justice, and I aim to see it done." He patted the buckskin parfleche containing the Bible. "I know that somewheres in the Good Book it says that vengeance is mine, sayeth the Lord. Well, I'm a-fixin' to relieve You of that burden for a time. Now, if You don't cotton to me doin' that, You best fling down a mighty lightnin' bolt to strike me dead. 'Cause that's the only thing that's gonna stop me." Preacher closed his eyes tightly and braced himself for a bolt from Heaven. When none came, he expelled air and said, "Thank You kindly. Now if You'll excuse my language, Lord, I'm a-fixin' to go kill me some sorry sons of bitches."

Thirteen

Bones had figured Preacher would come after him, and he had prepared for the visit. The fort in the middle of the pretty little valley had been reinforced with rocks and logs and dug up earth. Every bush had been pulled up, every tree cut down for hundreds of yards all around the stockade. Grass for several hundred yards all around the little fort had been repeatedly trampled down by horses and mules.

"You think you're smart, don't you?" Preacher muttered. "Well, you are, Bones. But you ain't near'bouts as mean as me. So that means I got it all over you."

After burying Eddie and the others, Preacher rode up into the high country to think things over and to clear his head. He knew better than to wage war when angry. Man has to be cold when he fights. Anger causes mistakes, and when outnumbered the way he was, Preacher knew he couldn't afford to make any mistakes.

Preacher sat his horse up on a ridge, in the timber, and ruminated for a time. Then he smiled and headed out. Maybe he couldn't get in that stockade, but he figured he sure knew a way to get them inside out. Might take him a couple of days to get it done, but he'd do it.

Willy Steinwinder limped down to the creek to get some water for coffee. He stood for a moment, looking rather

112

confused. He closed his eyes, shook his head, and opened his eyes again. Same thing. He walked back to the stockade and up to Bones.

"There is no water in the creek."

"What?" Bones asked, looking up.

"The creek is dry."

"I don't believe it. That's impossible!"

"Go look for yourself."

"Well, I sure will!"

Everybody walked out to look. The creek had dried up to no more than a tiny trickle in the center. Dark Hand sat on the bank and chuckled.

"You find this funny, Injun?" Jack Cornell asked.

"Yes. Most amusing. Preacher has dammed up the creek. Now what are you going to do?"

Jack Cornell wasn't going to do anything. Not ever again. Preacher didn't think he could make the shot, but he did. He had Jon Louviere's fancy hunting rifle and it was about the best rifle Preacher had ever had his hands on. It was handmade for Jon, that was evident. The workmanship was flawless. So Preacher loaded 'er up, sighted in, and let 'er bang.

He held high because of the distance and dead centered Jack Cornell in the chest. Cornell was stone dead before he hit the ground, his spinal cord severed. The others scattered for the protection of the stockade or hit the ground.

But no more shots came. Preacher worked his way out of the valley by following a ravine when he could and bellying the rest of the way. He figured he had at least three weeks before the others came back from Bent's Fort, and since he was sure they'd bring back some more ornery ol' boys with them, Preacher had decided to whittle down those that stayed behind.

He figured he had a right good start this morning. He was aimin' to whittle down one or two more come this evenin'.

Bones sat behind the earth and long walls and cussed Preacher. Van Eaton sat on a pillow and joined in. Willy Steinwinder had a few choice words to say about the mountain man, but he soon recognized the futility of that and fell silent. The men knew they had to move; without water they could not last long.

"We could go up stream and tear down that dam," Jimmie Cook suggested.

"You want to volunteer to do that?" Bones stopped cussing long enough to ask.

"I reckon not," Jimmie replied.

"That's what I figured." Bones stood up. "Come daylight we're splittin' up into five man teams and takin' out after Preacher. I ain't havin' no more of this."

"Oh, good show!" Sir Elmore said, clapping his hands. "Good show."

Bones almost shot the man right then and there. But he had found out that the gentry might be a tad foolish, but they weren't stupid. The bearer bonds, or bank notes, or whatever in the hell they were, weren't worth a damn unless the signature matched up with the one on record back in St. Louis. And since Bones could just barely write his own name, there wasn't a chance in hell he could copy any of the gentry's handwriting, and he knew it. Torture was out, for the royalty would guess they would be killed anyway and just scrawl their name, making the certificates worthless. So they had to be kept alive and escorted all the way back to St. Louis. And that really irritated Bones.

"We managed to bring enough water up to water the stock and have some for ourselves," George Winters said.

"Will we come back here for the evenin' tomorrow?" Bones was asked.

He shook his head. "No. We'll meet up over yonder in the timber west of here. This place is worthless to us now." He walked to a gun slit and looked out. The sun was going down.

"You reckon Preacher will be back and try to Injun up on us tonight?" Spanish asked.

"He will return this night," Dark Hand said. He had not gone with the men on their raid against Wind Chaser and his band. Wind Chaser had befriended him one time, and he could not bring himself to do harm to one who had been his friend in a time of need. He wished desperately to convey that fact to Preacher.

And Dark Hand had already, several times, prayed to Man Above that the group he was with did not run into any Utes. He had watched from a distance as Preacher very cleverly hid the evidence after the night raid. But he knew, as Preacher surely did, that it would not fool a determined search.

Dark Hand stood peering through a gun slit in the logs. He could sense Preacher's presence, ever more strongly as the last rays of the sun began to fade.

"You think he's out there, don't you, Dark Hand?" Robert Tassin asked.

"Yes."

"Well, he's a fool then!" a man called Cobb snapped. "What does he think he's gonna do? Attack this stockade? That would be stupid."

Dark hand smiled as he turned to face the man. "It is dark now, Cobb. Do you wish to be the first to leave these walls to relieve yourself?" Cobb said nothing. "No?" Dark hand said. "I thought not."

Preacher was working closer as the night fell softly all around him. He stopped his stealthy advance at the far side of the creek bank. He took his bow, strung it, and selected an arrow from the quiver. He waited, watching the stockade. Those inside had lit candles or lamps and they had a fire going. Stupid, Preacher thought. The gun slits were lit up like a chandelier: rectangular pockets of light in the darkness. Ever so often the shape of a head would appear briefly, then pull back.

Preacher calculated the distance. Easy shot. He waited with the patience of a stalking panther.

Davidson walked to a slit and peered out. Everyone inside the walls heard the wet smack and turned. Davidson stood on his boots for a few seconds, the shaft of the arrow protruding from his forehead. Then he toppled over and fell on his back. When he hit the ground the pistol in his hand discharged and the ball just missed Bones's head by a few inches. Bones stretched out on the cool earth.

"Douse them candles and lamps!" Bones yelled, cold sweat covered his body. "Put out them fires."

"Drag Davidson's body out of here and heave it over the walls," Van Eaton ordered. He had watched Davidson put the money given him by the gentry into his pack. He'd get it before they pulled out in the morning. Easy money.

There would be nine teams and then some pullin' out, Van Eaton thought. That meant the odds of Preacher trailin' any particular team was one in nine. Not the best odds in the world but better than nothin'.

Van Eaton knew what Bones was planning. With nine teams working the area, there was a good chance they could box Preacher in and end this manhunt. But they would all have to be very careful. Preacher was like a ghost in the woods.

Percy lit the stub of a cigar and another arrow came whizzing through a gunslit, this time on the other side of the stockade. The arrow thudded into a log, just missing Spanish, and the man yelped and flattened out on the ground.

"Good God!" Bones yelled. "Don't fire up no more matches."

"Isn't this exciting?" Sir Elmore whispered to his friend, Prince Juan Zapata.

Zapata's eyes were shining with anticipation of the upcoming hunt. "I cannot wait until the morning," the Spaniard replied. "The mountain man is indeed a worthwhile adversary."

"We'll have to do this again sometime," Rudi Kuhlmann said. "It is fraught with danger but very exhilarating."

"Oh, quite," Burton Sullivan agreed.

"Igits!" Van Eaton thought, listening to the royalty whisper amongst themselves. "I ain't never in all my borned days seen such a goofy bunch all gathered up in one spot."

Preacher had worked closer, passing through the horses in a crude corral. He calmed them with touches and whispers and made his way to the log walls of the stockade. Bones had placed no guards outside the stockade. Not very smart of him, Preacher thought. Then he stopped cold.

No way! No way that Bones would not put guards outside the log and rock and earthen walls. He wouldn't leave the horses unguarded. He wasn't that stupid. "Damn!" Preacher thought. "I been boxed. Unless I was awful lucky."

Preacher did not move, remaining as still as a rock. Only his eyes shifted, searching the darkness. And when his eyes touched a shape he almost jumped out of his moccasins. The man was no more than ten feet away. Preacher could make out the shape of the man's head, and the long barrel of his rifle. Fortunately for Preacher, the guard had his back to him. The night had turned cloudy, and there would be no moon. Already a few large drops of cold rain had fallen. If the dark building clouds held true, in a very few minutes this night was gonna produce a rain that would be a real toad-strangler.

Preacher pulled out his razor-sharp, long-bladed knife and held it close to one leg, so no stray glimmer of light would reflect off the blade.

"You see anything, Cleave?" the whisper came from a gun slit about a foot from where Preacher stood.

"Nothin'," the guard replied. "But the wind is freshenin'

117

and it's gonna pour down any minute. That's when Preacher will make his move. Bet on it."

"I just spoke to MacNary on the other side. He ain't seen or heard nothin' neither. I'm bettin' Preacher has done his deed and got gone back to his camp 'fore the rain comes."

"I just want to kill that Preacher and get back to civilization," Cleave said. "I don't like these mountains."

"Knock off the talk!" Bones called. "You'll give away your position."

Cleave muttered something about Bones under his breath and leaned up against the logs, still with his back to Preacher.

Preacher cut his throat and lowered the body to the ground. He began working his way around to the other side of the stockade, moving very slowly. John Pray had told him about MacNary, and MacNary was a bad one. A thug and a brigand through and through, a man who would do anything to anybody, man, woman, or child, if the price was right. Preacher had come into the cleared area to stampede the horses, but Bones had used a length of chain to fasten the crude corral gate, and Preacher had to nix that plan.

Thunder began to rumble in the distance and that covered any slight sound that Preacher might make. The clouds began dumping a very light rain and Preacher decided he'd pushed his luck enough for one night. When the shape of MacNary came into view, Preacher shot him and then jammed the muzzles of those terrible pistols into a gun slit and began firing as fast as he could.

Inside the log walls, the sound and fury was enormous. The lead balls were slamming into the logs, whining off of cook pots, and terrorizing those who had thought themselves to be safe and secure. A thug called Dutch screamed as a ball took him in the side. An Arkansas man known only as Wilbur began choking on his own blood as a ball took him in the throat and put him down. The flashes from Preacher's multi-barreled pistols blinded those inside the logs and before their eyes could once more adjust to the darkness, Preacher was gone, running through the night.

The men rushed outside of the stockade. But the darkness of the night and the now heavy-driving rain obscured the fast fading form of Preacher.

About two hundred yards from camp, knowing he could not be seen, Preacher stopped and turned around. "I am Preacher!" he shouted. "The Indians call me Ghost Walker. White Wolf. Man Who Kills Silently. None of you will ever leave these mountains. You will all die. I have given you all the chances you will ever get. Make your peace with God. Some of you will die tomorrow."

"I was under the impression the man was a near cretin. Illiterate," Sir Elmore said. "That was a very eloquent little speech."

"Now how does he propose to carry out that rather ominous threat?" Rudi Kuhlmann asked, stuffing snuff up his nose. He sneezed explosively several times in a row and the bounty hunters standing close to him, their nerves stretched as tight as a guitar string, almost shot him.

Dark Hand was the only one who had not rushed outside. The Pawnee squatted near the gate to the stockade. "Preacher means what he says," Dark Hand said. "It is my suggestion that we all leave these mountains at first light and do not look back."

"Yeller," Tatman said, his arm in a sling, easing the pressure on his wounded shoulder. "I knowed you was yeller all the time."

Dark Hand did not reply. He had moved back from the door and was packing up a few belongings. He had made up his mind. He was going to look up Preacher and make his peace with the man. If Preacher would accept it, the two would never again make war against the other.

The Pawnee was very swift in packing. He was through before the others even thought about reentering the stockade. Dark Hand was not missed until the next morning.

Fourteen

Preacher saw Dark Hand coming from a long way off. He got out his spy glass and scanned the country behind the Pawnee. No one else in sight. Then he noticed that Dark Hand was riding with his rifle in a boot and his pistols nowhere in sight. His bow was in his quiver, and not strung. He was riding with his big knife sheathed and hung by a cord around his neck.

"Wants to palaver," Preacher muttered. "That's odd."

Preacher stepped out from his camp into a clearing on the slope and waved his arms. He watched Dark Hand straighten on the horse's back, and then angle toward him. About fifteen minutes later, Dark Hand was reined up in front of him.

"Light and set, Pawnee," Preacher said. "I got coffee and bacon and bread if you feel like partakin' of my grub."

"You would feed me?"

"Sure."

"I accept. But watch closely my backtrail. There are a few in that bunch of blood-hungry fools who have the ability to track well."

"You left 'em?"

"Forever and ever." He dismounted and led his horse into Preacher's camp, picketing the animal with Preacher's stock. He squatted down by the fire and took the plate of food and the cup of coffee Preacher handed him. "It is one thing to make war against men. But not women and babies. I took no part in that."

"I didn't see your moccasin tracks nowheres about there. I knew that Wind Chaser had befriended you a time or two. Eat. We'll talk when you're done."

When the Pawnee had finished, Preacher poured them both more coffee and they smoked. Dark Hand said, "It is one thing to hate when there is reason for it. But my hatred for you had become unreasonable. My brother attacked you. You did not attack him. I attacked you, twice. You did not attack me. My hatred was stupid." He abruptly stuck out his hand and Preacher smiled and shook it. Dark Hand said, "From this day forward, we do not make war against the other. Is that agreeable with you?"

"Sure is."

"Good. Now I will tell you something. I was scouting the other day . . . two days ago . . . and came up on two Cheyenne. They were young men, and I have seen enough blood. I made peace and they did the same. We ate and smoked and talked. They had spoken with some Kiowa a few days before who had spoken with some Delaware who had just left the trading post on the river. A very large group of white men were there. They had just come in from the East. Far to the east. The Delaware told the Kiowa and the Kiowa told the Cheyenne and the Cheyenne told me that the men were buying huge amounts of supplies and they were all well armed. They also were a loud talking bunch and smelled bad. They did not bathe and the odor from their bodies was awful, the Cheyenne told me what the Delaware had told the Kiowa who told the Cheyenne. I believe these men will join Andy Price who should be at the fort by this time buying supplies for Bones and his people and the arrogant men with them.

"Preacher, my heart is very sad about the little sick boy

who was killed. I saw where you buried him with his horse. That was a good thing you did. He will need his pony to cross to the other side of life. But his grave will not fool the Utes when they return to find out what happened to Wind Chaser. And they will return, Preacher. After the hunt. Listen, I have what I think is a find idea. Why don't you ride to the strong Ute camp and tell them what happened? They will see to the fates of those who did that terrible thing?"

"No," Preacher said with a shake of his head. "I can't have Utes killin' ever' white man who comes along. We're not all bad, Dark Hand."

Dark Hand grunted at that and Preacher understood and had to smile. The white man had not given the Indians many reasons to trust them. But the Indians hadn't exactly welcomed the white man with open arms, either. Preacher understood that there was right and wrong on both sides. There always is when two strong cultures clash. What was considered barbarism and savagery to the white man was an accepted way of life to the Indian.

"Well, if Bones has more men comin' out to join him, I reckon I best get on with whittlin' down the odds."

"I would say that you have made a fine start toward that," Dark Hand said, a distinct dryness in his tone.

The eyes of the Indian and the white man met, and both of them chuckled. Most whites felt the Indian did not have a sense of humor. They were wrong. The Indian had a fine sense of humor. They just didn't show it very often around whites.

Dark Hand finished his coffee and stood up. "I go now, White Wolf. You will not see me again while this silly war is going on. Months from now, should we meet again, remember that you will always be welcome in my camp."

"And you in mine, Dark Hand," Preacher said, extending his hand.

Dark Hand shook the hand and walked to his horse. He was gone seconds later.

Preacher stood for a moment. "First Pawnee I ever really made friends with," he muttered. "Damned if he didn't turn out to be a right nice feller."

"Tracks lead off yonder," Van Eaton pointed, reporting back to Bones. "I betcha that Injun went straight to Preacher."

"No matter," Bones said. "I'm glad to be shut of him. I never did really trust him."

The teams of men were packed up and ready to mount. The royalty had been separated at Bones's orders. He wanted to keep as many alive as possible. He wanted his money, and the gentry were no good to him dead.

"Let's go," Bones said, swinging up into the saddle. "We'll meet an hour before sunset."

One team was to head straight for the new camp and get it ready. The other teams were to concentrate on tracking and finding Preacher. They didn't know that Preacher was, at that very moment, making the search very easy for them.

"Got him!" Spanish called out. "He ain't near'bouts as smart as he thinks he is. Look here."

The team members, including Robert Tassin, gathered around. The tracks were plain as could be. They didn't know that Preacher had been laying down sign all morning, trying to get them to see the tracks. For this sign, Preacher had jumped up and down in one place, broke off a branch, and built a small fire. He figured if this didn't work he'd have to find him a white rag and stand out in the open and wave it at the men.

"We've got him!" the French aristocrat said excitedly. "Let's press on, men." He spurred his horse and entered the timber.

"No, you don't," Spanish muttered. "Preacher is mine." He jumped ahead of Tassin and unknowingly and certainly unwillingly, saved the Frenchman's life.

Preacher's rifle boomed and Spanish went down, leaving the saddle like a sack of potatoes as the big heavy caliber ball blew a hole in his chest and shattered his heart.

"Merde!" Tassin said, jumping from the saddle and taking cover behind a tree. He looked all around him, but could see nothing. He looked over at Spanish. The man lay motionless on the ground, his shirt front bloody.

Tassin lifted his rifle, looking at where he'd seen a faint puff of smoke. If the Frenchman had been the man-hunter he thought he was, he should have guessed that as soon as Preacher fired, the mountain man would shift locations. The only thing that saved Tassin's life was the turning of his head as one of the team, a large, big-bellied, rather obnoxious fellow called Percy, stepped on a branch and it popped. Preacher's rifle crashed and the ball blew bits of bark into the side of Tassin's face, stinging and bringing blood. Had he not turned at the sound of the branch breaking, the ball would have blown a huge hole in his head.

Badly frightened, Tassin bellied down on the ground, presenting as small a target as possible. This was just not turning out well at all.

"You boys made a bad mistake," Preacher called from the brush. "You best say your prayers."

"Hell with you, Preacher," a thug called Hubert yelled. "We got you now."

"Then come get me," Preacher challenged. A second later he changed position, moving several yards to his left. Rifles boomed, the balls whizzing harmlessly to the position where Preacher had been.

"Oohhh!" Preacher moaned, trying to keep from laughing. "You got me, boys. Oohh, it hurts somethin' turrible. Damn your eyes, you've kilt me. Tell my poor ol' ma goodbye for me, boys." He managed to suppress a giggle.

Hubert gave out a loud shout of triumph and lurched to his feet.

"Get down, you fool!" Percy hollered.

Hubert suddenly realized he had made a perfectly horrible error in judgment. He froze in wild-eyed and open-mouthed fear and panic. Preacher dusted him, shooting him from side to side, the ball making a huge bloody hole as it exited. Hubert fell dead to the ground.

"Get out of here!" Percy yelled. "Work your way back. He's got us cold in this brush."

Paul Guy made a jump for his horse and Preacher's rifle boomed again. Paul's leg buckled under him and he collapsed to the ground, crying out in pain.

Preacher slipped quietly away. He'd dealt this bunch enough misery. He figured rightly that all the shooting would bring the others at a gallop. Preacher was a brave man, but no fool. He'd fight this group of man-hunters on his own terms, not on theirs. He slipped over the crest of the rise and jumped into the saddle. He had him a brand new little hidey-hole all picked out.

Bones took one look at the sign that Spanish had found and snorted in disgust. He looked at what was left of this team of men. "He suckered you all."

"Whatever in the world do you mean by that remark?" Jon Tassin shouted, holding a bloody handkerchief to his face. "I demand an answer!"

"Tricked you, that's what I mean. Preacher deliberately left this sign, hopin' you'd be dumb enough to follow it. And Spanish was dumb enough." He savagely kicked the dead Spanish in the side. "Stupid igit!"

"Let's proceed with the hunt!" Willy Steinwinder shouted. "After him, men!"

"Just hold on, hold on!" Van Eaton said. "That's what Preacher wants you to do. He's layin' up in the brush or behind some rocks just over that hill yonder. Now just settle down."

"Van Eaton's right," Bones said. "We got to sit down in a safe place and plan this out, carefully."

"I'm for that," Percy said. "I've helped hunt down a lot of men. But I ain't never seen no human bein' like this here Preacher person."

"Yeah," Paul Guy said through clenched teeth, as he wrapped a dirty rag around the wound in his leg. "Preacher is more like a wild animal that somehow got as smart as us."

A huge ignorant lout called Doyle said, "Preacher said last night that some of us would die this day." He looked nervously around him. "He was shore right."

Bones sensed the moment was getting spooky to some of the men. Down on the flats, he could see the rest of his party riding toward the ridges. He already had too many of the royalty gathered here. "Evans, you take Doyle and head off those other men. Preacher would love to catch us all bunched up near the timber."

Doyle and Evans didn't need a second invitation to leave this scene of blood and death.

Bones took off his hat and scratched his licy head. "We got to start actin' like an army and thinkin' like generals."

"I am a general!" Rudi Kuhlmann said.

"I thought you was a prince?" a man called Falcon said.

"I am. I'm a general too."

"Me, too," Wilhelm Zaunbelcher said. "And so is he." He pointed to Juan Zapata. "Well, why don't you start generalin', then?" a man called Flores asked.

Sir Elmore Jerrold-Taylor smiled. "We thought you

127

would never ask. Catching this Preacher person is easy. We'll show you how."

"Oh, yeah!" Bones said belligerently.

"Oh, yes," Tassin said. "Just watch and learn."

Fifteen

"That's odd," Preacher muttered, watching the man-hunters through his spy-glass. They were all packed up and riding away. He watched the riders until they were no more than tiny dark dots in the distance. He collapsed his glass and tucked it away, then squatted down and gave this some thought.

"Them ol' boys want me to think they're pullin' out, when I know damn well they ain't doin' no such of thing. Now, why would they want me to think that? Ummm." After a moment, he smiled and said, "So's I'd follow them and ride right into an ambush, that's why. Well, I ain't a-gonna do that."

Preacher thought a while longer and then began to break camp. He figured they would take the same route back that they took comin' in, so he'd just make a wide circle and see if he could get a few miles ahead of them. He'd be right there to greet them.

"This ain't a-gonna work," Flores grumbled. "We ain't seen hide nor hair of Preacher."

Bones and party, now led by the royalty, were on their third day of travel, and the thought was creeping into the minds of many of the man-hunters that Preacher had not taken the bait and was not going to fall into the trap.

By late afternoon of the third day, the man-hunters had

traveled about sixty miles from their last contact with Preacher. They had not seen one living human being. They did not know that most of the Indians were far to the north, hunting buffalo.

"Yeah," Bobby Allen said. "I'm a-gettin' hongry. I hope Mack finds us a good spot to camp pretty damn quick."

"Right purty," Mack Cornay said, looking at the coolness provided by the shady trees that lined both banks of the little creek. "This'll do just fine."

The man-hunters were in a long and narrow flat, running north to south between the snow-covered peaks of the Rockies. Cornay waited until the main body was in sight, and then began waving his hat. Rudi Kuhlmann, riding point, spotted the signal and angled the column off toward Mack and the creek.

Rudi could not understand why one minute he could see Mack, and the next instant he could not. He did not know the terrain ahead of him; did not know it was very deceptive, with ravines and gullies and wallows on the east side of the creek. And Mack Cornay was in no condition to be aware of anything. Preacher had thrown a fist-sized rock at the man, the stone slamming into the back of Mack's head and knocking him from the saddle. Mack lay on the ground, unconscious. Preacher had taken the man's weapons, his powder horn, and his shot, and vanished into the bog across the creek.

A knowledgeable man can traverse a bog, but he'd better know where to put each step, for there was mud there that could take a man down to his waist, or beyond. The bog ran for about fifteen hundred yards one way and was about half a mile across. Indians avoided the place, knowing it could be a death trap for both man and horse. Venomous snakes lay above the shallow water on clumps of grass, sunning themselves.

Rudi rode up to the creek and sat his saddle for a moment, looking down at Mack, thinking the man certainly chose a strange time and place to take a nap. Preacher's rifle barked and Rudi was slammed from the saddle, the ball tearing through his shoulder and almost blinding him with white-hot pain. He hit the ground on his belly, knocking the wind from him.

Bones and Van Eaton and a few of the others immediately left the saddle and bellied down in the knee-high grass. A few of the less-experienced, including all the royalty, raced their horses toward the wounded Rudi.

Preacher fired again from the bog and a man called Scott did a back-flip out of the saddle, dead before he impacted with the earth.

Wilhelm Zaunbelcher, shouting oaths in a guttural tongue, threw caution to the wind and galloped his horse through the creek. But the horse had more sense than the Baron. He refused to enter the bog, stopping quite abruptly. Zaunbelcher went flying out of the saddle and landed in the mud at the edge of the bog. He sank about six inches. Zaunbelcher thought he was in quicksand—he wasn't, but there was quicksand in the bog—and immediately panicked. He began screaming in fright, kicking his feet and waving his arms and flinging mud in all directions.

Sir Elmore Jerrold-Taylor drew a short saber from a saddle scabbard and shouted, "Charge, men!"

"Charge?" Bones said.

"I think that's what he said," Van Eaton replied.

This was the day of horse-sense. Elmore's horse refused to step into the bog, putting on the brakes and sliding to a halt. Like Baron Zaunbelcher, Sir Jerrold-Taylor left the saddle and went flying through the air, slowly turning as he flew. A Red-breasted Nuthatch flew past the Englishman and gave the huge creature a very strange look.

"Yna, Yna, Yna," the Nuthatch chirped, and flew on to tell his mate there was something very weird going on in the bog.

"My word!" Sir Elmore said. He landed right next to the Baron and when he impacted with the mud, the point of his saber jabbed Zaunbelcher in the ass and the Prussian came roaring up out of the bog, looking and sounding very much like some terrible monster from a swamp.

Benny Atkins realized he had made a bad mistake by following the nutty foreigners up to the creek and had jumped from the saddle, heading for the trees. Preacher's rifle sang its deadly song and Benny took a ball in his hip, turning him around in a haze of pain before he collapsed to the ground. He tumbled into the creek.

Preacher let himself sink into the mud until only the top of his head and his nose remained above the surface. He was behind a clump of grass and could not be seen. His one rather fervent wish was that there was not a big rattler sunning on the clump. The sun would be cycling soon, shadowing the valley in darkness. Preacher would mud swim out of the bog under cover of night. He rather hoped that some of the men would step into the bog, but he knew that was not very likely.

Sir Elmore reached up and jerked Zaunbelcher back into the mud and safe from rifle shot and they lay quite still for several long moments before they began cautiously working their way back to solid ground.

"Oh, drat! I lost my saber," Sir Elmore said.

"Excellent," Zaunbelcher said. "I hope you never find the damn thing."

The rest of the man-hunters waited until shadows began casting long pockets of darkness before they moved. And even then, they did so very cautiously. None of them had been able to spot Preacher and they did not know whether he was still out there in the bog.

"Creep out of that swamp or whatever it is careful-like," Bones called to Elmore and Wilhelm. "Stay low leadin' your horses back here. We got to get gone," To Van Eaton he said, "Have the boys start draggin' the wounded out."

"Right."

"What about Scott?" a man called.

"Leave him," Bones said, cutting his eyes to Van Eaton.

"You boys get gone," Van Eaton said. "I'll see to Scott."

Preacher heard the calling back and forth and let the men leave, noting which direction they took. Just in case they were trying to set up a trap—something he doubted— Preacher remained in the bog for an hour after they'd left. Then, at full dark he carefully worked his way out of the bog and back to his camp, about three miles away. He washed himself at a tiny run-off and brushed the now dried mud off his buckskins. Something was nagging at his mind but he could not bring it to full light. He shook his head and gave it up. It would come to him.

He cooked his supper and boiled his coffee over a tiny fire. As he ate and drank, he tried to figure out what was nagging at him. He knew it was something he'd seen, and seen that day, but whatever it had been remained elusive to him. He laid out his blankets and with rifle and pistols fully charged and close to hand, Preacher sighed and went to sleep.

He awakened with a grunt of anger about an hour later. Scalps. That's what he'd seen. There had been scalps tied to the manes of the horses of them silly foreigners.

And one of them had been Eddie's.

Sixteen

"So much for the generals leadin' us anywhere," Van Eaton groused that evening. "I told you it was a bad idea."

Van Eaton shrugged that off. He already knew it was a bad idea. He glanced around at his shot-up men. They were a pitiful-looking bunch and a lot of the enthusiasm for the hunt had been knocked out of them by Preacher. Bones had never before encountered such a man as Preacher. What Bones didn't know about any number of things would fill volumes, but just about any experienced mountain man would have behaved pretty much the same as Preacher as far as fighting ability went. Most mountain men would have been content to just run Bones and his so-called man-hunters out of the mountains, and then they would have gone on about their business. But there were a few who would have done just exactly what Preacher was doing.

"We got to find us a hidey-hole and stay low 'til Andy gets back," Bones said. "The men just ain't in any shape to go much farther and they damn shore ain't in any shape to mix it up with Preacher."

"You mighty right about that," Van Eaton said.

Up until almost that very moment, if Bones and his bunch had really wanted to give up the hunt, Preacher just might have let them go. But not after seeing Eddie's scalp

134

tied onto the mane of that horse. That snapped it with Preacher.

Preacher lay for a long time in his blankets after the nagging thought had awakened him in all its horror. Bones and them knew that was a white boy they dragged and scalped . . . or scalped and then dragged, the dread thought came to him.

The dirty scum! He didn't give a damn if those that went for supplies came back with a hundred extra men. Anybody who joined up with Bones Gibson, Van Eaton, and them silly and savage foreigners was dead meat.

The longer he thought about that previous afternoon, the more scalps he could identify. Wind Chaser had a streak of gray right down the center of his hair. Preacher had seen that one tied to the mane of Van Eaton's horse. Wind Chaser's woman's hair had a sort of auburn tint to it, since she was the daughter of a mountain man. Bones had been displaying that one. And their kids had taken after their mother, with lighter hair than the others in the tribe. Preacher had seen their scalps, too.

Preacher looked up at the starry heavens. This high up, the stars seemed so close he could almost reach out and touch them. But Preacher was in no mood to appreciate the beauty of the night. He had something else on his mind.

Killing.

Preacher picked up their trail about mid-morning. And for a moment, it confused him. The trail led south and east. Dismounting, he studied the tracks. There was still the very faint outline of older tracks, and he recognized those as being the men who had left for supplies and returning from Bent's Fort. Horses and mules. Then he realized what Bones was doing. His bunch was pretty well shot up and hurtin'. So he was tryin' to link up with his other party, hopin' they was bringin' reinforcements. Preacher figured

135

that when they joined up, they'd hole up for a time, and then come after him with a vengeance.

"Suits me," Preacher muttered. "Just fine. The more the merrier, Bones. Bones. Somebody shore named you right. 'Cause your bones is gonna bleach white as snow in these mountains, you kid-killer. I swear it."

Preacher didn't follow Bones and the others. He turned around and headed back north. He wanted time to kill a couple of deer, make some pemmican, smoke and jerk some meat, and just lounge around and eat some venison steaks. He'd found him some wild peas and prairie turnips and wild taters. Mix all that up with some pieces of venison and toss in some rose hips and sage and a body had him a lip-snackin' good stew. Preacher got all hungry around the mouth just thinkin' 'bout it.

The weary and bloodied bunch linked up with Andy Price and the gang of men he was bringing back from Bent's Fort. Bones eyeballed the bunch and figured about half of them would turn back once they took a good look at the Rockies. Fifteen or twenty more would pull out after the first sneak attack by Preacher. Those that stayed would be lean and mean and hard and tough.

"They's another bunch comin' up behind me," Andy told him. "I tole 'em to head on back. This ain't no game. But they're still comin' on. They're city toughs. Some of them come all the way from New York and Philly and Boston and them places. I don't understand how they've made it this far. They don't appear to know north from south. And you never in your borned days seen so many different kinds of guns. One of 'em's got two pistols. Each has a cylinder that holds six rounds and revolves. He called them revolvers. Strange lookin' things."

"They're what?" Van Eaton asked.

136

"Revolvers," Andy repeated.*

"How do they work?" George Winters asked.

"Damned if I know," Andy said. "But I don't think they'll ever catch on."

"Did you hear anything about the hunt back at the fort?" Bones asked.

"Oh, yeah. That's about all that folks talk about. And that's strange, too."

"How so?" Van Eaton asked.

"Well, they was a goodly number of mountain men there, but none of them seemed to be a bit concerned about Preacher. Near'bouts all of them said the joke was gonna be on us. One big mountain man told a bully boy from New York—let's see, how did he put it? Oh, yeah. "Ye'll nar leave them mountains ifn ye go yonder with a blood lust for Preacher. Ye been warned by us who knows White Wolf. Heed our words."

"How about Jim Slattery and them writers who left us?"

"They never showed up, Bones. Nobody there has seen hide nor hair of them."

"Injuns got them," Van Eaton opined.

Bones was thoughtful for a moment. "That mob comin' up behind us just might be what we need. Preacher will be so busy tryin' to figure out what to do, mayhaps some of us can slip off durin' the confusion and kill him."

Sir Elmore had walked up. He said, "Say now. That is an excellent thought. By jove, I believe you've quite probably stumbled upon the solution to our problem." He patted Bones on the shoulder. "A very admirable bit of

*A Nichols and Childs belt model revolver. About .34 caliber. Only a very few were made. Manufactured about 1838 or '39. The cylinder revolved using a mechanical device called a pawl that was attached to the hammer.

ruminative prowess, my good man." He smiled and walked off to share the good news with his fellow adventurers.

Andy shook his head. "I was hopin' them fellers would learn to talk right whilst I was gone."

"No such luck," Van Eaton said. "They's even worser than before."

Preacher spent his time relocating his caches of supplies, jerking a goodly amount of meat, resting and eating and getting ready for war. He was completely unaware of the second band of men hunting him. While Bones was waiting for the wounds of his men to heal, and Preacher was preparing himself mentally to dispose of the entire worthless, no-count, disagreeable lot of them, summer came to the mountains in full bloom. The valleys were pockets of color in all hues.

Utes had returned from a very successful hunt and were puzzled by the disappearance of Wind Chaser and his small band. Warriors from Wind Chaser's village were frantically and desperately searching for their families. But so far they failed to search the little valley where Eddie and Wind Chaser and his band had met their deaths. But they would. The wilderness was vast, and it was impossible to look everywhere. The warriors from Wind Chaser's village mistakenly headed north and west in their search, and the little valley, now covered with summer's blossoms, remained untouched, for the time being.

Had they run into Dark Hand, he could have and would have told them what had happened, but Dark Hand had traveled north and east, to rejoin his own people, who were camped over in the unorganized territory that lay just south of the Missouri River.

Sir Elmore had found his saber but wisely kept it sheathed and out of sight because Baron Zaunbelcher had threatened to break it if Elmore ever drew it again.

138

Most of Bones's men were healed up enough to ride, and those that weren't properly healed could either suffer the discomfort and ride, or stay and be left behind. All chose to ride.

The second band of man-hunters was just about the most disreputable looking bunch of ne'er-do-wells that Bones had ever seen. And when the likes of Bones Gibson thought somebody was trash, they couldn't get much lower if they crawled under a snake's belly.

Bones had ridden back to eyeball the second bunch, to see if there might be any men in there that he could use. He found a few possibilities, but for the moment, would stay with what he had. He was back up to strength, just over forty men.

This bunch, he thought sourly, would not last a week in the mountains, not if just one of them made a hostile move against Preacher. Preacher would turn on them like a wild animal and run them all back to the Mississippi. If they made it that far. Bones wisely decided to distance himself from this mangy looking pack of so-called man-hunters.

"You there!" the gruff shout stopped Bones as he was just riding off.

Bones turned to stare at the burly lout who was striding toward him. "What do you want?"

"Where's this here murderer called Preacher?"

Bones laughed at him. "You want him, you find him."

"I'm Lige Watson." The man acted as though that was supposed to mean something.

"So?"

"I'm the toughest man in all of Pennsylvania."

Bones laughed at him. "Then you best head on back to Pennsylvania, Watson. 'Cause out here, you're nothin'."

"We'll see about that."

"Not for very long, you won't." Bones left it at that and rode away.

"Holy jumpin' elephants!" Preacher said, peering through his spy glass. He took a second look just to make certain his eyes weren't deceiving him. They weren't.

It looked to him like about forty or so in the first bunch, and that would be Bones's men, for he could pick out Bones in the lead. Another forty or so in the second bunch, layin' back about a mile behind Bones.

"I shore am gettin' to be a right popular feller," Preacher muttered, putting away his glass. "Damned if that ain't a regular army down yonder. Forty in one bunch and forty in the other. They gonna be fallin' all over one another 'fore this is through." He smiled a wicked curving of his lips. "I'm gonna have me some fun come the night."

What was fun to Preacher could be downright unsettling to others . . . and sometimes lethal.

The floor of the long narrow valley was dotted with camp-fires, with a dark space about a mile in length between the two camps of man-hunters. Lige Watson, the self-appointed leader of the second bunch, walked through the camp, inspecting 'his men,' as he liked to call them.

To Lige, they looked like a very formidable army. In reality, they were about as sloppy a rag-tag bunch of losers as had ever gathered anywhere. The group was made up of those types of people who are constantly out for an easy dollar, who expect the world to give them a handout, who always blame others for their problems, who could never keep a job because the boss 'picked on them.' Among the second group were strong-arm boys, thieves, hustlers, pimps, forgers, murderers, rapists, and every other kind of no-good anybody would care to name.

Really, the social and moral difference between Bones's group and Lige's bunch was minuscule. There wasn't a man in either group worth the gunpowder it would take to blow his brains out.

"Lookin' rale good," Lige said to his friend, Fred Lasalle, after completing his walk-through of the camp. "I'd put these boys up aginst just about any group twicest our size."

"Did you git to talk to any of them royal highnesses?" Fred asked.

"Well, sort of. I spoke to one and he tole me that in all his years he had never stood so clost to such an odorous cretinous moronic specimen of foul humanity."

Fred blinked. "Well, you done good, then, din you?"

"I don't rightly know. I reckon so."

"What do all them words mean, Lige?" Derby Peel asked.

"Means we all right, I guess."

"Thought so."

With the exception of the rendezvous of the mountain men, which had now ceased to be, never had such a large gathering of white men occurred in the Rockies. The stench of unwashed bodies could be smelled for hundreds of yards. No self-respecting Indian would get within an arrow's range of such a group. The smell alone probably contributed to saving their lives from Indians looking for a scalp.

"Whew!" Preacher muttered, as he drew closer to the encampment. His nose wrinkled at the stench of unwashed bodies. A buzzard would have a tough time competing with this bunch, he thought.

Preacher lay on his belly in the tall grass less than fifty yards from Lige's camp and looked over the scene that unfolded before him. It was only slightly less than incredible. The fools had fires blazin' that were big enough to roast a whole buffalo. The big ugly bully-lookin' man someone had called Lige was probably the leader of this skunk-pack, Preacher reckoned. He looked like a man who had a real high opinion of himself the way he strutted around. Preacher took an immediate dislike to him. He'd seen men like Lige before, men who'd come to the mountains and tried to fit in with other trappers. They had not lasted long. Mountain men were hard to impress.

"Well, boys," Lige said to his friends who'd come west with him. "Tomorrow we start huntin' down this Preacher person. I don't figure on it takin' no more than a week. Prob'ly less than that."

Preacher smiled and moved closer until he reached a pocket of darkness. Then he stood up and slipped into the camp. Many of the men were dressed in buckskins so no one paid any attention to Preacher as he walked through the camp and straight up to Lige.

"Howdy," Preacher said. "I got a message from Bones if you be Lige."

"I'm Lige. What's on your mind?"

"Well, Mister Lige, don't get mad at me, I'm just deliverin' the message. Bones said for your men to bring your cups and come on over. They's whiskey a-plenty and food for all. Says both our bunches had best get to know one another. But he said for me to tell you to keep your butt out of his camp. Says if you show up he'll stomp your gizzard out."

"He said *what?*" Lige hollered.

"Oh, he said a lot, Bones did. But I dasn't repeat most of it. It was right insultin' and personal."

"You tell me, mister!" Lige growled the words, as a large crowd gathered around.

"Well, now, don't get mad at me," Preacher said.

"I'm not gonna get mad at you. You just tell me what Bones said."

"Well, he said you smelled worser than a skunk and prob'ly had about as much sense as a jackass. And he called your mamma some real turrible names, he did. I just

142

won't repeat them slurs aginst a good woman. I just won't do it. God might strike me dead."

Lige was so mad he was hopping up and down.

"If you don't mind," Preacher said. "I'd like to leave that bunch of name-callers over yonder and join up with you, Mister Lige. I think Bones is settin' up an ambush for your boys. That's what it looks like to me. Besides that, I just cain't abide a man who'll call another man he don't even know a low-down, no-good, buzzard-puke-breath, dirty son of a bitch like Bones said you was."

Lige's eyes bugged out and his face turned red. His ears wriggled and his adam's apple bobbed up and down. "You stay here," he said to Preacher, finally finding his voice. "I think you a good man. Let's ride, boys. We got a nest of snakes to clean out."

Within seconds, the camp was deserted. Preacher grinned and began wandering through the camp, picking up what supplies he felt he might need. "Gonna be real interestin' over at Bones's camp in about five minutes. Real interestin'." Chuckling, Preacher faded into the night.

Seventeen

"Riders comin', Bones," a guard called. "Looks like that new bunch."

"Now, what you reckon that pack of ninnies wants?" Van Eaton asked.

"They certainly are coming in quite a rush," Baron Zaunbelcher remarked.

Lige and his group rode right through the camp, knocking over pots and scattering bedrolls and sending men scrambling to get out of the way.

"What the hell do you think you're doin', you half-wit?" Bones yelled to Lige.

Lige and his men jumped off their horses. "I got your message, you big mouth no-count!" Lige yelled, marching up to Bones. "And this is my reply." Lige rared back and flattened Bones with a right to the mouth.

Lige's men jumped at Bones's men and the fight was on.

Preacher could hear the shouts and yelling and cussing more than a mile away. Carrying several huge sacks filled with powder horns, food, weapons, candles, matches, and what-have-you, Preacher walked away toward the high-up country. He would have taken several blankets, but they all had fleas hopping around on them.

Bones jumped up and popped Lige right on his big

snoot. The blood and the snot flew and Lige's boots flew out from under him and he landed on his butt.

Bob Jones had tied up with Mack Cornay and the two men were flailing away at one another. Derby Peel had squared off against Van Eaton and the men were exchanging blows, each blow bringing a grunt of pain and the splattering of blood. Fred Lasalle looked around for somebody to hit and his eyes touched on Sir Elmore Jerrold-Taylor, standing beside a fancy wall tent. Fred walked over to the clean shaven and neatly dressed Englishman and without a word being said, slugged him right on the nose. Elmore hollered and grabbed at his busted beak. He drew his hands away and looked at the blood. "I've been wounded!" he yelled.

Jon Louviere jumped on Fred's back and rode him to the earth while Stan Law busted Baron Wilhelm Zaunbelcher in the mouth. With a roar, the Prussian drew back one big fist and sent Stan rolling through the dirt, then turned and kicked Fred Lasalle hard in the belly with a polished boot. That put Fred out for the duration.

Will Herdman jumped on Andy Price and went to pokin' and gougin' and kickin' and bitin' until Andy threw him off and began stomping on him. That went on until Cantry, a good friend of Will's, ran over and hit Andy on the head with a club. Andy's eyes rolled back, he hit the ground, and he didn't wake up for an hour. Will, battered and bloody, said to hell with it all and stretched out beside Andy.

The men in the camp, with the exception of the nobility, who quickly retired to their tents and tied the flaps closed, fought until they were exhausted. Almost to the man, they fell down to the ground and lay there, chests heaving.

Finally, Bones, lying flat on his back in the grass, managed to gasp out to Lige, "What in the hell brought on all this, you igit?"

"Don't you be callin' me no igit, you low-life," said

Lige, who was also stretched out on the cool grass. "And you know what brung it on."

"I don't neither!"

"Do too!"

"Don't!"

"Does!"

"I do not!"

"You think about it. You know!"

"I don't know! Why the hell do you think I'm askin'?"

Even though he wasn't a very smart man, that managed to get through to Lige. He thought about it for a moment. "You sent a feller over to our camp to see me and he said you said a lot of bad things about me."

"I never sent no feller over to see you! And I ain't said no bad things about you. I *thought* a bunch of bad things, but I never said 'em aloud."

Lige ruminated on that for another moment. He raised his bloody head and looked around. "Say, where is that feller anyways?"

"Back yonder at our camp, I reckon," Sutton said, holding a rag to his bloody mouth.

A tiny spark of suspicion entered Bones's head. He raised up on one elbow, the eye that wasn't blackening and closing because of a right cross from Lige's fist narrowed. "What did this here feller look like, Lige?"

"Wal, he were dressed in buckskins. Sorta tall and you could tell he was muscled up right good. He were clean shaven 'ceptin' for a moustache. And he moved real quiet like. Come to think of it, and I just thought of it, he had the coldest meanest eyes I ever did see."

Bones flopped back on the ground. "You igit! That there was *Preacher!*"

"*Preacher?*" Lige hollered. "You mean the man we're a-huntin' come a-struttin' and a-sashshaying bold as brass right up into the big fat middle of our camp and tole me them lies?"

"Yeah." Bones heaved himself up to a sitting position. "Now you might git some idea of the type of man we're huntin.' "

"Nervy ol' boy, ain't he?" Lige muttered around a swollen mouth.

"You could say that," Bones replied.

When Lige and company returned to their camp, Lige found a note written on a scrap of paper and stuck on a tree limb. He laboriously read the missive.

"What do it ay, Lige?" Fred Lasalle asked, peering over Lige's shoulder.

"It says, 'Git out of these mountins. I won't warn you agin. This here is yore only warnin'. Preacher."

"The man must think he owns these here mountains!" Hugh Fuller said.

"Yeah!" a man called Billy said. "To hell with him."

A huge hulking monster of a man whose hands extended past his knees, giving him a distinct ape-like appearance, said, "I don't like this feller Preacher. I'm a-gonna tear his arms out when I find him and beat him to death with 'em."

"Way to go, Lucas," a much smaller man, only about five feet tall yelled. "That'll be fun to watch."

Lucas grinned at the man. What teeth had not rotted out were green and his breath could cause a buzzard to faint. "You and me, Willie. We'll catch this Preacher and be rich."

"All right, boys," Lige hollered. "Gather round. Come on, come on. I got things to say." When the camp had quieted down and the men gathered in a circle, Lige said, "At first light we start huntin' this murderin' no-count. And we'uns is gonna be workin' side by side with them ol' boys over yonder in the other camp. I think . . ."

"Hey!" a man hollered. "My powder horn's gone. Jeff, didn't you lay out a side of bacon to slice."

"Yeah. Why?"

"Well, it's gone too."

The men all ran to their bedrolls and blankets and tents. Soon, many of the men were cussing and stomping around.

"Preacher stole all the stuff," Bob Jones said. "He took enough powder to blow up half these mountains."

Preacher wasn't at all interested in blowing up the mountains. He had other things in mind.

The Cheyenne war chief called Bear Killer sat on his horse and looked down at the huge body of men in the valley below. He, along with representatives from the Ute, Arapaho, Kiowa-Apache, and the Southern Comanches were all traveling east, to make peace with each other. The location was about seventy-five miles east of Bent's Fort. The gathering of various tribes and the making of peace between them had been the idea of High Backed Wolf, a Cheyenne chief, a very famous warrior, and a man known for his diplomatic skills. He felt it was foolish to fight amongst themselves. After the historic meeting, which history only skims over very lightly, those tribes never again made war against the other.

Bear Killer looked down at the white men and shook his head. "Preacher cannot fight so many men and win. Perhaps we should wait until darkness comes and slip into the camp of the white men and help Preacher," he said to one of his warriors.

But the warrior shook his head. "No. Standing Bull said that Tall Man of the Arapaho told him that Preacher wants no help. This is a personal matter."

"Ummm. Yes. I remember. Preacher is indeed a brave warrior. I hope we never have to fight him again."

"Little Eagle told Stands Alone that the white men down there smell terrible. They do not wash their bodies and are very loud and vulgar. They kill animals and birds and leave them to rot on the ground. They do not dig proper places to dispose of their waste. They are not good people. They are wasteful and ignorant."

"I hope Preacher kills them all. If there are any left upon our return, we shall give Preacher some help in ridding our land of these worthless men. Without his knowledge, of course."

The Indians waited until the whites had passed and then rode on to their historical meeting on the Arkansas.

Several miles away, watching from near the timber line, Preacher could just make out the long double line of riders as they headed north. Preacher mounted up and headed south, staying in the timber far above the valley floor, no more than a shadow as he worked his way along.

He saw Bear Killer and his warriors and they saw him. The men passed within a few hundred yards of each other, lifted right hands, palms out, and rode on without speaking. Preacher picketed Thunder near water and began working his way toward the sprawling camp of the man-hunters. Using his spy glass, Preacher studied the camp. It was just about like he'd figured. Bones had left no guards behind. Only the cooks and servants were there, and Preacher wanted them gone. So far they had taken no part in the man-hunt, and Preacher held no animosity toward them. He spent the better part of an hour working his way up to the camp.

Preacher almost scared one of the servants out of his shoes when he suddenly rose up out of the grass about a yard from the man and said, "Howdy!"

The man dropped a load of tin plates he'd just washed and clutched at his chest, his mouth open and his eyes wide with fear. The others stood still and stared at Preacher. None of them made any move toward the rifles that had been placed around the camp in case of hostiles attacking.

"Relax," Preacher told the cooks and servants. "I ain't here to do none of you no harm. Y'all dish me up a plate of that good-smelling grub and a cup of coffee and we'll talk." Preacher sat down on the ground while a cook quickly served up a heaping plate of food.

Preacher thanked the man and said, "You boys reckon you could find your way out of these mountains?"

"Certainly," a man-servant replied. "I served in the British Army before gaining employment with the Duke. My experience with rugged terrain is vast."

"Is that a fact? Well, was I you boys, I'd busy myself packin' up and then I'd get the hell gone from here. Y'all ain't tooken no part in huntin' me, and I'm obliged to you for that. Your bosses is miles north of here, lookin' for me in all the wrong places, as usual. Now boys, when they do catch up with me, it's gonna get right nasty. Start packin'."

The servants and cooks exchanged glances. One said, "What about the savages?"

"They ain't gonna bother you none. They got themselves a big pow-wow down on the Arkansas. The four main tribes is gonna make peace with each other. 'Sides, they's enough of you and y'all's well armed. It would take a powerful big bunch of Injuns to attack you. When you get down to Bent's Fort, you ask around and hook up with supply wagons headin' back east and tag along with them for extree safety."

Several of the men turned and began packing. The others soon followed suit. One said, "The horses do not belong to us. There will be warrants issued for our arrest."

Preacher smiled. "There ain't nobody gonna be alive to issue no warrants, boys. There ain't none of that bunch gonna leave these mountains. Or damn few of them. So y'all take whatever you feel like takin'. Now, y'all seem like right nice fellers. So I'm gonna give you some advice. Y'all are all foreigners. You don't know nothin' about the West, and the men who has spent their lives out here. Look at me."

The cooks and servants stopped packing and looked.

Preacher patted the stock of his rifle. "This is the law out here, boys. No fancy robed judges or high-falutin' lawyers or badge-totin' lawmen. This is all there is. Now y'all hooked up with some mighty bad company. Maybe you didn't know what you was gettin' yourselves in for. I'll think that. 'Cause if you give me reason to think otherwise, I'd not look kindly upon you."

"We were told it was a hunting expedition," one said. "We had no reason to think it was anything else. We did not learn the truth until we were far from civilization back in Missouri—if civilization is the right word—and were in the middle of all that vastness."

"Pack and git!"

When the men had left, Preacher began gathering up all the blankets, tents, food, clothing, and medical supplies. He piled everything up and then went to the other camp and did the same. Then he set fire to the mess and began running across the valley floor to the slopes. When Bones and the gentry spotted the smoke, they'd come gallopin'. Preacher smiled as he ran effortlessly across the meadow. There was gonna be some mighty irritated folks when they saw what he'd done. Mighty irritated.

BOOK TWO

I can be pushed just so far.

Harry Leon Wilson

One

"The dirty, rotten, no good . . ." Bones went on a rampage, cussing and jumping up and down and throwing himself about like a spoiled child in the throes of a temper tantrum.

The men had managed to save quite a number of articles from the fires. But their tents were gone as were many of the blankets and spare clothing.

To heap insult upon injury, Preacher had left another note reading:

I WARNED YOU

A dozen men from Lige's bunch exchanged glances and without saying a word, mounted up and rode out. If they had any luck at all, they could catch up with the cooks and servants and ride back east with them. They wanted no more of Preacher.

Bones and Van Eaton and the royalty watched the men leave without comment. They were glad to be rid of them. Lige cussed the deserters and shook his fist at them and shouted dire threats until he was hoarse, but that was all he did.

Unbeknownst to Lige's people, at the orders of the royalty, Bones, Van Eaton, and men had buried a great deal of supplies carefully wrapped them in oilcloth and canvas.

"That was good thinkin'," Bones said to Sir Elmore after he had calmed down.

"Naturally," the Englishman replied.

No man among them had any way of knowing that a small group of settlers and a few missionaries had already left Bent's Fort, heading for the Rockies to establish a settlement and a church. The problem was, they were being guided by a man who was so inept he would have trouble finding the altar in a church.

"I am thrilled beyond words," Patience Comstock said to her sister, Prudence, as they bounced along in a wagon. "This is such a grand adventure. We'll be doing the work of the Lord by bringing God to the savages."

"Yes," Prudence agreed, tying her bonnet strap under her chin. "And won't Father and Mother be surprised to learn about that Preacher man they told us about back at the fort? Just think, Sister, a man of the Cloth so well-known and so devout, so ... so, strong in his faith and loved by all that even the savages call him Preacher."

"Yes, sister. But I wonder why the Methodist Board of Missions didn't tell us about this man?"

"Well, he might be of another faith, dear."

"Of course. I'm sure that's it. No matter. We're all doing God's work." Patience tucked a few strands of auburn hair back under her bonnet. "I'm sure he's a fine gentlemen."

"That dirty son!" Bones muttered, looking at the scorched boots he'd managed to pull from the smoldering mess. "I paid good money for these back in St. Louis." He tossed the ruined boots aside. "Preacher. *Preacher?* How did a man like that ever get the name of Preacher?" he questioned with a snarl.

As it turns out, early on Preacher was captured by Indians and while they were mulling over whether to kill him outright or torture him to see how brave he was, the young man started preaching the gospel—sort of—to them. He preached for hours and hours and hours until the Indians finally reached the conclusion that he was crazy and turned him loose. Once the story got around, and that didn't take long, he was known as Preacher.

Preacher did nothing for several days except watch. He had been sure that once he burned the supplies of the man-hunters, they'd all give up and go home. He'd told the cooks and servants that he was going to kill all those after him just to get them moving. The truth was, Preacher's deep grief and hot anger over the death of Eddie and Wind Chaser had tempered somewhat. He could kill ten times the number of those men after him and that wouldn't bring the dead back to life.

He just wanted this over and to live his life in peace.

"Damn," Preacher said, lowering the spy glass. "What's it gonna take to discourage them fools down yonder?"

Some of the men were real woodsmen and frontiersmen. They'd been smoking fish and meat and making jerky and really eatin' pretty high on the hog. And Preacher had seen where a whole passel of supplies had been dug up. He had stung the man-hunters some, but that was about it.

Preacher didn't know it, but his troubles were only just beginning.

"Oh, sister," Patience said to her twin, Prudence. "Aren't they magnificent?"

"Breathtaking, sister."

They were gazing at the Rockies.

One of the settlers, a good solid, sturdy young man of

German stock, named Otto Steiner, walked up to the twins' wagon. "Quite a sight, ja, ladies?"

"Oh, Mister Steiner, they are just beautiful!" Patience cooed.

"Ja, ja. All of that. Well, I just want to see those lovely rich valleys and lakes in those mountains where a man and his wife can raise kids and vegetables and have cows and fish and hunt. We go on now." He waved at the scout, who was now sober, having exhausted his supply of whiskey. "We go, man. Take us through the mountains."

The scout, known only as Wells, nodded his head and picked up the reins. "I ain't gar-enteein' nothin'. But we'll give it a shot."

"What do you mean, sir?" Patience demanded. "We were told back in Missouri that you knew this country."

"Wal, they lied. I ain't never been this far a-fore. And to tell you the truth, I ain't real thrilled about goin' no further, neither. So I don't think I will."

"What does that mean?" Otto asked.

"Means I quit." Without another word, he rode away, heading east. He did not look back.

The four wagons and eight people suddenly looked awfully tiny with the majestic mountains looming in front of them.

"Well now," Frank Collins said, walking up with his wife of only a few months with him. "This sort of leaves us in a pickle, doesn't it?"

"The Lord will see us through," Jane Collins said, smiling up at her husband.

Hanna Steiner joined the group, as did Paul and Sally Marks. "I didn't like that Wells person anyway," Hanna said bluntly. "He was a very untidy man who did not bathe enough and he cussed. I cannot abide a man who swears."

"Ja, Hanna," Otto said. "You are right about that, you surely are."

"Well!" Patience said, flouncing on the wagon seat. "We

158

must press on." She picked up the reins. "The Lord is with us and surely He will hear our prayers this evening and send His man of faith in the wilderness, Preacher, to guide us through. I am certain of that. Onward, people. We'll lift our voices in Christian song as we travel through the wilderness." She popped the big rear mules on the butt with the reins and off they went, creaking and lurching and singing across the plains, only a few miles from the Rockies. The faint sounds of song could be heard as the young pioneers headed bravely into the unknown.

The fare in the camp of Bones had decidedly gone downhill with their cooks leaving and much of their supplies destroyed. It was now mostly venison and beans. And not one sign of Preacher had been found by the daily patrols. It had been two weeks since the cooks and servants left and Preacher had burned their camp.

"I think the man has fled," Robert Tassin said.

"I concur," his countryman, Jon Louviere agreed.

Bones and Van Eaton, sitting on the ground a few yards away, listened but said nothing. It really made no difference to either man. The longer they stayed out, the more money they made. The rules and rates of this 'game' had changed. With the exception of Bones and Van Eaton, each man was being paid five dollars a day, a very princely sum for the time. Bones and Van Eaton were receiving substantially more. In addition, when, or if, Preacher was found, and the aristocracy killed him, each man in the group would receive a cash bonus. The entire group could have the reward money posted on Preacher's head. Literally. For the reward money could only be claimed by bringing Preacher's head back as proof. A carefully packed glass jug and pickling solution had been brought by the second group.

Up near the timber line, Preacher was getting bored. His hopes that the hunting party would go away and leave him alone had been dashed. On this clear and crisp mid-summer morning, just as dawn was lighting the horizon, Preacher reckoned it was time to open this ball and he was going to lead the band. He picked up two rifles and headed out.

Patience and Prudence and party had broken camp and were on the move. They were about eight miles away at dawn.

The camp of the man-hunters had shifted, the unwashed multitudes crawling out of their blankets, shaking out the fleas and various other bugs and headed for the creek for coffee water.

Bones was squatting by the fire, warming his hands and waiting for the water to boil. He was always surly in the mornings and this morning he was surlier than usual. Even Van Eaton did not dare to speak to him. The gentry were gathered together, as usual. They preferred their own company to that of the unwashed.

Bones reached for the coffee pot just as a rifle ball banged against the big iron kettle and ripped off, the flattened and ragged ricochet striking a man-hunter in the center of the forehead and dropping him dead on the ground. Bones kissed the earth, flattening out on his belly.

One of Bones's original group, Joey York, was a tad slow in reacting and Preacher's second shot ended his man-hunting days forever. The ball from the fancy hunting rifle punched a hole in Joey's chest and knocked him into a cookfire, setting his clothing and greasy hair ablaze. The ensuing smell was not exactly conducive to a good appetite.

"Did anybody spot the smoke?" Van Eaton yelled, from his position behind a tree near the creek.

"Do we ever?" Tom Evans called.

"Somebody pull Joey out the fire," Bones said. "The smell is makin' me ill."

One of the second party, a man called Stanley, jumped up and made it halfway to the smoldering body of Joey before Preacher nailed him, dusting the man from side to side. Stanley stumbled and fell dead without making a sound.

"He's got to be in that little stand of trees over yonder," Cal Johnson yelled, sticking his head up and peering over the log he was hiding behind. "But that's a good three hundred yards off. Man, he can *shoot!*"

Preacher's rifle boomed and Cal lost part of an ear. He fell back behind the log, squalling in pain as the blood poured. "Oh, God, he's kilt me!" Cal screamed.

Falcon glanced at him. "Naw. You'll live. But you gonna be wearin' yore hat funny from now on."

"Jesus!" Stan Law yelled, "Joey's stinkin' something fierce. Cain't nobody haul him outta there?"

"You want him out, you haul him out," Horace Haywood called. "I ain't movin'."

A man called Hoppy, because of the way he walked—one leg was shorter than the other—jumped up and hip-hopped toward the fire. Preacher fired again and now Hoppy's left leg was equal to his right. The ball took off about half of his left foot. Hoppy flopped on the ground, screaming to high heaven.

"Charge, men!" Sir Elmore ordered. "Into the fray!"

"Charge yoresalf!" Derby Peel told him.

"By God I will!" Sir Elmore said. "Where's my saber?"

Baron Zaunbelcher quickly scurried away from Elmore.

"Stay down!" Bones yelled. "Don't be a fool. Preacher's got us cold."

"He's movin'!" Jimmie Cook yelled. "Headin' off to the south. If he makes the crick, he's gone for sure."

Sir Elmore jumped up, waving his saber. Baron

Zaunbelcher was keeping a good eye on the Englishman. "Now's our chance. Charge, men!" Elmore ran toward the creek, waving his saber. Burton Sullivan and Willy Steinwinder right behind him.

"Oh, Lord!" Bones said, crawling to his boots. "Come on, boys. We can't let nothing happen to them silly people."

En masse, the entire camp—those who were able—came to their feet, all running after Preacher, waving rifles and pistols and yelling and cussing. But Preacher had left the creek and was hiding among the trees that lined the bank. He caught sight of the sun flashing off of Elmore's blade and sighted in. The ball clanged against the polished steel and Elmore's entire body experienced the sensation of a railroad spike being hit with a sledge hammer. For a moment, before Burton hauled him down, Elmore looked like a man with a bad case of the twitches.

Using his second rifle, Preacher took aim and put a ball into a man's belly and the man tumbled to his knees and then slowly fell into the creek, face first. Two minutes later he had drowned. Preacher watched the entire running human wave hit the ground and he took off running, zigging and zagging through the grass and brush, heading for the ridges. Very quickly Preacher was out of rifle range and gone. He reached his horse and headed south.

Back at the camp of the man-hunters, they were busy patching up the wounded and seeing to the disposal of the dead. Elmore's right hand had stopped its twitching. He was looking sorrowfully at his slightly bent saber.

"Throw it away," Zaunbelcher urged.

"Indeed not! It's only bent a little. My father carried this sword during the War of 1812."

Baron Zaunbelcher almost said he now knew the reason the British lost, but thought better of it at the last second.

Preacher had put several miles behind him and the now scared, shook-up, and bloody band of man-hunters. He wasn't worried about them following him; not this soon anyway. He threaded his way through the timber, topped a ridge, and looked down into one of the prettiest valleys in this part of the country. He stared hard at the scene before him. He blinked. But the scene remained unchanged.

Four wagons, a half a dozen cows, one of which was probably a bull, and riding horses.

Four wagons? Here? Now?

Preacher rode down the grade and across the meadow just as the pilgrims were climbing down to the lush grass and flowers of the valley floor. Preacher had not had a bath in several days and it had been a couple of weeks since he'd shaved. His buckskins were stained and his hat had damn sure seen better days. He knew he looked rougher than a cob and meaner than a bear, but at the moment, he didn't much care. He rode right up to the wagons and got himself a jolt. Two of the finest-lookin' women he'd put eyes on in a-while stood side by side. Twins, with no difference he could spot in them at all.

"Howdy, folks!" Preacher called. "Y'all ain't got no drinkin' whiskey with you, now has you? I feel the need for a little Who Hit John."

"Sir!" one of the twins piped right up. "I'll have you know we are on a mission for God. We do not sanction with the partaking of strong drink."

"Do tell. Well, I'll be damned."

"And we do not hold with swearing, either!" Hanna said, standing with hands on hips. She was a trifle ample across the beam for Preacher's liking, but still a handsome woman.

"You don't say? Well . . . dip me in buffalo crap and call me stinky."

One of the twins stepped closer and stared at him. "Sir? Are you a mountain man?"

"I reckon. I been in these mountains ever since I was

163

knee-high to a frog. What are you folks doin' out here all by your lonesome?"

Everybody started talking at once in a babble of voices. Preacher dismounted and stood silently before them until they settled down. When quiet prevailed, Preacher said, "I was just kiddin' y'all 'bout that whiskey. I got me a couple of jugs stashed up in the brush that I stole from some guys."

"You . . . *stole* some whiskey?" Prudence asked.

"Yeah."

"Why?"

"So's I could drink it."

"There are other people close-by?" Otto asked.

"Oh, yeah. I'd guess near'bouts seventy or so about five miles yonder way." He pointed.

"Seventy?" Patience blurted.

"Yeah."

"What are they doing?"

"Doin' their best to kill me, ma'am."

"Kill you!" Sally shrieked. "Why?"

"'Cause I been killin' as many of them as I could, that's why."

The men and women all wore stunned looks on their faces. "You have been . . . killing them?" Frank Collins asked.

"Oh, yeah. I reckon up to the moment I've kilt . . . well, oh, fifteen or twenty, I reckon. But it's all right, 'cause they started it."

"You have personally killed fifteen or twenty men in your life?" Prudence asked, her face pale.

"Oh, no, ma'am. That's just in the last few weeks. I lost count on how many men I've kilt over the years. White men, that is."

"What . . . what is your name?" Patience asked.

"Preacher."

Patience paled.

"How many other men out here are called Preacher?" she asked in a tiny voice.

"Just me."

Patience fainted.

Two

Otto caught the woman before she hit the ground and gently placed her in the shade of a wagon.

"What's the matter with her?" Preacher asked. "She comin' down with the vapors?"

Prudence glared up at him. "You . . . you . . . brute!"

"What did I do?" Preacher questioned, looking at the men and women.

Frank Collins said, "Really, nothing, sir. We all were under the impression that you were a man of God, that's why Patience fainted."

Preacher was clearly puzzled. Something was all out of whack here and he couldn't figure out what it was. "A man of God? I been called a lot of things over the years, but damned if I've ever been called that."

"Sir," Hanna said, looming menacingly before him. "I must insist that you refrain from swearing."

Preacher sighed. Before he could tell Hanna what was foremost on his mind, and after doing that would probably have to shoot her husband, Patience moaned and sat up.

"I had the most terrible dream," she said, her face flushed. 'I dreamt that we were confronted by a horrible man who drank whiskey and ran around killing people." Her eyes began to focus and they focused on Preacher. "Oh, my word! It wasn't a nightmare."

"Now, I have been called that a time or two," Preacher admitted. "Y'all splash some water on that female's face and get her up. I got to talk to y'all. This just ain't no place for pilgrims to be at any time, most especially right now." He looked at Hanna. "You make some coffee and put on some grub. I got a case of the hongries flung on me. I'm goin' over yonder to that crick and take me a wash and a shave. I'll be back."

"Well!" Hanna flounced about as Preacher turned his back to her and swung into the saddle.

"Do it," Otto told her. "I think that, if I understand correctly his quaint way of speaking, we are in trouble here. I want to hear what he has to say."

Prudence helped Patience to her feet and got her unflustered. Fifteen minutes later, Preacher reappeared. His buckskins were still stained, but he had taken a short bath and shaved the heavy growth of beard from his face.

"He really is a very handsome man," the woman all silently concurred.

"He really is a very dangerous man," the men all silently concurred.

Preacher poured a cup of coffee and squatted down. The coffee was weak for his tastes, but he made no mention of that. "Now listen up, pilgrims. I got to tell you what's goin' on. Then you make up your own minds 'bout what kind of man I am. Not that your opinion means a damn to me. But I don't like to be judged wrongly."

While the bacon and fried potatoes were cooking, Preacher took it from the top, beginning with him and Eddie leaving civilization back east and the reasons why. When he finished telling about burying Eddie and his little paint pony, the only dry eye in the bunch was his. A couple of minutes later, he said, "Well, that's it, folks."

"I wonder why we heard nothing about the bounty on you?" Frank Collins asked.

"Prob'ly 'cause y'all don't frequent taverns and saloons

and the like," Preacher told him. "Nor do you associate with them that does." He smiled. "Them mountain men back at the fort who told you I was a preacher of the gospel . . . you 'member any names?"

"Well," Hanna said. "There was this huge fellow called Horsehide Jack."

Preacher started grinning.

"Yes," Patience said. "And there was another gentlemen with the unsightly name of Pistol Pete."

Preacher's grin spread.

"And one great bear of a man they called Papa Griz."

Preacher laughed. "Them ol' boys was havin' a high ol' time puttin' you folks on, was what they was doin.' Don't feel hard toward 'em. They didn't mean no harm. They was just funnin'. Humor gets sorta dark out here in the wilderness. 'Cause a lot of the time, they ain't a whole hel . . . heck of a lot to laugh about."

"I fear that because of my insistence that we press on," Patience said, "I have placed us all in great danger."

Preacher thought about that. "Maybe," he finally said. "But not if y'all will play along with a lie I'm dreamin' up right now."

"Whatever in the world do you mean, sir?" Prudence asked.

Preacher grinned and told her.

Preacher had carefully stashed the pilgrims and their livestock and wagons in a little canyon on the east side of the valley and told them not to light fires nor venture past the tree and brush lined entrance of the canyon. Then Preacher set out to find some man-hunters. Only this time he didn't have killing on his mind. Well, not much anyway.

"Look!" Van Eaton cried out, pointing.

The small group of men looked at the man with a white handkerchief tied to the barrel of his rifle.

"By the Lord!" breathed Sir Elmore. "That's our quarry."

"He wants to talk," Bones said. "He's comin' under a white flag. We'll honor it."

The gentry with him looked at Bones as if he had gone mad. "You can't be serious, sir!" Robert Tassin said.

"I'm serious. A white flag is a white flag. We'll honor it."

Preacher rode slowly toward the six man team, stopping about ten yards from them. Bones and Elmore rode out to meet him. "You boys got another problem facin' you," Preacher said. "Not near 'bouts as dangerous as me, but a problem nonetheless."

"And what might that be, sir?" Elmore asked.

"The Methodist church sent out a flock of missionaries to bring the gospel to the heathens. They're holed up over yonder in a valley. I run into them some time back and told them what was goin' on here, 'tween us. The scouts that brung them in has gone back with a message to the church board and the President of the United States. They tooken all your names back on paper to give to important folks back east. Anything happens to them missionaries, and you'll all have federal warrants out on you. The war 'tween us is still on, but them Bible-shoutin' folks had best be left alone."

Sir Elmore Jerrold-Taylor's back straightened. "Sir, no harm shall come to those missionaries. I am a Christian myself and believe strongly in the Lord."

Preacher had no immediate comment on that, but his thoughts were grim. If this fool really believed himself a Christian person, then Preacher could pass for a duck. "Fine." He looked at Bones. "How about your boys?"

"They'll stay clear."

"Them missionaries, over my objections, has volunteered to set up a make-shift hospital and take care of the wounded. That all right with you?"

"Fine with me."

"That's wonderful," Sir Elmore said. "That's very gracious of them. But you destroyed all our medical supplies," he added with a pout. "That wasn't very sporting of you."

"Well, shame on me," Preacher said sarcastically. "My goodness! You just can't depend on nobody nowadays to be a good sport, can you?"

"Oh, quite true. Quite true."

Preacher shook his head at the Englishman's words. He couldn't figure out if the man was serious or just a teetotal damned fool. He backed Thunder up some twenty feet or so. "Now you boys do the same," he told the men. When they were about fifty feet apart, Preacher said, "Next time we see each other, you best start shootin'. 'Cause this is the last time I aim to be cordial with you."

"We'll do that, Preacher."

"Head on out," Preacher ordered.

"Don't you trust us?" Sir Elmore asked.

"Hell, no." He leveled his rifle. Bones and Elmore turned their horses, rejoined their group, and they all got gone.

"Do you trust these bounty hunters to keep their word, Preacher?" Otto asked.

Dark in the missionary's camp. The women had cooked up a fine meal and Preacher was laying back against his saddle, drinking coffee and smoking his pipe. "'Bout as far as I can pick up a grizzly bear and throw it."

"You said one of the nobility was called Zaunbelcher, is that correct?"

"Yeah. He's a baron. Whatever the hel . . . heck that means."

"It's a fine old family," Otto said. "But starting about a

century back, they began marrying very closely. I'm afraid insanity is running in their blood now."

"I don't doubt that a bit. But you don't have to worry about that no more."

"Oh? Why?"

"'Cause I'm a-fixin' to stop his clock, that's why."

Paul Marks stared at Preacher across the fire. "You are going to fight seventy-odd men all by yourself?"

"They was close to a hundred or better when I started. And they'll be about ten less this time tomorrow."

"You say those deadly words so . . . casually." Patience said. "Doesn't human life mean anything to you?"

"Them folks huntin' me ain't human, Missy. You think about that."

A coyote pack started up, lifting their voices to the sky. The women shivered at the sound.

Preacher smiled. "The Injuns call them Song Dogs, ladies. They're sacred to some tribes. Coyote won't hurt you. Neither will a wolf if you leave the poor beast alone."

"Song Dogs?" Prudence questioned.

"Shore. Just listen to 'em. They's makin' pretty music. Just listen and enjoy it."

"You ever been married, Preacher?" Frank asked.

"The Injun way, yeah. I got kids. Y'all prob'ly frown on that, but that's the way it's done out here. And don't think Injuns take marriage lightly, 'cause they don't. Injuns is human people. Their ways is just different from ours, that's all. I don't agree with a lot of what they do, but then, I do agree with a lot they believe in and practice. When this little trouble of mine is all cleared up, I'll sit you down and try to convince you to head on back east. The Injuns don't want your religion, and they don't need it."

"Whatever in the world do you mean by that?" Patience cried. "They're poor unsaved heathens."

"They ain't no such of a damn thing, Missy. They worship the same God you do . . . in a way, that is. Their God has many names, but they all amount to the same thing. Man Above, Wakan Tanka, Grandfather Spirit, Great Mystery Power, Heammawihio—The Wise One Above. The God of the Pawnees is Tirawa, and they sacrifice a human to that God. And it's a terrible sacrifice, too. Now, I don't hold with that a-tall." Preacher picked up a handful of dirt and let it slowly dribble to the ground. "This is Grandmother Earth. The earth is life. The Injun respects the land and the critters on it.

"No, folks, the Injun has their own religion. When an Injun dies, his soul, tasoom, in Cheyenne, travels up the Hanging Road." Preacher smiled again. "That's the Milky Way to us. The Injun believes that after death everything is good; there is no reason to fear death. And that only those who take their own lives won't never rest in a peaceful village in the Land Beyond. Now as far as I'm concerned, that pretty much goes along with what's in the Good Book."

"But they must be baptized in the blood to be saved!" Patience said.

"I don't believe that, Missy. And I don't believe a person's got to congregate, neither. I think if a body accepts that there is a higher power over us all, and tries to live right, that person ain't gonna be denied entrance to the Land Beyond. You think there ain't gonna be no horses and dogs and cats and coyotes and wolves in Land Beyond? If that's the case, I don't want to go."

"You don't mean that, sir!" Hanna almost shouted the words.

"That's blasphemy!" Sally said.

"I just figure it's the truth," Preacher replied. "Be a mighty sorry damn place without critters to make friends with." He stood up and stretched. "Y'all sleep sound. I'll be around. But I'll be pullin' out 'fore dawn. Y'all might not see me for a few days." He walked off, quickly lost in the darkness.

"The man is either a simpleton and a fool, or a highly complex person," Frank Collins remarked.

"He's no fool," his wife said softly.

"He certainly is a very confident man," Paul Marks said.

"I . . . don't believe I have ever met a man quite like him," Patience admitted. "He is . . . delightful."

He was also gone when the pilgrims awakened the next morning. While they slept soundly, Preacher had built up the fire, made coffee for them, and left them a rather ominous note.

YOU FOLKS BEST TAKE TO SLEPIN LIGHT. OR YOU GOIN TO WAKE UP SOME MORNIN AND BE DAID.

While Hanna, the self-appointed cook for the group, was slicing bacon, the sound of a single shot came faintly to the gathering of young men and women.

"Oh, dear," Patience said. "I hope nothing has happened to Mister Preacher."

Hanna looked at her and smiled.

Prudence looked at her and frowned.

The men glanced at one another and winked.

Their wives said to their husbands, "Now, you stop that!"

About three miles away, Bones squatted down in the brush and looked at the dead man. He was one of Lige's group who had gone into the woods to take care of his morning's business and instead got him a bullet in the head.

Bones was extra cautious this day as he crouched behind a tree, presenting no target at all. There had been something in Preacher's voice yesterday that told him game time was all over. The mountain man was through playing; from now on, it was going to be a deadly business.

"Is the wretch dead?" Duke Burton Sullivan yelled.

"Yeah."

"Oh, drat!"

Bones inched his way back to the edge of the camp he would have sworn was as secure as a fort. He knew damn well that Preacher, as soon as he fired, had changed position. He was probably on the other side of the camp now. Waiting as silently and as menacingly as a big puma. Watching through those cold hard eyes. It was not a real comfortable feeling.

"Everyone turn around," Bones said. "Until we're in a circle. Preacher'll have no choice but to stand and fight and die, or leave. Now move out."

But Preacher had already left the area. He had slipped in a ravine a few hundred yards from the enemy camp and snaked over the lip a few hundred yards later. He'd had him a hunch that sooner or later Bones would wise up and do something smart for a change. It was about time for him to start using his noggin.

"Preacher!" a man shouted from the camp. "I know you ain't gonna answer me, but just listen. Me and two others want out. We're through. We quit."

"You yeller skunks!" Lige yelled.

"Call us whut you will, Lige. We're quitting this here hunt. Preacher! We're ridin' out. We're done. Don't shoot for God's sake."

God, Preacher thought. How come when the goin' gits tough, sorry low-lifes like them yonder start to callin' on God when they never give Him a thought 'fore now? Preacher remained still and silent and waited.

The men took a chance that Preacher wouldn't shoot and quickly packed up, saddled up, and rode out.

Cuts it down some, Preacher thought, watching the three men until they were out of sight.

The men in the camp began their fanning out in an ever broadening circle and Preacher pulled out. He figured they'd be looking for him all morning, and he had some things he wanted to do. He began leaving a very faint trail, knowing that some of those in Bones and Lige's camp

174

were real woodsmen and wouldn't fall for too obvious a trail. He laid the trail winding out of the valley and up into the mountains. He left a broken branch here, a scar on bare ground there, as he left the valley and headed for the high up. He'd already done all the work for the surprise he had in mind. Now if Bones and them would just come to the party.

Three

"He's gettin' tired," Van Eaton said. "I tole you we'd wear him down after a time."

"I do believe you're right, old boy," Burton Sullivan said. "Come, come. Let's press on."

Not using his spy-glass for fear the sun would reflect off the lenses, Preacher squatted up near the tree line and watched the tiny, ant-like figures pause for a time, and then move on, following his faint trail. "That's right, boys. Just like the spider, I'm a-waitin'. So come on."

Preacher moved over to his already picked out and readied position and waited. Those below had sense enough to know they'd kill a horse trying to ride up, so they dismounted and were spread out, coming up in a single stretched out line, about a thousand feet wide.

Preacher made himself comfortable and settled down for a time. He knew it would take the men below him thirty minutes or so to get where he wanted them.

"He slipped and cut himself here!" Tige shouted. "He's hurt and headin' for the high up, jist like a damn animal."

Bones and Van Eaton inspected the blood. And it was blood. Preacher had found where a big puma had killed a deer and hid the carcass after eating. He carefully looked around him, for the deer was still warm, and then put the heart and liver in a piece of the animal's hide and got the hell away from that place. He didn't want to have to fight no mountain lion . . . not just yet anyways.

"You mighty right about that," Bones admitted. "He's hurt bad, too. Look at all that blood. Come on, boys. We got him."

"Superb!" Jon Louviere said.

"The blood trail goes right up this grade," Falcon said. "I don't know how bad he's hurt, but he's leakin' some."

High above them, Preacher put his back against the rock wall behind him and both feet against a huge boulder. Once he got that rock rollin', it would pick up hundreds of other rocks and give Bones and them some grief . . . a lot of grief, Preacher hoped. While all the dust was fillin' the air, Preacher would shift over to another spot he'd inspected and rigged up, and supplied with a few goodies.

The men grew closer and Preacher smiled. "Bye, bye, boys," he whispered, and laid into the boulder.

There was no place to run. This high up, only a few scrub trees grew in their weird twisted shapes. They offered no protection against the tons of rocks coming down the grade at avalanche speeds.

One thing could be said about the nobility. They were all excellent mountain climbers and all had a healthy respect for the mountains. All were uneasy about this high-up, long, and ragged, rocky grade. They'd seen terrible accidents in the Alps, and this smelled like a tragedy about to happen. They lagged back and to one side.

Willy Steinwinder heard it first, and experienced the ground begin to tremble under his expensive hand-made boots. "Slide!" he yelled, and started running for safety, the others in his party right along with him.

The other men looked up, horror and fear in their eyes, their dirty and unshaven faces paling at the furious sight tumbling toward them.

A man from Tennessee glanced over at his friend, Webber, just as a melon sized rock, traveling at great speed, slammed into Webber's face and took his head off. The blood spurted a good three feet into the air. The Tennessee man had about two seconds to scream before the rock slide buried him.

Bones ran soundlessly to one side, Van Eaton right beside him. They got clear of the major slide, but both were pelted with fist-sized rocks and both were bloodied and bruised.

Lige Watson lost his footing as a rock slammed into his head and sent him sprawling ... but knocked him safely out of the major portion of the slide.

Jimmie Cook was flattened by a huge boulder and bloody bits and pieces of him were scattered all the way down to the valley floor.

Four men from Lige's group were pinned down and could do nothing except scream in fright and stare in horror and wait for death to clamp its cold hand around them, which it did, leaving no trace of the men behind.

The men were running for their lives, knowing it was hopeless; for many this was to be their last race. Behind them, shattered and bloody arms and legs were sticking grotesquely out of the dirt and rocks.

Preacher had shifted positions as soon as the dust began to rise from the tons of rocks tumbling down the grade, and was belly down, watching the massive slide snuff the life from the bounty-hunters.

It was over in a less than a minute. But the dust was so thick it restricted visibility for several minutes. A man from Maryland known only as Teddy staggered out onto the now barren slope and stood dumbly for a moment. Preacher's rifle barked and Teddy began rolling down the grade, a big hole right in the center of his back.

"The dirty son!" George Winters cussed Preacher. "He ain't even givin' us time to tend to the dead and wounded."

Bones gave the man a disgusted look and said nothing.

Van Eaton looked at George. But like Bones, he kept his mouth shut.

Lige's bunch were the ones who had taken the real beating as far as loss of men. They had been so eager to trap and kill Preacher, they had forged ahead of the others and taken the brunt of the rock slide. Counting himself, Lige had about twenty men left. At least that's what he figured. Lige wasn't a very good counter.

High above them, Preacher's rifle cracked and Lige had about nineteen men left. A Delaware man dropped like a stone and began rolling down the grade. Several dozen horrified eyes watched the body slowly gain speed and finally land with a thud on the valley floor.

Bones, Van Eaton and his men, and the dusty and the now grime-faced nobility, knew better than to try to move. They all had witnessed Preacher's precision with a gun and knew that as long as it remained daylight, to move was to die.

"Stay down!" Rudi Kuhlmann yelled.

"I cain't take no more of this!" a man from Illinois screamed. "Spencer was kin of mine. I seen them rocks knock his brains out. Damn you, Preacher!" he shouted, standing up. "I'll kill you, Preacher. I'll . . ."

Die. Preacher's rifle sang its deadly song and the Illinois man slumped to the rocky grade, on his knees, a large stain appearing on the front of his shirt. The man had a very puzzled expression on his face. "No," he spoke for the last time. He finally fell over on his back, head pointed downward. He slid for a few yards, stopped, and was still.

"This is the way it's gonna be, boys," Preacher's faint shout reached the men. "You better face facts, you birdbrains. I know these mountains, you don't. I know ever' stream, ever' crick, ever' valley, ever' box canyon, and ever' cave. I could have kilt all of you a hundred times over, but I was hopin' you'd come to your senses and clear on out and leave me be. Now what's it gonna be?"

"I'm through, Preacher!" a man yelled. "You let me go and I'll never come back."

"Go on, then."

"Nelson," Van Eaton said.

"Let him go," Bones said. "More for us when the end comes."

"If we're alive when the end comes," Van Eaton replied.

"You and me got no choice in the matter. This is personal with Preacher, now."

"This ain't worth no five dollars a day," another man yelled. "I'm headin' out with Nelson."

"Fine," Preacher said.

"Sal," Van Eaton said.

"I've had it!" one of Lige's men shouted. "You hear me, Preacher? I'm haulin' my ashes back to New York State."

"Git gone, then."

"I'll see you in hell, Preacher!" another of Lige's men shouted. "But I don't want no more of this."

"Tell your mommy hello and stay close by her side," Preacher yelled. "I 'spect she'll be glad to see her wanderin' boy come home."

"You mighty right 'bout that."

"Anyone else?" Preacher questioned.

No one else chose to leave. Preacher knew that these staying behind were the hardcases. There would be no give in them and no quittin'. They were in this until the end.

Lige slowly counted his men. Near as he could figure it, counting himself, out of the original bunch, sixteen were all that was left. He shook his head. "I wouldn't have believed it possible," he muttered.

"Did you say something?" Wiley Steinwinder questioned the man.

"It just ain't reasonable that one man could do this much damage," Lige whispered.

"I will admit it is somewhat incredible," Sir Elmore

180

joined the conversation. "But this just makes it all the more exciting. Gads, what a formidable foe we face."

"Idiot," Van Eaton muttered. "I wish to God I'd never got mixed up with this pack of ninnies."

"You want to quit, Van?" Bones whispered.

"We cain't, Bones. Dark Hand is shore to have tole Preacher that you and me was in the bunch that tortured that kid. We got to see this thing through or elsest we'll be lookin' over our shoulders 'til the end of time."

That was the feeling among those of Bones's group who stayed. They had to finish this. For, to a man, they felt that Preacher would spent his life tracking them down. They were wrong. They could have left and Preacher would have gone on his way.

After a moment of silence, Preacher told them that. "Go on home, boys. If you say it's over, it's over. I mean that. They's been too much killin'. Let's stop it right now."

"He's lyin'," Bones told his people, having to shout across the barren slope, over the rocks and dirt that would forever cover many of his men.

"I ain't neither!" Preacher yelled. "I ain't never knowin'ly broke my word. Leave and don't come back and we'll call this even. You got my word on that."

"The hospital of the missionaries is safe ground for us all!" Bones yelled. "Any there is safe. You agree?"

"Does that include me?" Preacher hollered.

"Tell him yes and when he makes his appearance, we'll kill him," Sir Elmore urged.

"I agree to that," Tassin said.

But Bones shook his head. "No. Think about it. Maybe one of us will get wounded and have to go there for patchin' up. We'd be fair game."

"Unfortunately, he's right," Baron Zaunbelcher reluctantly said. "The camp of the missionaries must be declared neutral ground."

"All right, Preacher!" Bones yelled. "You got a deal."

"Let me hear the gentry say that. I want their word. They claim their word is damn near holy, so let me see if they got the class to keep it."

That made the nobility angry. One by one they shouted their agreement to Preacher's terms.

"Pick up your wounded and tote 'em out of here," Preacher yelled. "Long as you don't make no funny moves, I'll hold my fire."

"Give us your word on that!" Juan Zapata shouted.

"You got my word on it."

The man-hunters cautiously left their hiding places and began seeing to the wounded. Preacher held his fire, content to watch. It took most of the afternoon to carry the bone-shattered men down the slope to the valley and get them in the saddle or on quickly made travois.

What they did not know was that Preacher had left the scene about fifteen minutes into the gathering and hauling off of the wounded. He packed up the supplies that he had cached and went over the top of the mountain.

Several miles from the slide area, Preacher stopped at a spring and washed the sweat and grime from his body and hair. Before the first wounded were on their long and painful way to the 'hospital,' Preacher rode into the neat little camp of the missionaries. They had rigged up several lean-tos as shelter for the wounded.

"Them rickety-lookin' things ain't near 'bout gonna be enough," Preacher told them, walking over to the fire and pouring a cup of coffee. "But I don't care if you lay 'em out on the ground for the varmints to chew on. Just 'member, y'all agreed to this scheme."

"We are sworn to serve our fellow man," Hanna said. "We follow the teachings of the Bible. Sometimes it is with an effort, and sometimes we fail, for we are mere mortals and therefore shall never attain perfection, but it is our duty."

"Mighty noble of y'all," Preacher said, sitting down

with a sigh and relaxing. "Does my heart good to know they's people like y'all in the world. But if it's all right, I'll jist lay right here and watch y'all do all this good work."

"You are coming close to blasphemy, sir," Patience told him.

"I ain't neither. I'm tellin' the truth, that's all. Beats a lie, don't it?"

Patience flounced away, but not before stealing a flirtatious glance at Preacher.

Preacher ignored it.

He was dozing when Otto's frantic yell brought him awake and reaching for his rifle. He relaxed when he saw it was the wounded men from the slide.

Patience, Prudence, and the others in the group stared at Preacher in disbelief. "You . . . one man . . . did all *that?*" Frank Collins asked.

"And a heap more that's comin' up behind this first sorry-lookin' bunch," Preacher said, pouring himself a cup of coffee and stretching out. "And they's a goodly number of others all dead and buried under tons or rock and dirt. I done a purty neat job of it if you ask me."

"Incredible," Hanna said. "You behave as if you are proud of all the pain and suffering you have inflicted upon your fellow human beings."

"Oh, I am!"

"Disgusting!" Prudence said.

The first batch of wounded rode in and reined up. They stared at Preacher in wonderment and ill-disguised hate and hostility.

"Howdy, boys!" Preacher called cheerfully. "Looks like y'all run into some trouble. My goodness, what happened to y'all? Did you tangle with a whole passel of grizzly bar or get in the way of a buffalo stampede?"

"Very funny," Van Eaton said, painfully dismounting and limping back to the travois behind his horse.

"What's the matter with your head, Van Eaton?" Preacher asked. "How'd you git all them bumps on your noggin?"

Van Eaton lost his temper and reached for the pistol in his belt. A hard hand clamped down on his wrist and squeezed. Van Eaton thought for a second his wrist was going to be crushed. He looked into the broad peasant face of Otto Steiner.

"This is neutral ground, friend," Otto said. "But don't cause me to lose my temper. Back before I found Christ, four men came out of the darkness one night to rob me. I broke the back of one, the neck of another, and smashed the brains out of the other two. And I do not joke. I do not have much of a sense of humor."

"Neutral ground," Van Eaton hissed through clenched teeth reeling from the pain in his wrist. "I give you my word. And I'll shoot any man who violates it."

Otto released his wrist and Preacher called out, "Have some coffee, Van Eaton. Supper'll be on in a few minutes. You best partake. It might be your last one."

Four

Preacher had to hand it to the men and women who had wandered west to serve their God. They did a bang up job when it came to fixing up the wounded.

"We've all had medical training," Hanna told him.

Later, when Bones and Lige and most of their people had left, Preacher sat by the fire drinking coffee. He became conscious of eyes on him and looked up. Patience was staring at him.

"You think I enjoy all this killin', don't you?"

"Frankly, yes. I do."

"Well, you're wrong, Missy. 'Cause I shore don't. I've done given them ol' boys out yonder a dozen chances to back off and let me be. They could ride out of here tonight and I'd not give them another thought. Hell, Missy. I give them all another chance to leave this day, up on the slide."

"He ain't lyin' 'bout that, ma'am," a man with two busted legs spoke up. "He done it."

"More'un oncest," another wounded man said. "And I shore wish I'd a took his invite."

"And he's let some go," a third man offered up. "I tell you this, Preacher. When I can ride, you've seen the last of me."

Most of the bruised, banged-up, and broken men in the camp agreed, except for one loudmouth brute.

"Not me. I aim to kill you, mountain man. I'm gonna track you down and skin you alive. Then I'm gonna cut off your head, pickle it, and tote it back east to claim my reward."

"Why?" Patience asked him, a horrified look on her face.

Preacher smiled into his coffee cup and said, "That's Ed Crowe, ma'am. He's a murderer, a rapist, and a brigand through and through. But he claims to have re-pented his evil ways. Now he's a bonney-e-fied man-hunter workin' with Bones and Van Eaton. Two of the sorriest men on the face of the earth."

Ed cussed Preacher until Otto showed up and said, "If you do not stop that filthy language, I will gag you. If that doesn't stop your vulgar mouth, I just might rip out your tongue with my bare hands."

"Otto!" Hanna cried. "Please. Do remember who we are and what we represent."

"Be still," he told her. "There is a time and place for all things. Including violence."

Ed Crowe must have believed the big man, for he shut his mouth and after that, as long as he was in the camp of the missionaries, when he spoke, it was free of profanity.

"I ... guess I've misjudged you, Preacher," Patience said. "I apologize for that."

Preacher waved it off. "I just wanted you to know that I ain't no heartless savage, Missy. And that I really didn't want all this killin' and did try to stop it." He stood up. "I best be goin'. Bones and Lige and the gentry and the rest of that pack of no-counts will be gunnin' for me at first light. I don't want no shootin' around this camp."

Before she could form a reply, Preacher had vanished into the night.

* * *

Bones and his bunch had pulled themselves into a tight little camp right next to a fast runnin', spring-fed stream. And there they stayed. They posted guards that stayed alert and were changed often. Each day, under a white flag, an unarmed man would ride to the camp of the missionaries to check on the wounded, and then ride back. Other than that, they did not leave camp. Preacher had no way of knowing what they were planning, only that it would probably be better than any previous plan. So far, everything they'd tried had failed miserably. For now, all he could do was wait and watch and see.

Preacher was determined that he would not start the next round of gunfire. He had given some thought to just picking up and moving on. But he knew the man-hunters would just come after him ... after they did—God only knew what they would do to the—missionaries; and Preacher had him a pretty good idea what they'd do to the women.

The mountain man felt that he was in between that much talked about "rock and a hard place."

He had not been back to the missionary's camp and make-shift hospital. He felt that would be just too dangerous for those good folks.

On the fifth day of inaction, Preacher got lucky. Just as dusk was spreading its first shadows all over the valley floor, Preacher sat in the brush on a slope viewing the scene below him through his spy glass. About a quarter of a mile from the camp of the man-hunters, a covey of birds suddenly shot up into the air.

"Now what's all that about?" Preacher muttered, shifting the glass and studying the area in question. But he could see nothing. Then he spotted a very slight movement in the tall grass. After studying the area for a moment, he collapsed the pirate's glass and smiled.

"Very good, Bones," he muttered. "Yes, indeed. You got more sense than I gave you credit for havin'." He picked up his rifle and moved out. Preacher thought it was a good thing he'd taken a long nap that afternoon, for it looked like it was shapin' up to be a long night.

The night was black and the air was heavy with moisture. A bad storm was building, and if a body has never been in the high-up country when a thunderstorm hit, you just can't imagine the sound and fury. The pounding of the thunder is unbelievable and the lightning so fierce it'll stand your hair up on end.

Preacher studied the sky and figured he had about an hour before the full brunt of the storm struck. He also figured he could do a lot of damage in an hour.

Mack Cornay froze like a rock when he felt the cold edge of a Bowie knife touch his throat. He started sweating in the coolness of the night air when Preacher said, "You just never learn, do you, boy?"

Mack was so scared he was afraid to reply. He remained stone-still as Preacher shucked his pistols out of his belt and laid them to one side.

"Are you gonna kill me?" Mack whispered, his voice a tremble in the darkness.

"I shore ought to. You would if you was in my moccasins, wouldn't you?"

"I reckon. Can we deal?"

"What do you have that I want?"

"Information."

"Talk."

"Me and Frenchy is on this slope. Cobb is about a quarter mile to the south. Pyle is acrost the valley with Hunter. Flores is closin' the box north and Percy is comin' out later this night to put the lid on to the south."

"That's right interestin' news. What is your name, boy?"

"Mack Cornay. Please don't kill me, Preacher. I'll git gone ifn you'll let me. I swear that on my mother's head."

Preacher thought about that. "How you figure on gettin 'your horse away from the camp without bein' seen?"

Sweat was running down Mack's face. He thought hard

for a moment. "I cain't. But I can slip into the missionary camp and take one of the wounded feller's horse. And I'll do it, too. You bet I will. For God's sake, Preacher. I'm beggin' for my life, man."

Preacher removed the razor sharp knife from Mack's throat and the man was so relieved he slumped face down on the cool earth. "Thank you, Jesus," Mack whispered. "I'm comin' home to see you, Mamma."

"Get gone, Mack," Preacher told him. "And you know what I'll do if I ever see you again."

"You'll kill me." Mack didn't put it as a question. He knew the answer.

"You got that right. Move! And be damn quiet in leavin'. You hear me?"

"Yes, sir, Mister Preacher. I'll be like a ghost."

"I ever see you again, you gonna be a ghost. Now get the hell gone from here."

Mack Cornay turned and looked at Preacher. "Thank you, Preacher."

"Take your rifle and pistols and clear out," Preacher told him.

Mack slipped quietly into the night. The odor of his fear-sweat lingered sourly for a few seconds and then the wind carried it away.

Preacher moved out. He would save Frenchy for last, for the man from Louisiana was known to be a bad one to tangle with. Preacher began working his way south. He'd heard some about Cobb, but nothing that impressed him.

Preacher laid a sturdy stick up 'side the head of Cobb and the man dropped like a stone into a well. Preacher trussed him up and waited for the man to come out of his addle.

"Oh, my dear sweet God!" Cobb said when he came to and his eyes began to focus.

"How come people like you always call on God or Jesus

when you get in a tight?" Preacher questioned. "You damn shore don't pay no heed to His words 'til you do."

"I be good from now on," Cobb whispered, like he never heard Preacher's question. "Dear sweet Mamma, pray for me."

"Disgustin'," Preacher said. He popped Cobb across the face with a big hard hand. That got Cobb's attention. "Didn't your mamma whup you none whilst you was growin' up?"

"She beat me some."

"'Pears to me she didn't beat you enough. What am I gonna do with you, Cobb?"

"Turn me a-loose, I hope!"

"So's you can run tell Bones and them silly uppity folks what I'm doin' this night? Not likely."

"I wouldn't do that!"

"I think I'll just truss you up real good and let the bears eat you."

"Oh, Lord, Lord, please save me from this heathen!" Cobb cast his supplication to the heavens.

"Heathen? You call *me* a heathen?"

"I didn't mean it, Mister Preacher. I swear I didn't. You got me so bumfuzzled I ain't thinkin' straight."

"I tell you what I'm gonna do, Cobb. I'm gonna test you right good. I'm gonna see if you're a man of your word."

"I'm an honorable man, Preacher. You just ax anybody. They'll tell you."

"I bet they will," Preacher said drily. "I'd bet at least a penny on it. Cobb, I want you gone from these mountains. And I mean gone and stayed gone. I'm tired of all this fuss and bother. You know that ravine that cuts 'crost this valley?"

"Oh, yes, sir. I do for a fact. Runs all the way 'crost it. Comes within a few hun'red yards of the missionary camp. I know it real well. I bet I could . . ."

"Shut up an' listen. You beginnin' to babble. I want you

to work your way down this slope and git in that ravine and over to the missionary camp. Then I want you to take one of them spare horses over yonder and git gone. I unloaded your weapons. So don't even think about pointin' any of 'em at me."

"I wouldn't. I swear it."

"Cobb, listen to me. I don't never want to see you again. You hear me?"

"Yes, sir. I do. I really do. And you ain't never gonna see me again."

"I better not ever see you again," Preacher said menacingly. "'Cause if I do, I'm gonna strip you buck-ass nekked and stake you out over an ant hill. Then I'm gonna pour honey all over your neck and head and sit back and watch whilst the ants gather and eat your eyes."

Cobb shuddered and crapped in his pants.

"Whew!" Preacher grimaced and fanned the air with a hand. "Git outta here!"

Preacher smiled as Cobb scurried away. Maybe he had missed his calling; he should have been an actor. He was sure convincing this night.

But he wasn't quite that lucky with Frenchy. Frenchy turned around when Preacher was about five feet away from him. Lightning flashed and Frenchy's eyes widened and his mouth dropped open. It took him about one second to recover and grab at the pistol behind his belt.

One second was the time Preacher needed. Preacher closed the gap and slugged Frenchy just as his hand closed around the butt of his pistol. Lightning flashed again and a cold rain began falling, slicking over the already treacherous footing on the rocky slope. Preacher lost his balance and fell down, dragging Frenchy with him. The two men hit the ground hard, with Preacher landing on top of Frenchy, knocking the wind from him. Preacher slammed a fist against the side of Frenchy's head, causing his hands to loosen their grip on Preacher's shirt. Preacher hit him again just as hard as he could and Frenchy's fingers lost their grip altogether, and his hands fell to the ground.

Preacher caught his breath and then quickly trussed the man up. Already the Louisiana man was moaning and twitching. Preacher had just set the man up, his back to a rock, when Frenchy came to and opened his mouth to yell. Preacher jammed a handful of dirt into the man's mouth.

"You yell and I'll cut your throat," Preacher warned. "You understand?"

Frenchy believed him, for his eyes widened at the thought of that prospect and he nodded his head. Frenchy spat out the dirt and said, "What do you want, Preacher?"

"To give you a chance to get gone, Louisiana Man."

"You gittin' soft in your old age, Preacher?"

Preacher chuckled as the cold rain pelted them both. "You think I am, Frenchy?"

"No," Frenchy was quick to reply. "But you won't kill me while I'm tied like this."

Preacher hesitated. That was a fact and somehow Frenchy either knew it or had sensed it about the mountain man. "That's right, Frenchy. But what I can do is knock you silly, tote you up the mountain, strip you down to the buff, wedge you up under a run-off, and then let the weather do the rest. And I'll do that, boy—don't you doubt it for a second. I'm used to the high country. This cold rain don't bother me none. But you now, well, pneumonia'll kill you shore. Think about that."

Frenchy's eyes told Preacher he didn't doubt that at all. When he spoke, Preacher sensed he had won. Maybe. "All right, Preacher. You cut me a-loose and I'm gone."

Preacher freed the man's wrists and stepped back. "Frenchy, don't even think about makin' no funny moves or goin' 'back on your word. This will be the last chance you get. I mean that, boy. When I get done with this night's work, I aim to hallo Bones's camp in the mornin'.

If they ain't packed up and pulled out by noon, the killin' starts."

Frenchy nodded his head. "You put Mack and Cobb on the run, didn't you?"

"Yeah, I did."

Frenchy shook his head. "They was both weak sisters. I didn't figure they'd last this long. You won't put no more on the run, Preacher. You best know that now."

Preacher sensed then that he hadn't won this one. Frenchy was going to make his try. "Then they're fools, Frenchy. Don't you be one."

"Oh, I ain't no fool, Preacher. I just don't like you."

"That's your option, boy. But it ain't worth dyin' for. You best take heed to them words. I'm givin' you a chance to go on back to Louisiana. Take it, Frenchy. I been there. The women is pretty, the wine is sweet, and the food is the best there is. Hell, Frenchy, you don't even know me. I'm offerin' you your life. Think about it."

"What you say is true."

Frenchy stood up slowly, a strange smile on his lips. He faced Preacher. He didn't say a word as his hand flashed for his knife.

Preacher's right hand clamped around Frenchy's wrist just as the blade came free of the scabbard. Preacher twisted and shoved the big-bladed knife to the hilt in Frenchy's belly, just under his rib cage. Frenchy gasped in pain and staggered back. He stopped just as lightning flashed and looked down at the handle of his knife. He raised his head and looked into Preacher's eyes.

"No man has ever bested me with a blade. No man ever done that."

"They's always someone better, Frenchy. You should have had enough sense to know that."

Frenchy sank to his knees. He screamed just as thunder rolled and pealed and echoed around the mountains. His mouth filled with blood and he toppled over.

Preacher gathered up his weapons, powder, and shot. He looked down at the dead man and thought about his night's work so far. "Well, I reckon two out of three ain't all that bad."

Five

Preacher took Frenchy's words to heart about there being no more who would quit and called it a night. He began carefully making his way back to his camp—a hidden cave-like overhang that nature had concealed so well Preacher doubted that any living being had ever before set a foot in the place. The storm was full-blown now, a real rip-snorter. Preacher built a small fire for coffee and food. He saw to Thunder and then stripped down to the buff and dried off, changing into another set of buckskins. He sat by the fire, deep in thought.

After tomorrow, when Preacher would tell those remaining man-hunters that if they didn't give up this foolishness and ride on out, it would be shoot-on-sight, he knew he would have to back up his threat with action. Problem was, he just didn't want to do that.

"What else can I do?" he muttered, as the bacon sizzled in the pan and the water started to boil for coffee.

The flames danced silently, offering him no answer to his question.

"Just do it, I reckon," Preacher said.

When the missionaries awakened, Preacher was sitting under the canvas over the cooking area, drinking coffee. It gave them only a slight start, since by now they had accepted that Preacher could move like a ghost.

"I hope y'all brought a whole bunch of medical supplies," Preacher said without looking up. "This here war is fixin' to get real nasty."

"How did you know we had awakened, sir?" Otto asked.

"I heard you open your eyes."

"That is ridiculous!" Prudence said.

Preacher shrugged.

"I believe him," one of the wounded men said.

"I suppose you left this lovely valley littered with dead and dying men last night," Hanna said.

"Just one. And I give him a chance to ride out 'fore I done the deed. Just like I'm a fixin' to give the rest of that pack of hyenas out yonder ample warnin'."

"And if they don't heed your warning?" Paul Marks asked.

Preacher turned his head and stared at the man. The look in the mountain man's eyes made Paul queasy in the stomach. Without realizing he had done so, he backed up a couple of steps.

"I'm tired of foolin' around with these people. I'm tired of bein' hunted. I'm just by God tired of it. And I ain't gonna put up with it no more. I can't just leave. I do that, you folks will be in for a real bad time of it. And I think you women know what I mean. And it ain't y'all's fault. You just happened to come along at a real bad time." He shook his head and poured more coffee. "I just don't see no other way out of this mess."

"There ain't no other way out, Mister Preacher," the man with broken legs spoke up. "I'd make a bet that you convinced Cobb and Mack to leave last night. If so, that's all that's leavin'. The rest will stay to the last man."

"You done some good guessin'," Preacher said. "I met

up with three last night. Frenchy decided to play his hand. His cards run out."

Ed Crowe opened his mouth. "I don't believe you kilt Frenchy, mountain man. I say you're lyin'."

Preacher glanced at the mouthy man. "When you get on your feet, Crowe, you and me is gonna go 'round and 'round. So you got that to look forward to."

"You don't scare me none!" Ed sneered.

"I'm real glad to hear that. Now shut up. Your whiny voice is gratin' on me."

Ed wanted to say something else. He wanted to pop off real bad. But the look in Preacher's eyes warned him silent. Ed dropped his gaze from Preacher's cold stare and shut up.

Patience and Prudence set about making breakfast—pan bread and bacon—and Preacher ate in silence until one of the wounded men called his name. He looked over at the man.

"You know them fancy gents is all 'bout half tiched in the head, don't you?"

"I figured it."

"Crazy as ever seen," another wounded man said. "And I've seen some crazies in my time."

"And both Bones and Lige has some real crazy folks ridin' with them," the first man continued. "Lucas and his buddy, Willie, they're 'bout two boards shy of a straight picket fence, if you know what I mean. But they're dangerous."

"They like to kill, you mean." Preacher did not put it as a question.

"Yeah. I believe so."

Preacher nodded his head. "Preciate it." He rinsed out his plate and placed it on a table. "I'll see you folks later on. You best get some bandages ready. You gonna be needin' 'em."

He mounted up on one of the horses of the wounded

men and rode out. Otto had told him about Cobb and Cornay. The two men had staggered into the camp late the night before, both of them frightened out of their wits. They hadn't even paused for coffee. Just went straight to the picket line, saddled up, and rode out. They headed south. Said they were leaving the mountains and it would be a cold day in hell before they ever returned.

Otto had volunteered to ride over to the man-hunter's camp and tell them that Preacher wanted to speak to the men, all of the men. Preacher told him where to have the men meet him.

Preacher was sitting on a ledge overlooking the valley when the men rode up. En masse. He was taking a chance that one of them might take a shot at him, but it was a risk he was willing to take to put an end to this foolishness.

"All right, boys," Preacher called from the rock ledge. "Gather in close and perk your ears up good. By now you prob'ly found Frenchy and you know that Cobb and Cornay is gone. Here's the deal. Listen up, 'cause I ain't gonna say this but one time. You boys has wooled me around long enough. I'm done playin'. You can ride on out of here right now, and live to tell your grandkids about this stupid hunt. Or you can stay and die. If you ain't packed up and gone from here by mid-afternoon, I'm gonna start killin' you wherever and whenever I find you. No more deals after this one. That's all I got to say. Git the hell out of these mountains." Preacher turned and vanished from the sight of those below him.

The group of men sat their horses for a moment. No one spoke.

Tom Evans broke the silence. "You think he means all that, Bones?"

Bones thought for a moment and then nodded his head. "Yeah, I do, Tom. I think this hunt just took a bloody turn."

The royalty twisted in their saddles and looked the men over. Sir Elmore called out, "Any of you men want to leave?"

Slowly, the men began shaking their heads. They were all making more money on this hunt than they could possibly make back where they came from. And they all stood a chance of making a small fortune. They weren't about to give that up.

"Preacher'll be on the prowl come the night," Van Eaton opined. "We best get back and get ready for him."

But Preacher had changed his tactics. He wasn't about to enter that valley after the man-hunters. They were going to have to come to him. He'd taken his pirate glass and studied the man-hunters' camp late that same afternoon. "Fools," he muttered. "Plain damn fools. You was warned, boys. Now you gonna learn these mountains is *mine!*"

A man named Jeff, from Lige's bunch, found that out the hard way the following afternoon. He decided he'd go kill him a deer, for they were all tired of smoked fish and jerky. He hadn't gotten five hundred feet off the valley floor when Preacher's rifle boomed. Jeff tumbled out of the saddle and hit the ground hard. When he opened his eyes, he was in a world of pain and looking up into the cold eyes of Preacher.

Those back at the camp had heard the single shot and exchanged wary glances. They all knew what it meant, and it didn't mean that Jeff would be bringing in any venison.

"Don't . . . leave me here to die alone!" Jeff gasped.

"Why not?" Preacher asked, a hard edge to his voice. "You come a-huntin' me, not the other way 'round."

"I got . . . information."

"Then you better talk fast, boy. 'Cause you ain't got long."

"Them down yonder is . . . gonna take you alive and . . .

torture you. Then when they's had their fun ... they's gonna turn you a-loose nekked and hunt you down."

Preacher shook his head in disgust. "How did you ever agree to go along with something like that?"

"It was my idee!"

Preacher could but stare at the man for a moment. "Anything else?" He asked wearily.

"Yeah. Them good-lookin' wimmin is gonna get used hard. After ... we ... them ... is done with you. Pass 'em around 'til we git tarred of 'em. Kill the men slow to make 'em holler."

"Them fancy-pants foreigners go along with that plan?"

"Oh ... yeah. They lookin' forward ... to it." Jeff closed his eyes and died.

Preacher went through the man's pockets and found a handful of gold coins. He kicked a few rocks and leaves over the body and took Jeff's horse. He rode straight to the missionary camp. First thing he noticed was that Ed Crowe was gone. There were six men still out of action due to broken bones. Preacher gathered the men and women around him, within earshot of the wounded men, and laid it on the line for them. He was blunt and left nothing that Jeff said out.

"No, by God, they won't!" a man spoke up, his voice angry. "We would have died if it hadn'ta-been for these good folks here. I done a lot of mean things in my life, but I ain't never put a hand on no good woman nor gentlemen like these men is. We got our guns and ample powder and shot and patches. You go on and don't worry none about these folks. Bones and them will have to kill us to get to them. Right, boys?"

The three other men were very vocal in their defending the missionaries. Preacher eyeballed each of them, finally concluding that they meant it. It takes a sorry type of man to molest a woman, and these men were several cuts above that. No angels, mind you. But not gutter-slime either.

200

"You boys'll do," Preacher told them.

"You'll stay for food?" Patience asked Preacher.

The mountain man shook his head. "Too risky for y'all. By now, Ed Crowe's done told Bones and the others about these boys here talkin' hard aginst this hunt and their decision about not comin' back to their camp." Preacher held up a finger and thought for a moment. "But I tell you what I'll do to tip the balance some. I'll just wing me four or five tomorrow and then they can't do nothin' to y'all if some of their own men is here bein' taken care of by us. How's that sound to you?"

Patience stared up at him. Finally she found her voice. "Well, that certainly is an idea that none of us would have ever thought of."

"Good. Tomorrow I'll go bust some arms and legs and such and they'll have to bring them here. You make damn sure you get their guns from them and hide them good, you hear?"

"Whatever you say, Preacher."

"Y'all get ready for some new patients 'bout noon tomorrow." Preacher turned and left the camp.

That night, Preacher crept up close to the camp of the man-hunters and began taunting them. He cussed them loud and long and then he shifted locations, slowly circling the camp. He traced the ancestors of the nobility back to apes swinging from vines in the jungle and got them so mad they had to be physically restrained inside the camp.

"All of you is lower than a snake's belly!" Preacher shouted out of the darkness. "You couldn't whup a bunch of old women—none of you. I never seen such a bunch of yeller-livered cowards in all my borned days. Man-hunters, my butt! Ain't none of you ever fought a man 'til you come up on me. And you're all so skirred of me you can't

201

sleep at night. I've bested ever' one of you so many times I'm feelin' plumb ashamed of it. I'm gonna go cut me a switch to use on you when I catch you. All of you act like a bunch of foolish children."

"Tomorrow you die!" Baron Zaunbelcher screamed out into the night.

"Stick it up your nose," Preacher told him. "You better leave these mountains, buzzard-breath. You best tuck your tail 'tween your legs and run on back to mommy and daddy in the castle and hide under the bed. That is, if you have enough sense to find the bed."

Zaunbelcher was so furious he was jumping up and down and screaming out oaths.

Preacher then started in on the other gentry until the blue-bloods were livid.

Then Preacher started in on Lucas and his friend Willie, comparing them to an ape and a monkey. And that was the nice thing he said about the pair. Willie grabbed up weapons and fired blindly into the night while Lucas, trembling with rage, beat on the ground with his huge fists and roared out curses and threats until he was hoarse.

Preacher laughed and taunted the men until he had nearly the entire camp of man-hunters in an uproar of anger. Then he faded into the night. He had a hunch that come the morning, they'd be out looking for him.

"Damnit, it's a trick!" Bones said to the royalty. "Can't you see that? Preacher was tossin' insults at us to make us mad. He knows if we get mad we'll do somethin' stupid. And we can't afford to do nothin' stupid."

But his friend Van Eaton sided with the others. Preacher had been especially hard on Van Eaton, calling the man some terrible names.

"That mountain man dies tomorrow," Van Eaton said, pushing the words through clenched teeth. "That's it, Bones. He dies tomorrow."

But a lot of people had spoken words along the same lines. Preacher had buried them. If he felt like burying them, that is.

Six

The man-hunters left ten guards at the camp, chosen by drawing lots, and the rest pulled out just after dawn. They were all angry to the core but most had tempered their wild anger down to a hot bed of coals. Bones had prevailed upon them to cool down: don't go after Preacher unless they had a clear head.

Preacher had laid down sign, albeit not too obvious, for he knew there were some real woodsmen in the bunch, and was waiting. He figured they'd come up on him sometime about mid-morning. He had chosen his spot with caution, taking pains to insure himself several ways out. And he had made up his mind that if he got even the smallest opportunity, he was going to put a ball or two into some of those blue-blooded snooty-nosed gentry. Right in the butt, if he could. 'Cause that's what they'd become to Preacher: a royal pain in the butt.

Preacher was under no illusions. He knew he was in terrible danger. He knew that the slightest miscalculation on his part, and he'd be dead. Or worse, taken alive for torture. If anyone were watching, it would seem that he was taking this manhunt much like a game. They would be very wrong in that assumption. Preacher worked out in his mind every move in advance. He was confident, but only because he'd lived and survived by his wits and skill ever since he was a young boy.

Preacher waited.

Bones had spread his group out into teams, a good tracker with each team. He alone felt in his gut that Preacher was up to something. But he'd asked the trackers if the sign was too obvious and to a man they had agreed it was not.

"He ain't doin' this a-purpose," one had said.

"It's just that he ain't as good as he thinks he is," another one had opined.

But Bones still had his doubts. By now he had reached the conclusion that Preacher really wasn't as good as people said he was—he was *better!*

"I'm going over there to scout!" Prince Juan Zapata shouted, pointing toward a rise just at the edge of the valley, before the earth began to swell into mountains.

Before Bones could yell for him not to leave the group, the rich, spoiled Spaniard had spurred his mount and was gone at a gallop.

"Fool!" Bones muttered.

Juan topped the rise and dismounted to stretch his legs. He looked all around, and then bent over to pick a flower to place in his hat. Preacher's rifle boomed and the Prince took a heavy caliber ball right in one fleshy cheek of his royal butt.

Zapata jumped about three feet into the air and commenced to squalling loud enough to wake the dead.

Preacher had not been sure he could even make the shot because of the long distance, but he held high and was right on target. It surprised the hell out of the mountain man. Because of the distance, the ball had lost much of its power when it impacted with Zapata's regal ass, but it still had enough zip to imbed deeply in his rear end.

Preacher never in his life saw so many people leave so many saddles in that short a time.

"Sure a bunch of skittish folks," he muttered, reloading the fancy hand-made rifle that had once belonged to one of the Frenchmen. He tried not to remember which one it was. "Fine shootin' rifle. Be a damn shame to shoot a feller with his own rifle," he said with a grin.

He watched as the men began moving through the grass to the aid of the still-squalling Prince. Preacher took a chance that he might hit something and sighted in just ahead and above the head of a growing snake-like path in the tall valley grass. He gently squeezed off a round.

A man jumped up and grabbed at one leg. Preacher grinned. Looked like another one of those fancy-pants folks.

"My leg!" Duke Burton Sullivan screamed. "He shot me in the leg!" he yelled as he fell down to the ground.

"Smart, Preacher," Bones muttered, his face pressed against the coolness of earth. "Now I know why you done what you did last night. Fill up the hospital and we have to keep the missionaries alive to treat the wounded. You no-good, miserable ..." He cussed for a moment, then added, "For an ignorant mountain man as I was told you was, you sure have a headful of smarts."

For reasons known only to him, Bates foolishly jumped up and made a run for the wounded Prince and Duke. He came close to making it.

"We'll sure give it a try," Preacher muttered, pulling his rifle to his shoulder.

The fancy hunting rifle banged and Bates had a leg knocked out from under him. He did a flip and hit the ground, hollering to the high heavens.

"Now that was a lucky shot," Bones muttered.

"You got lucky on that one, boy," Preacher muttered. "Let's get gone from here."

After five minutes or so had passed, Bones crawled to his knees. He sensed, more than knew, that Preacher had done his work and was gone. "All right, people. Let's gather up the wounded and get them to the gospel-shouters."

Bones looked over at Zapata, lying on his belly. "He can't ride, so some of you rig up a travios."

"This sorta knocks our plans in the head, don't it, Bones?" Van Eaton spoke softly.

"Yeah."

"And I was lookin' forward to dallyin' some with them women over yonder. I like 'em with some meat on their bones. That there Hanna hottens up my blood something fierce."

"Go find a cold crick and jump in it," Bones suggested.

"Hell, I took a bath last month!"

When the dejected and bloodied bunch of man-hunters reached the site of the make-shift hospital in the middle of the wilderness, they were quick to note that not only were the missionary men armed, and armed well, so were the wounded. Even the women had shotguns strategically placed. Took Bones about one second to understand that if they made a try for the women, a lot of men were going to die, for several of the wounded were more than fit to travel. That meant they were staying behind deliberately to act as guards.

Bones cut his eyes to Van Eaton. His right hand man had picked up on it, too. He nodded his head slightly.

"I must have medical treatment!" Prince Zapata yelled. "I demand it."

"Put him over there," Otto said, pointing and trying to hide his smile. "I'll see to his wound."

"I demand you stop that smiling at me!" Zapata shouted. "I am seriously wounded."

"You don't demand anything from me," Otto bluntly told him. "And I never heard of anyone who died from being shot in der butt."

Bones, Van Eaton, and those who helped bring the wounded to the make-shift hospital took their leave and being careful to stay in the center of the long valley, made their way back to camp. It was a weary and dejected bunch of man-hunters. Even the shoulders of the nobility slumped at bit as they rode. Nothing had turned out the way they planned. But the thought of calling off the hunt was nowhere in their minds.

For the others, over coffee and hot food, the talk was, surprisingly, not of quitting, but of what to do next.

"Corner him and burn him out," Pyle suggested.

"Corner him?" Flores looked at the man. "How? Most of the time we don't even *see* him."

"I wish we had some cannons," Falcon wished aloud. "We could blow him out of the mountains."

No one chose to respond to that. But a few of the men did smile at the ridiculousness of the remark.

"I got an idea," Sam Provost said. "Let's do to him like he done to us. Let's insult him and make him mad. Then he'll lose his temper and do something stupid."

"He'd see through that charade," Jon Louviere said. "Whoever told you Preacher was a stupid man was very badly misinformed. He is very intelligent and cunning. Which makes this game all the more exciting."

Van Eaton looked at the man. "Game? This is a game to you?"

"But of course.'

"Man," Van Eaton said, shaking his head, "I can't figure none of you all. We got people dead all over these mountains. That Preacher has put lead in near'bouts all of us at one time or the other. He's destroyed our camps, burned our supplies, stampeded our horses, ambushed us, caused rockslides, thrown snakes at us, made fools of us, and he ain't even got nicked one time. And you think it's a game?"

Bones poured more coffee and sat back down. "It's done got personal to me now. The money aside, it's a matter of honor. If we don't corner Preacher and bring his head back in that there jug, we're all done as bounty hunters. We'll never be able to get another job. News of this will get out. You can just bet that them that quit and headed back east has done told the story to anyone who'll listen. Folks is laughin' at us all over the place. I can't have that. I won't tolerate it. I ain't leavin' these mountains 'til Preacher is dead and we got his head. I'll die first."

Bones had finally expressed what had been in the minds of the rest of the men; the constant thought that silently nagged and dug at their pride. One man was making fools of them all. That just wouldn't do. To a man, they couldn't allow it. The hunt had to go on. The men didn't have a choice, or so they thought.

"We got to leave the valley and take to the mountains," Tatman spoke up, raw hatred for Preacher burning in his eyes. "We got to stop thinkin' like this was Back East and start thinkin' like a mountain man."

"By jove!" Sir Elmore piped up. "I think you've got it!"

"Maybe so," Bones said. "Maybe so. It's worth a try. We'll leave ten men behind to guard the horses and the camp, and we'll strike out on foot. We'll each take supplies for three days and fan out in the mountains." He looked at Tatman. "Good thinkin', Tatman. Real good thinkin'."

"What are them igits doin' now?" Preacher muttered, peering at the men through his pirate glass. "Looks like a bunch of ants scurryin' about down there," He studied the activity for a moment longer, then put away his glass and shook his head. "They're comin' after me on foot. They done lost what little sense they had left. They're comin' right at me, in my country, on foot. Lord have mercy!"

With a smile that would have caused a savage alarm, Preacher picked up his rifle and moved out. Now he'd show them how this game was really played. "Ants to a honey trap," Preacher muttered.

Tom Evans was the first to discover how far out of his class he was. Something smashed against the back of his head, dropping him into darkness. When he came slowly swimming out of unconsciousness, he thought for sure he was dead. He might as well have been. Preacher, and he was certain it was Preacher who'd hit him with something, had taken his shot bag and his powder. He'd busted Tom's rifle and pistols and snapped the blade off his fine knife. He had peeled him right down to the buff, and had even taken his boots. "Halp!" Tom hollered. "Somebody come halp me."

About a half a mile away, Homer Moore was waking up. He had a fearsome headache and a big lump on the side of his head that hurt like the devil when he gingerly fingered it. And he didn't have a stitch on. He looked wildly around him. His weapons were gone, as were his clothes. He was as defenseless as the day he'd been born. "Oh, Lord!" Homer said.

Cliff Wright heard a noise behind him and turned. He caught a rifle butt under his chin that knocked him cold. When he came around, he was hanging upside down from a tree limb by his bare ankles. Like the others, he had been left bare-butt nekked and could see where his weapons had been rendered useless by somebody. Preacher, he was sure. Cliff started hollering for help. He didn't know how he was gonna live this down. Come to think of it, he didn't know how he was going to *get* down. "Halp! Halp!" he yelled.

Tatman came charging through the brush and Preacher busted the man's right knee with the butt of Homer's rifle. He smashed the knee to pieces and Tatman was out of the game for a long time. The big man passed out from the pain. When he awakened, his weapons were gone. He began crawling for safety, moaning and cussing and dragging his knee-broken leg.

Derby Peel turned around about three times and got himself lost as a goose in the dense forest and underbrush. He panicked and began running and yelling. He fell into a ravine, landed on his rifle, busted the stock of his rifle and broke several of his own ribs in the process. He passed out from the pain in his side and chest.

The men were so widely separated, and the country so rough and heavily timbered and thick with brush, the cries of the totally embarrassed men could not be heard. It was only by accident that Derby Peel was found, lifted out of the ravine, and toted off to the missionary's hospital.

"The ignorant fool fell into the ravine and landed on his rifle," Lige remarked. "How damn clumsy can you get?" He turned around just as Preacher hurled a fist-sized rock that caught the big man in the center of his forehead and knocked him sprawling to the ground.

Jeremy King, one of Lige's bunch, whirled around, lifting his rifle. Preacher blew a hole in his chest and Jeremy landed on his back, dead eyes open and staring at nothing.

The woods erupted in wild gunfire, but Preacher had dropped to the ground an instant after he fired and the balls hit nothing except air, leaves, branches, and thudded harmlessly into the timber.

Tom Evans and Homer Moore, who had been wandering about trying to find their clothes, chose that time to blunder into the clearing . . . bare butt shining.

"My God!" Fred Lasalle blurted. "Them boys ain't got no clothes on."

"I always did wonder 'bout them two," Bob Jones said.

"What's all the shootin' about?" Tom asked.

"Git down, you fools!" Stan Law hollered. "It's Preacher up yonder."

"Don't get over here next to me," Bob warned.

Their worries were needless, for Preacher was a good

quarter of a mile away, running through the timber. He spotted movement ahead and stopped, bellying down on the ground. He smiled when he recognized Van Eaton as one of the men.

Van Eaton moved just as Preacher squeezed off a shot. The ball slammed into a tree and Van Eaton got a face full of splinters that bloodied him and scared him. He dropped to the ground, sure that he'd been mortally wounded.

Preacher quickly reloaded and wriggled into a better spot. Sam Provost raised his head up and took the last look of his life. Preacher shot him between the eyes.

That was enough for Van Eaton. Leaving Sam's body behind he and the other man with him, Horace Haywood, ran from the area. They'd gone about two thousand yards when they came up on Cliff Wright, dangling butt bare and all from a tree limb. One side of his face was bloody and scratched something awful. The men stood and stared in disbelief for a moment.

"Y'all want to stop that bug-eyed gawkin' and cut me down and find me something to wear!" Cliff hollered.

While Horace was cutting him down, Van Eaton asked, "What happened to your face? Did Preacher do that?"

"No!" Cliff snapped the word. "A big bear did. He come by about an hour ago and reared up two-three times a-sniffin' at me. Like to have scared me half outta my wits, let me tell you. Then he rared up on his back legs, reached up and slapped the pee outta me and just wandered off. I hate these mountains, Van Eaton. I mean, I really, *really* hate these mountains. I hate these mountains nearly 'bout as much as I hate that mountain man. And I *do* hate Preacher."

"All your guns is ruint," Horace told him. "And I can't find your clothes nowhere." He took off his jacket and handed it to Cliff. "Wrap that around you."

Van Eaton held up a hand. "Wait. Let's go back and peel

the clothes offen Sam. He shore ain't got no more need for them. And his boots'll fit you too, Cliff."

"Suits me. I'll get his guns, too."

But Preacher had smashed Sam's guns, leaving them useless, and taken his powder and shot.

"Crap!" Van Eaton said, as Cliff removed the dead man's clothing. "Now I see what he's doing. If this keeps up we'll be throwin' rocks at him."

Lige and his dwindling bunch came cussing through the timber, dragging a moaning Derby Peel on a hastily made travois. Lige's head was bloody and there was a huge knot in the center of his forehead.

"What happened to you?" Van Eaton asked.

"Preacher," Lige said, a surly note to his voice. "He flung a rock at me."

Van Eaton sighed and muttered, "Now he's throwin' rocks at us. Good Lord Amighty." He pointed to Peel. "All right, all right. What about him?"

"He either fell into a ravine or Preacher throwed him into it. He's stove up pretty bad. Busted some ribs, I reckon," Homer said, red-faced. He was wearing Jeremy's jacket which wasn't quite long enough to cover his essentials, and Tom was wearing the dead man's pants.

"Where's your guns?"

"Busted up. Gone. I don't know. Preacher took all our powder and shot, too."

"Halp!" The shout came faintly to them. "Somebody come halp me. Over here."

"That's Tatman."

Van Eaton rubbed a hand over his unshaven face. "I hope to hell he's wearin' his britches. I done seen enough men's bare butts this day to last me a lifetime!"

Seven

The missionaries were amazed and somewhat amused that one man could inflict so much damage on so many. And to a person, they all realized something else about this legendary mountain man called Preacher. He could have easily killed all these men who now were straining their meager medical facilities and knowledge. But despite his tough talk and dire threats, he had elected to injure most and not kill.

If the missionaries were secretly amused, the man-hunters certainly were not. The nobility were livid with rage, and Bones and Van Eaton and Lige were so mad they could scarcely speak.

No plan they had conceived thus far had worked, and Preacher had made fools of them—again—toying with them as if they were little children.

"This is mighty fine venison you cooked up, ma'am," Tom Evans said to Patience. "One of your men shot this today, did he?"

"You might say that," she replied.

"Huh?" Tom said.

"Preacher brought it in about an hour before you gentlemen arrived," Prudence told him.

Tom's face turned beet-red and he almost choked on his food. He suddenly lost his appetite.

Duke Burton Sullivan was tempted to hurl his plate into the fire, but thought better of it. That would be very bad manners on his part. Prince Juan Zapata muttered some curses in his native tongue and laid his plate to one side. Derby Peel shook his bruised head and wished he had never left home. Tatman, his knee set and immobilized, was the first to admit—to himself—that the whole bunch of them were outclassed. None of the newly wounded men had any idea that Preacher was less than a hundred yards away, watching the scene through very amused eyes. After a time, Preacher picked up his rifle and slipped away. Bones and his men would not be expecting an attack on their main camp this soon after their fiasco in the mountains. Preacher thought he'd just go stir things up a bit.

Back at their own camp, Bones and Van Eaton sat to one side and looked over what was left of their group. It sure was a pitiful sight. Beat-up, bloodied, bruised, and embarrassed, the men were silent and sullen this late afternoon. But incredibly, almost to a man, there was no thought of giving up.

Joe Moss, one of Lige's group, got up from the ground to pour a cup of coffee. On his way to the fire, he paused to speak to Alan James, a man from his home state. Joe turned and Preacher's rifle boomed from the dusk and the shadows, the ball shattering Joe's left knee and knocking him screaming and thrashing about on the ground. Alan leaped for his rifle and brought it to bear. But there was no target. Only the darkness presented itself.

"Oh, Sweet Baby Jesus!" Moss hollered, jerking in pain. "I'm ruint for life."

Before the echo of the shot had faded, every man in camp had bellied down on the ground. Every man except Alan. He stood crouched, rifle at the ready. Preacher's rifle boomed again, and Alan was spun around like a top, the big ball breaking his hip bone. He fell across Joe's shattered knee and Joe screamed and dropped into unconsciousness. All over the camp, men were cussing and casting about dire threats. But nobody got up to carry any of them out.

Preacher slipped across the valley and headed for his own camp. Somebody would be transporting the newly wounded over to the missionaries, and true to his word, Preacher would not ambush anyone doing that. He knew the man-hunters would not honor that if he was the one wounded, but that was their rock to mentally tote around. Preacher's conscience was clear and he planned on sleeping well that night.

The next morning, Sir Elmore, Baron Zaunbelcher, Willy Steinwinder, Bones, Van Eaton, and Lige rode over to the camp to see about their friends. They almost went into apoplexy when they saw Preacher, lounging comfortably and drinking coffee.

"Howdy, boys!" the mountain man called cheerfully. "Did y'all get a good night's sleep?"

"Just remember, this is a neutral zone," Frank Collins reminded the men.

"We'll honor it," Bones said. He looked at Preacher. "You got more than your share of nerve, Mountain Man."

"I reckon." He pointed to the several bouquets of wild flowers that now brightened the camp. "But I wanted to show the ladies how much I 'preciated them bein' here. So I picked them a bunch of flowers. Purty, ain't they?"

Willy Steinwinder's face became ugly and mottled with rage. When he got his anger under control, he said, "You . . . picked those flowers?"

"Well, they shore didn't leap out of the ground and into my hand. I think y'all ain't bein' very gentlemanly 'bout this here situation."

"What do you mean, sir?" Baron Zaunbelcher demanded.

"Y'all didn't bring nothin' for the ladies, did you?"

Steinwinder turned his back to Preacher and looked up at the blue of the sky. He muttered darkly under his breath.

Preacher wouldn't let up. With a straight face, he said, "Here I am, havin' to hunt game so's the very men who was doin' their dead level best tryin' to kill me will have somethin' to eat. Now, that don't seem real fair to me. Seems like y'all would see fit to contribute somethin'."

The men stared at Preacher. A thousand thoughts were running through their heads but they were speechless. Stunned into silence. All of them.

Tatman hollered, "Kill him for me! Just hammer back and kill that smart-aleck for me!"

Bones found his voice. He looked at Preacher. "Took their guns, did you?"

"It seemed a smart move at the time, yeah."

Bones had also noticed that Preacher had a sawed-off shotgun lying across his lap. Bones knew what a sawed-off shotgun could do. He'd seen men cut in two with them. So he was very careful to keep his hands as far away as he could from his pistols. "So what now, Preacher?"

"Y'all can pull out and I'll forget all about this."

Van Eaton said, "You know can't none of us do that, Preacher. And you know why."

"Pride's a terrible thing sometimes, Van Eaton. You really figure it's worth dyin' for?"

"When you're in our line of work, yeah, I do."

"Maybe so. But y'all could change your line of work, you know?"

"My good man," Sir Elmore piped up. "I have a sporting proposition for you."

"I just bet you do. What is it?"

Your mummy and daddy still living?"

"Yeah. My mum . . . mother and father is alive."

"Could they use ten thousand dollars?"

"Who couldn't."

217

"Well . . . there are some of us who . . . never mind. My proposition is this: As soon as Juan and Burton are up to it, we shall put up bank notes worth ten thousand dollars. We'll, ah, let the good missionaries hold the notes. Then the eight of us hunt you. In an area that can be worked out. If we kill you, your parents are richer by ten thousand dollars. I mean, face facts man, we're going to kill you eventually. Why not make your parents' lives a bit easier?"

Preacher blinked, then blinked again. This fool really believed what he just spouted. Preacher chuckled softly. "No, mister high falutin' mucky muck. I think I'll pass. But I will take this time to try to get somethin' through your heads. I've tried before, but perhaps this time I can get through to you. You boys ain't gonna kill me. I may get bit by a rattler or a hydrophobia skunk; my horse might step in a hole and toss me and break my neck. I may get mauled by a puma or kilt by a grizzly. Some Injun might get lucky and do me in. All sorts of things can happen to a man out here in the Lonesome. But I'll tell you all what ain't gonna happen: you boys ain't gonna kill me. You best understand that."

"Oh, that's piffle!" Elmore said with a wave of his hand.

"No, it ain't neither piffle," Preacher said. "Whatever that means. It's pure fact. Now, boys, I mean what I say. This ain't fun and games. Whilst you're in this camp, you're safe. But out yonder," he pointed to the valley and beyond, "you're fair game to me."

Sir Elmore looked down his aristocratic nose at Preacher. "I must say, sir, that there is little distance between you and a fool."

Preacher smiled. "You mighty right about that. I figure five feet at best."

Before he left the missionary's camp, Preacher had asked if they had any kind of opiate to knock Tatman and a couple of others out? Otto assured him they did, and they most certainly would do just that.

Preacher left the camp feeling better. Otto was not a real trusting man when in the company of brigands and thugs. And the man was ox-strong. Had arms on him 'bout the size of Preacher's thighs. If Otto ever got his hands on a body, it would be all over 'ceptin for the buryin'. And Hanna wasn't no delicate bloomin' flower herself.

Preacher awakened in the wee hours of the morning. No sense of danger awoke him. It was the workings of his mind. For years Preacher had prowled the mountains and ridden the country in relative peace. He had run-ins with Indian and whites alike, all mountain men did. Indians who resented the coming of the white man and trashy whites who raided trap-lines and the like. Preacher had never been known as a trouble-hunter. And he tried to shy away from those who did want trouble. But the past two or three years had been rough on him. As his reputation grew, so did the people who came looking for him to make a name. Seemed to him the immigration of eastern folks heading for a new life out west had brought him nothing but headaches.

Preacher sighed and reached out to feel the coffee pot. The coffee was still warm enough to taste good. Without getting out of his blankets, he reached for the cup and poured it about half full. The coffee was just right. Black as sin and strong enough to bend nails. Good.

Preacher lay back, his saddle for a pillow, and tried to figure out the best thing he could do. If not for the missionaries, he thought he'd just pull out and hole up 'til winter.

But he couldn't do that with the gospel-shouters in the valley. Bones and his men would have their way with the women and the men. Preacher did not want to go through life with that on his conscience.

So, he concluded, he had to see this fight to the end

whether he liked it or not. So all right. But he thought he knew a way to do it without any more killing ... or at least keeping it to a minimum.

With that issue settled in his mind, he went back to sleep.

Eight

The man fetched water from the creek, returned to the camp, and squatted down in the dim light of pre-dawn. He laid twigs on the coals, then added heavier sticks when the kindling burst into flames. He lifted the coffee pot and his right hand and arm went numb when a heavy caliber rifle ball punctured the pot and tore it from his hand. The early riser leaped for the safety of darkness and away from the campfire. The entire camp of man-hunters was awake and belly down on the cold ground. They watched through startled eyes as a fire-arrow arched its fiery way through the air and landed on a pile of dirty, flea-infested blankets just vacated by Lige Watson. The blankets burst into flames and tall shadows lept around the murk of the camp. Another fire arrow landed inside the crude corral and the horses were spooked. They smashed through the flimsy barricade and spilled out into the valley, running wild.

Sutton leaped to his bare feet and Preacher cut him down with a ball in his leg.

Preacher had carried four rifles and his bow with him that morning, determined to put as many men out of action as possible, hopefully without killing any of them. If he could get enough of them wounded and unable to ride, he would take the missionaries and lead them away from this place and then maybe he could go on with his life and live in peace.

"Anybody see where he is?" Bones tossed out the question.

"No," Van Eaton replied from a few yards away. "It wouldn't make no difference no how. He moves as soon as he fires."

With the light increasing, Preacher ruined another big coffee pot, the big ball sending the pot flying.

"Two pots left," Tom Evans said sorrowfully. "And them horses are still runnin'."

"It'll take us the better part of two days to round them all up," Fred Lasalle said.

"You uncouth savage!" Jon Louviere yelled. "Stand up and fight like a man."

Bones shook his head and muttered, "I swear them people get dumber and dumber with each passin' day."

"I challenge you to a duel!" Sir Elmore screamed. "Meet me in honorable combat!"

"Sure he will," Van Eaton mumbled.

Another fire arrow soared gracefully through the air and landed in the grass behind the camp and flames began licking their way higher and higher. Bones had ordered the camp built inside a lazy half circle of the creek, so the flames had but one way to go—straight into the camp.

"We gotta put out that fire!" Bones yelled. "It'll burn ever'thing we got if we don't."

Hugh Fuller jumped up and grabbed a bucket of water. Preacher broke his arm with a ball. George Winters ran for his saddle and his sleeping blankets and Preacher cut his leg from under him. Preacher fired at another running man and missed him clean. Using his last loaded rifle, he shot Ray Wood in the side. Preacher gathered up all his empty rifles and began working his way around to the rear of the camp. The flames were leaping into the air and the smoke was thick.

"Stay on your belly and toss water or beat blankets on the ground in front of you!" Bones yelled. "Beat it out with your hands if you have to."

"Get shovels or use your blades to dig a break!" Van Eaton added, panic in his voice.

The smoke was so thick none of the man-hunters could see the single, odd-shaped arrow arch through the air and land in the middle of the flames. But they could all damn sure hear and feel the explosion as the bag of powder attached to the arrow blew, sending fire and sparks flying all over the place.

The concussion knocked one man down and stunned several others closest to the explosion. Another arrow landed and a second explosion rocked the smoky camp. Sir Elmore was only a few feet away from the second explosion and the explosion rendered him sillier than a happy lunatic for a few moments. He was wandering about the fire and smoke humming and playing patty-cake until Baron Zaunbelcher tackled him and brought him down.

Preacher figured he'd done a fair amount of damage and caused enough confusion for one morning. He ripped the hammers off three of the rifles, put them in his pocket and tossed the rifles aside. He took off at a run, circling the camp and heading in the direction of the running horses. He figured he'd have a good hour before any of the men came after him.

He managed to calm down and get hands on four of the trembling horses. He led them off into the mountains and turned them loose. They might return to the camp, and they might not. He left them on rich, belly high grass near water.

Several hours later, he watched from a distance as the wounded were taken to the already over-burdened, makeshift hospital. Near as he could figure, both groups combined had about thirty men still able to ride and fight. That was still too many for Preacher's liking.

He suddenly smiled. The deal was no shootin' or ambushin' whilst the wounded was taken to the hospital. There wasn't nothin' said about what might happen on the return trip.

"Now, that's sneaky, Preacher," he whispered. His smile widened. "Damn shore is!" he said aloud. "I'm proud I thought of it, too."

He counted the mounted men. Fifteen of them. They'd only managed to round up about a third of the horses.

He worked his way to the valley floor and made himself comfortable beside the creek bank. An hour later, common sense told him to abandon his plan. Bones had sent riders far ahead of the main group's return, riding on both sides of the creek bank with rifles at the ready. Preacher forded the creek, bellied down in the grass, and snaked his way clear. He smiled as he spotted the returning group. Bones was wising up. He'd split the group into two parties. One on the far side of the long valley and the other near the creek.

"You're learnin', boy," Preacher muttered. "But not fast enough to do you no good."

Preacher counted the men in the returning groups. He knew he'd wounded three, maybe four. He counted them again. One was missing. "Gettin' sneaky, aren't you, Bones?" Preacher whispered.

He stayed right where he was. Preacher could be more Indian than an Indian if he had to, and he figured this was a good time to do just that. He moved only his eyes. Birds soon became accustomed to the motionless presence and paid him no heed. It was a few minutes before dusk when Preacher sensed, more than heard, the man. Whoever he was, he was damn good. But Preacher knew there was no way the man could know where he was. What he had done was take a guess and it had proved out to be a good one.

The man, and it turned out to be a man Preacher had heard called Bobby, came within twenty feet of Preacher.

And Bobby was good. Real good. He moved as quiet as a mouse through a church. He moved so good that Preacher lost him. He couldn't see him, he couldn't hear him.

Preacher knew he was in trouble.

All right, Hoss, he thought. You played it smart and got yourself in trouble. Now what?

Bobby made the mistake of emitting a slight grunt when he jumped and that was the only thing that saved Preacher's life. He rolled to one side, leaving his rifle behind, and Bobby's tomahawk got buried in the dirt. Preacher kicked out, his foot catching Bobby on the knee and staggering him just long enough for Preacher to jump to his moccasins. Bobby immediately jerked a pistol out of his belt and Preacher's left hand shot out and clamped down on the man's wrist, preventing him from leveling the pistol. Locked together, the two men fought with fists. Preacher with his right, Bobby with his left.

Preacher slammed a big right fist again and again into Bobby's face, smashing his nose and pulping his lips. Bobby smashed a fist into Preacher's face and the blood from both men mingled in this death struggle. Bobby tried to back-heel Preacher but the mountain man had expected that and was ready.

Preacher heard the gun cock and finally managed to grab hold of his knife. He drove the blade into Bobby's side and twisted. The man-hunter screamed and pulled the trigger. Preacher felt a tremendous blow in his side and knew he'd been hit. How hard, he didn't know. But he knew it was bad. He jerked out the knife and cut Bobby from belly to backbone, then released the man.

Bobby fell to the ground. "At least I got lead in you," he gasped.

"You ain't gonna live long enough to enjoy it, though," Preacher spoke through gritted teeth against the throbbing pain in his side.

"I 'spect you be right about that, mountain man." That

was the last thing Bobby said. He shuddered once, then closed his eyes and died.

Knowing the shot would bring man-hunters at a gallop, Preacher got gone from there.

"All right," Bones said, staring at the two distinct blood signs. He had inspected Bobby's pistol. "We lost Bobby, but he got lead into Preacher, and judgin' from the blood, it's a bad wound. And this time it's real."

"Let us proceed at once!" Sir Elmore said.

"No!" Bones snapped with adamance. "Not in the dark. Think about it. Preacher gonna be holed up like a hurt panther, lickin' his wounds. A wounded animal is the most dangerous. We go blunderin' out there now, some of us ain't gonna be returnin'."

"At least with Preacher hurt, we can all get a decent night's sleep," Van Eaton allowed.

Preacher was weak when he arrived at his mountain camp. Before leaving the valley floor he'd grabbed up enough makin's for several poultices and now he set about boiling water. He took off his shirt and inspected as best he could the wounds. And there were two, one in the front, and the exit hole. Preacher had several bullet scars on his hide, and knew if the wound had been a killing one, he'd a been dead by now. But the bullet holes needed tendin', and the sooner the better. And he was already weak from the loss of blood. He made a broth from part of a venison haunch he'd hung up high and while that was simmerin' he cleaned out the wounds and applied the hot poultices. He added salt to the broth, for when you lose blood you crave salt. Then he drank two cups of the broth and felt a bit better. He put water on for coffee and lay back on his blankets to rest. Preacher was a realist, and he knew he was in real trouble. He was weak and in no shape for a fight. He'd heal quick—he always did. But he had to stay quiet for several days. As he lay warm by the fire, he reviewed his back trail. He'd left plenty of sign leavin' the scene of the death struggle, but he soon began erasin' his tracks. It wouldn't fool no Indian, but it might fool those with Bones. He had to have several days of rest. Preacher knew that wounds healed much quicker in the high up country . . . he didn't know why, but thought it probably had something to do with the cold, clean air.

He finally went to sleep just as the small fire was dying down to coals.

The trackers lost Preacher's sign less than two miles from the death scene in the valley. They started working in ever widening circles, but it didn't prove out. The mountain man had vanished without leaving a clue.

"They's got to be a drop of blood," Van Eaton insisted. "A broken twig, a bent leaf—something!"

"Look for yourself," Titus, the Kentucky man said matter-of-factly. "Wounded he may be, but it didn't slacken none his ability to hide a trail."

At that moment, Preacher was less than a half mile from the man-hunters. But people who are unfamiliar with the mountains fail to realize that there are literally hundreds of places to hide without detection. Preacher had left his horses at the missionary camp and on foot, left practically no sign.

And in hiding, Preacher never disturbed the natural look of the landscape, using nature at its purest for concealment. Preacher rested while Bones and the nobility stomped all over the place and accomplished nothing except for the raising of blisters on their feet.

Finally, Bones called a halt to the search for Preacher and pulled everybody back to the main camp in the valley.

There just wasn't any point in continuing. To the man-hunters, it seemed as though the mountain man had simply dropped off the face of the earth.

"Don't y'all be frettin' none about Preacher," Dirk, one of the newly converted men at the missionary camp told the women. "Hurt he may be, but that man is tough. And he knows ways to use what nature has provided to get hisself healed up."

"That's right," Will, another ex-man-hunter added. "That ol' boy is part wolf, part cougar, part bear, and all around mean when it comes to who flung the chunk. His kind is hard to kill. I seen a man up in the Blue Ridge one time take six balls in him and he still kept on comin'. He kilt them that was shootin' him and the last I heard, he was still alive and doin' right well, he was. There ain't no harder man in the world to stop than a feller who knows he's in the right and just keeps gettin' up and keeps on comin' at you."

Otto rode in and dismounted. "They've moved their camp," he told the group. "Over to the next valley west of here. This time they chose well. Preacher would be wise not to attempt any attack on this camp."

"If he's alive," Patience said, a gloomy note to her voice.

Otto smiled. "Oh, he's alive. I spoke with him not more than two hours ago."

Everyone started talking at once and Otto waited until the hubbub of voices had died down.

"He's still not a hundred percent, but very close to it. He's used Indian potions and poultices. We must learn those, people. Their healing powers are nothing short of miraculous. Preacher is fine."

Dirk gave Patience a friendly wink. "Told you," he said with a smile.

Nine

"We're just about out of everything," Van Eaton announced. "If we stretch coffee and beans and flour, we might last another ten days. No more."

"Them gospel-shouters has a-plenty," Dutch said. "I say we go take it and have our way with them women."

. Three weeks had passed without any of the man-hunters so much as glimpsing a track of Preacher. Preacher had moved very little. He had stayed alive by trapping rabbits, snaring mountain trout in fish-traps, and eating berries and tubers. After each rabbit, he would move the trap to a different location, sometimes no more than a few yards away. He was healed up and if anything, he was tougher and stronger than before. He was definitely leaner and meaner. He had killed a deer with bow and arrow and had passed the time by making himself a new pair of moccasins.

Now it was time to move.

Preacher had given up trying to understand the inner workings of the minds of those chasing him. He knew only that he was going to put an end to this hunt. He also knew that many of the men he had wounded would have by now left the missionary camp and rejoined Bones and his bunch. So much for trying to limit the killing.

So, on a fine morning in late summer, Preacher made his way to a place the Indians called Echo Point, the summit rearing up just over fourteen thousand feet in the thin air. It was a place where a shout could be heard for miles in all directions.

"I am Preacher!" the mountain man shouted, the words bouncing from valley to valley. "I am called Ghost Walker. White Wolf. Killing Ghost."

His words reached every human ear within miles. The Indians smiled and looked at one another in satisfaction, and the whites stiffened in shock.

"That cocky! . . ." Bones hissed.

"Magnificent!" Otto said.

"To those who hunt me, your time has come. You will not leave these mountains. Your flesh will rot and your bones will bleach under the sun and be scattered by the critters. You've hunted me and shot me and done your best to kill me. But I live. I live! Now I hunt. Now you will know the fear of the hunted. I will stalk you during the day and cut your throats while you sleep at night. You . . . all . . . will . . . die!" Preacher thundered.

"Big blowhard!" Tatman said, hobbling about the camp on a crutch. His knee was far from healed, but it was just about as healed as it was going to get with the time he had left to him. He hobbled over to where Joe Moss sat on a log, his own busted knee wrapped securely and stuck out in front of him, and carefully sat down. "We owe that mountain man, don't we, Moss."

"In spades," the man said bitterly. He pulled out a knife and began sharpening the blade on a stone, "I want to skin him alive; keep him screamin' for a long time."

"Yeah, yeah! That's a good idee, for shore."

Derby Peel walked over, favoring his healing ribs, and agreed with what Moss had to say. "Just let me be there when you do it, boys. I owe him too."

"Least you can walk," Tatman said. "Me and Moss is

crippled for life. It just ain't right what he done to us. It just ain't right. Cripplin' a man ain't no fair way to fight. It just by God ain't."

"Shore ain't," Moss agreed. "That man has con-demned me to be a cripple for the rest of my days. There just ain't no justice in this world, that's for shore."

Bones and Van Eaton had heard the words and ex-changed glances. "I ain't quittin'," Bones spoke softly. "I can't quit."

"I know," his friend replied. "I didn't say nothin' about quittin'. Just that we're soon gonna be out of supplies. Well," Van Eaton said with a sigh, "least we'll be together when the deed is done."

Bones gave him a sharp glance. "What the hell do you mean by that?"

"Aw, come on, Bones," Van Eaton whispered. "Look around you. Men all shot up an' limpin' an' crippled an' moanin' an' groanin'. One man done all that. One man, Bones. We ain't gonna beat that mountain man, Bones. And you know it well as me."

Bones made no reply. Just sat with his head down star-ing at his filthy hands.

Van Eaton stood up and put a hand on Bones's shoulder. "We been friends for nigh on thirty years, Bones. And we've made a right considerable sum of money chasin' wanted men. But I got me a feelin' in my guts that this here is our last run. Bones? We could always head west and change our names."

"No," Bones said firmly. "That mountain man ain't gonna make me turn tail like a whipped dog. Van Eaton?"

"Yeah?"

"You see me buried proper, all right?"

"All right. You do the same for me if I go first."

"You know I will."

On the other side of the camp, the nobility had listened to Preacher's words and promptly dismissed them as mere prattle. They had already discussed the matter of supplies and had decided that they'd give this hunt about ten more days and then head out of the mountains before winter. But they would return the next spring to resume the hunt. This had been the most exhilarating time of their spoiled, pampered lives.

Juan's butt had healed up well. Rudi's shoulder was a bit stiff but functioning. Burton's leg had healed up nicely as well.

They were ready for the hunt to resume.

Preacher strolled into the missionary's camp nonchalantly, as if he'd been gone for no more than an hour instead of three weeks. "Howdy, folks! Y'all got any vittles to eat?"

Everyone crowded around, inspecting him. Preacher looked to be better than he was the last time they'd seen him. Patience said so, speaking for all in the camp.

"It's the pure mountain air that done it. That and good clean Christian livin', of course," Preacher replied with a straight face. He looked around him. The area where they had housed the prisoners was empty. "What happened to all your patients?"

"Some died," John said. "They're buried in the meadow yonder. Most recovered and went back with Bones." He pointed to four clean-shaven and bathed men. "These four, Dirk, Simpson, Will, and Jim, have accepted Christ into their lives and are going to stay with us."

"Well, by golly, I think that's grand, boys." Preacher shook each newly converted hand and the former rouges and man-hunters grinned at him.

Dirk said, "You don't have to fret none about anything happenin' to these folks, Preacher. Me and the boys would give our lives for these fine people."

Preacher stared hard at the man, and silently agreed that Dirk meant it. "I believe you. You're a good man."

His plate of food was ready and Preacher sat down and dug in. He ate that and then ate another full plate before he was full. He leaned back with his pipe and a cup of coffee and sighed. "Y'all got any medicines left?"

"Some," Prudence said. "But not a large amount. Why?"

"Y'all better get ready for some more patients. 'Cause after I finish this coffee and smoke, I'm fixin' to go huntin' me some no-counts."

Otto said, "We offered them salvation. They refused. Some even openly scoffed at us. Since that time we have posted guards out at night and none of us ever go without our weapons. The women have all had firearms training."

"That's good. 'Cause if y'all plan on stayin' out here, sooner or later you women will have to pick up a gun and kill you an Indian or a brigand. I just hope that when the time comes, you won't hesitate none in the pullin' of that trigger." He paused to puff on his pipe. "When I get done with my business, I want to set you folks down and talk to you 'bout your plans on settlin' in this country. It ain't the wisest choice you could have made. But that'll wait 'til another day."

"Our mission remains clear and our course is unalterable," Patience told him.

"Uh-huh," Preacher said. "We'll see."

"Preacher," Otto said, quickly changing the subject, "I've seen the man-hunters' new camp. It's a good one for defense. The best they've chosen."

Preacher smiled. "I've seen it too. And they couldn't have picked no worser place. I'm headin' over there now. I'll see you folks tomorrow or the next day. Bye."

Preacher lay in the rocks above the camp and studied it more closely through his glass. Bones couldn't have

233

picked a worse spot if they'd all got together and held a stupid contest.

The camp had good water and there was graze for the horses, but the whole place was surrounded by timber. And Bones had built permanent watch shelters for the lookouts. Preacher memorized their locations and then stretched out for a nap. He planned on a busy evening.

Twice he'd lined up Tatman in his sights and twice Preacher had let the man live. He just couldn't pull the trigger. He just could not bring himself to shoot a man he'd made a cripple for the rest of his life. Preacher knew that if the conditions were reversed, Tatman would shoot him without blinking . . . but maybe, he thought, that's one of the main things that separates us.

It would have seemed incredible to others, but for a moment, Preacher felt a twinge of pity for the group of man-hunters. He's never seen a more beat-up and raggedy-lookin' bunch of men in all his days. They looked plumb pitiful. And he knew from the meager rations they were dishin' up that the bunch was nearly out of supplies.

From his position in the timber, Preacher counted the men. He shook his head. 'Way too many of them. The missionaries wouldn't stand a chance of beating them off if the man-hunters attacked in force. And if they ran out of supplies, they would attack and take what food the gospel-shouters had, and preacher knew they had plenty.

Preacher experienced that old feeling of being "between a rock and a hard place" land on him again. Whatever he decided to do, he had to keep the safety of the missionaries foremost in his mind.

Damn! he thought.

He thought a lot worse than that when one of the men stepped out of the campfire lit clearing and into the woods and came within a few feet of peeing on him.

I do get myself into some predicaments, Preacher thought sourly. The man finally closed up his britches and walked back into the clearing.

Preacher slowly backed away from the clearing, carefully avoiding the wet spot left by the man-hunter. He could have killed several of those chasing him—and he knew he probably should have—but for the time being, he left them live. He also felt he would probably regret that decision later on.

But Preacher wasn't going to leave the vicinity of the camp without first raising a little hell, letting the man-hunters know that he could move unseen among them any time he liked. He paused and gave that some thought. No, he concluded. No, he wouldn't do that. As much as he wanted to, he finally realized that wasn't such a good idea.

Preacher was torn with indecision. He just didn't know what to do. He knew what he *should* do, but he couldn't bring himself to do it. For the hundredth time, he wished these people would just go away and leave him be.

Preacher had the same feeling now as when years back, his older brother had told him there wasn't no such thing as Santy Claus.

For two days, Preacher watched the man-hunter camp and waited for them to do something. But all they did was eat and sleep and lounge about and act like they didn't have a care in the world. But Preacher had some cares. He knew he had to get those missionaries out of there before the snows came. People who had never experienced a winter in the high country had no idea just how fearsome a thing it was. The temperature could fall to way below zero faster than anybody would believe possible. And the passes would be clogged with snow. A man who knew the country and was on a good horse could make it. A wagon? No way.

The next morning, early, Preacher was in the missionary camp. "Pack up," he told them bluntly.

"I beg your pardon, sir?" Prudence questioned.

"Are you hard of hearin', woman? I said pack up and harness up. I'm gettin' you people out of here."

"You don't understand, sir," Hanna said. "We . . ."

Preacher waved her silent. "I understand more than you do, lady. I know it's damn near autumn. And I know I can't allow you people to be trapped up here when the snow comes. All the signs—if you know how to read them, and I do—point to a fierce winter. Y'all just don't know what winter is like in the mountains. Folks, we're high up. Higher than you realize. You just can't imagine what it's like up here in a blizzard. I can't get it through your heads that once the snow comes, you're stuck. You can't get them wagons out. Personally, I don't see how you ever got 'em *in.* You think you've seen winters back in New York or Maryland or wherever the hell it is you come from? You ain't seen nothin' 'til you seen snows piled tree-top high and winds fifty mile an hour and temperatures thirty below and water froze so solid you can walk a horse acrost it. You'll die, people. And the ground will be froze so deep down, blastin' powder wouldn't even dent it and I'd have to wait 'til spring to dig your graves. Am I gettin' through to you? Good. Now pack up. We're leavin' and to hell with them foolish bounty-hunters. With any kind of luck we'll be gone two-three days 'fore they realize it. Now . . . move!"

Ten

"Gone!" Bob Jones yelled, jumping from his horse. "They're gone!"

"Who's gone?" Lige said, standing up.

"Them missionaries, that's who."

Everyone in the camp gathered around him. Bones grabbed him by the arm. "Are you sure?"

Bob gave him a dirty look. "Sure? Hell, yes, I'm sure. I just come from there. And the campfire ashes was so old and cold they didn't hold nary a spark."

"The ground around the ashes?" Van Eaton asked.

"Cold."

"Two days at least," Ed Crowe said. "How about tracks?"

"Plenty of them. Headin' south. I figure that's why ain't none of us heard nothin' from Preacher. He's leadin' them gospel-shouters out."

Bones was thoughtful for a moment standing amid the cussing and loud-talking group. The four men who had left his group to stay with the missionaries were seasoned fighters with no back-up in any of them. Otto Steiner, Frank Collins, and Paul Marks all looked to be capable and tough. And Bones had no doubts about the women being able to fight right alongside their men. Add Preacher to that list and it made for a group who would stand tough

237

and fight to the bitter end. True, Bones and company had them out-numbered about five to one, but sometimes numbers made little difference when the other men were fighting for their families and for God.

Sir Elmore Jerrold-Taylor had found his slightly bent sword and was waving it around. Zaunbelcher had moved quickly to the other side of the clearing. "Break camp, men!" Elmore shouted. "We follow and attack. To your steeds, men. Hurry."

No one paid the slightest bit of attention to him. By now the man-hunters had all come to the conclusion that his Lordship was crazy as a bessie bug, and those with him weren't that far behind. Sir Elmore finally realized that no one was listening to him and walked off to pout.

"Well, we'll follow, for sure," Bones said. "But before we attack, I want to look this situation over."

"You mighty right about that," Van Eaton agreed. "Dirk and them others is no pilgrims. And them gospel-shouter men didn't look like no pushovers to me."

"I just wonder where that damn Preacher is taking them?" Lige Watson pondered aloud.

Preacher was taking the missionaries just as far away from the valley of the man-hunters as he could, driving them hard.

In two and half days, Preacher had pushed the wagons over thirty miles. A phenomenal feat considering the country in which they were traveling. But there was just no way to hide the trail the wagons left in their wake.

Preacher wasn't too worried about any Indian attack, for the Indians would see he was taking the whites out of their territory, and that basically was what they wanted. But he was moving them out of Ute and Arapaho country and onto the edge of Cheyenne territory. Although Preacher had always gotten along fairly well with the Cheyenne, a body just never knew when a band of young bucks might happen along and take that moment to attack.

"Notional," Preacher told Otto as they rode side by side. "Injuns is notional people. I reckon I understand 'em 'bout as well as any white man, and I'll be the first to tell you even after all the years I spent out here I don't really know all that much. A man can ride into near'bouts any Indian village and get fed and put up for the night and treated right well. It's when you try to leave that it gets right testy. Don't ask me why they do that, 'cause I just don't know."

"Because they are savages," Otto said. "Uneducated, Godless savages."

"They're uneducated accordin' to the white man's point of view, yeah. Smart as a body can get in their own right. I done told y'all they ain't Godless."

Dirk rode up. The women were handling the reins to the teams, while the men ranged front and back and to the sides of the tiny train. Dirk had been lagging back about five miles. "No sign of Bones yet, Preacher."

"They'll be along. But I think I can get us down to the hot springs for a soak 'fore they catch up to us. The ladies is gonna enjoy these springs."

They sure did, and it was only with the greatest of effort that the men didn't try to sneak a peek at the ladies as they bathed and soaked and squealed and giggled in their birthday suits, splashing and playing in the hot water.

Dirk stuffed rags in his ears and wandered off to read the Bible. Simpson and Jim volunteered to stand watch about a mile from the springs, and Will rode off to see about shooting some game. When the ladies were done the men took turns washing off days of grime and soaking out the kinks and stiffness in weary muscles and joints. Upon their return from the hot waters, Prudence got to battin' her eyes something fierce at Dirk—who was a fine-lookin' man—and swishin' her bottom and sashshayin' about. Dirk got so flustered he walked into a tree and damn near knocked himself goofy. Preacher figured if he could get Dirk and Prudence together and toss a bucket of cold water on them, he'd have enough steam to run one of them big ugly and terrible soundin' locomotives he'd seen Back East.

Preacher finally had to take off into the hills to get away from Patience. There was nothing he liked better than a good roll in the blankets with a fine-lookin' filly. But this was neither the time nor the place for a romantic tussle. However, he had learned a few years back that missionary women wasn't no different from other women when the candle got snuffed out and they got cozy. Loud, too. Preacher couldn't hear out the one ear for two days after a night with one particularly fine-lookin' gospel-shouter lady, a few hundred miles west and north of where they was right at the moment.

Preacher moved the pilgrims out the next morning. He'd heard tell of a tradin' post about four days from the springs and though he'd never been there, he decided to make a try for it. The missionaries were sorely in need of supplies. By this time, there were over a hundred and fifty trading posts scattered through the West. In two years trading posts had sprung up all over the place as more and more people were leaving their homes east of the Mississippi and heading west.

"Don't expect no fancy place like y'all seen in St. Louis," Preacher warned the ladies. "And the men there will likely ogle you gals from toes to nose. White women is scarce out here."

It was the most disreputable looking place the missionaries had ever seen. But it was a right busy post, doin' business with Indian and white alike. Preacher spoke with a couple of trappers he'd met over the years and knew slightly, then went inside to get a drink of whiskey.

Damned if the first person he spotted when he stepped

up to the rough bar was a man who'd swore on his mother's eyes he'd someday kill Preacher.

Mean Pete Smith almost swallowed his chewing tobacco when he looked up and saw Preacher. His mouth dropped open and his eyes bugged out.

"Shut your mouth, Pete," Preacher told him. "Flies is uncommonly bad this year."

"You!" Mean Pete hollered.

"In the flesh."

Mean Pete stood up.

"Take your rough stuff outside," the owner of the post said. "I'll brook no trouble in here."

"Shut up," Mean Pete told him. "Me and this rooster here got things to settle 'tween us."

"Whiskey," Preacher told the man behind the planks, doing his best to ignore Mean Pete. "And don't gimmie none with no snake-heads in it."

The man looked hurt. "I serve only the finest of whiskey, sir."

"Right," Preacher said drily. "Aged a full two days at least. Put a jug out here."

The bar was separated from the mercantile part of the post by a log wall. A brightly colored blanket served as a door.

"You better enjoy that drink, Preacher," Mean Pete said. "'Cause it's gonna be the last'un you'll have."

Preacher poured and sipped and grimaced. "I was wrong. This here stuff was aged 'bout one day."

"Did you hear me?" Mean Pete roared.

"Oh, shut up, Pete," Preacher told him. "You said the same thing last time we hooked up and I left you on the floor. Now sit down and be quiet."

Mean Pete wasn't about to sit down and shut up. He had taken an immediate dislike to Preacher years back and challenged him to a fight. Preacher whipped him. For the last twenty or so years, every two or three years Mean Pete would come up on Preacher, challenge him to fight, and Preacher would tear his meat house down.

After gettin' his butt bounced off the floor six or eight times, Preacher figured Mean Pete was about the hard-headedest man he'd ever met. Now here he was again. Only now it seemed like he wanted gunplay. Preacher was tired of gunplay. Weary of it. And he didn't want to kill Mean Pete. He turned to face Pete.

Preacher asked, "Pete, where in the world did you ever get the name of Mean Pete?"

"Haw?"

"Your name. Who was the first to call you Mean Pete?"

"I disremember. What's that got to do with anything?"

"I was just curious. 'Cause I ain't never heard of no kick and gouge you ever won. And when them Kiowa come at us down on the Canadian that time all I 'member seeing from you was your big butt runnin' off. So how in the world can you be called Mean Pete?"

"Preacher," Mean Pete took a step closer, his hands balled into fists, "I just ain't a-gonna stand here and let you in-sult me. I'm a-fixin' to stomp your ugly face. And then I'm a-gonna shoot you."

"In that order?"

Mean Pete flushed and took another step. He was a couple of inches taller than Preacher, and maybe twenty five pounds heavier. Neither Preacher nor Mean Pete noticed when the blanket was drawn back and the missionaries all crowded into the opening, staring at the scene before them.

Mean Pete gave a whoop and a holler and jumped at Preacher. Preacher drew back and busted him smack in the face with the full jug of whiskey and Mean Pete hit the boards. Pete didn't even moan. He was cold out.

Preacher turned to the man behind the bar. "If the whiskey had been worth a damn, I wouldn't a-done that. And if you want pay for that snake-head poison, get the money

242

from him." He pointed to Mean Pete. "Now give me a good jug 'fore you make me mad."

Patience fanned herself vigorously. "My word!" she whispered to Prudence. "He is such a *forceful* man."

Patience and Prudence were awakened that night by Preacher's somewhat drunken singing. It was a ditty he'd learned from a boatman in St. Louis one time and it was about a Scottish lassie named Lou Ann MacGreagor and her red sweater. Seems she filled it out rather well. The ditty seemed harmless enough until Preacher got to the second half of the song. Those verses concerned themselves with Lou Ann's undies . . . or as it turned out in the next verse, her lack of them. Just as Preacher got all tuned up to sing a few more verses, each one raunchier than the other, Patience and Prudence immediately began singing hymns, loudly. As Preacher's singing became lustier, the other missionaries quickly joined in Christian voice.

By all accounts, it was a rather odd mixing of tunes. Somehow, between Preacher's bellering and the sweet harmonies of Patience and Prudence and the others, Lou Ann MacGreagor got to the promised land and got all mixed up with the prophets and everybody was girding their loins and dancing naked on the rock of ages with the angels and the meek.

A drunken Arapaho staggered out of the barn, where he'd been imbibing with some friends and joined in, singing in his own tongue about a lost love . . . which in this case was his horse.

Preacher woke up the next morning rather confused. He just could not remember ever hearing that ditty sung in quite that manner.

He finally put it off to bad whiskey. But he couldn't understand why Patience and Prudence and Hanna and Jane and Sally were all giving him such dirty looks.

By noon it appeared that Preacher had been forgiven for his night of drunkenness and people were once more speaking to him, not that it mattered one whit to Preacher whether they spoke or not. His head hurt anyway.

"That loutish fellow back there," Otto said, riding up beside Preacher. "Mean Pete. Will he be coming after you?"

"Naw," Preacher said. "He was drunk. He never does remember our fights . . . might be 'cause they're so short. The one thing he does remember is that he don't like me."

"Why?"

"I don't know. He took one look at me years back and decided he didn't like me. We been havin' these head-buttin's ever since. Mean Pete is kind of a strange feller."

"I'm sure he must have his good points."

"If he does, he sure keeps 'em hid right well."

"Where are you taking us, Preacher?"

"Bent's Fort."

"But, sir . . ."

Preacher shook his head. "Otto, you and the others is fine people. Good people, and you mean well. But ain't none of you needs to be out here in the wilderness. Come back in ten years. You want to save souls, practice on whites first, 'cause the Injuns don't want you. I told you the Injuns got their own religion and they're happy with it. You've told me time and again that you want to farm. Fine. Go to Arkansas or Louisiana or East Texas and farm. You and Hanna have kids and be happy. You can find heathens to convert anywhere. This whole country's gonna bust loose in a few years. The Injuns claim all this country as their own. They pretty much put up with us trappers 'cause I reckon we're all more Injun than white after all this time out here and we don't meddle in their affairs."

"But, sir . . ."

"Hush up an' listen to me. When we get to the fort, y'all hook up with wagons headin' Back East and go. Now, damnit, Otto, you know in your heart and your brain that I'm right."

The man sat in his saddle in silence for a time. He slowly nodded his head. "Yes, you're right, Preacher." He smiled. "But it has been a grand adventure."

"Tell your grandkids about it. Write a book about it. And think kind thoughts of me."

"Patience will be disappointed. She, ah, likes you, Preacher."

"She'll get over it. She'll find her some fine Christian man and get hitched up and I'll be just a fadin' memory in her mind. Now go tell the others what we're doin', Otto."

Patience and Prudence both let out a howl at the news, but they soon settled down as Otto convinced them that they could better serve their church in a more civilized area. Now all Preacher had to worry about was getting the pilgrims to safety. He knew a place about two days away where mountain men tended to gather for a ride to Bent's Fort. If he could reach them before Bones and his bunch caught up with them, the missionaries would be safe, for Bones and his man-hunters would never attack a dozen or so mountain men. If they were foolish enough to do that, it would be the last time they ever attacked anyone.

Preacher's luck held and two days later, a few hours before dusk, he led the wagons into the encampment of mountain men.

"Wagh!" a huge bear of a man shouted, rising from the ground upon spotting Preacher. "It's Preacher, boys. With a whole passel of pilgrims."

"That's the man who told us you were a man of the cloth, Preacher," Otto said.

"Horsehide!" Preacher hollered. "You big ugly moose!

Ho, Papa Griz. I brung you boys salvation. God knows you heathens need some."

"We was ridin' for the mountains to lend you a hand, Preacher," a man called.

"Hell, I don't need no help. But I'd like to prevail upon you boys to help these fine folks I got with me."

The mountain men took one look at Patience and Prudence and Preacher knew his worries were over. The missionaries would be safe. Preacher would resupply from his friends and then head back to confront and once and for all close the book on Bones and his man-hunters. Preacher wasn't lookin' forward to it, but it was something that had to be done. He sat down by the fire and stretched his legs out with a contented sigh. Most of the wild and woolly and uncurried mountain men were gathered around the missionaries, unhookin' the teams, helping the ladies down from the seats and ogling Patience and Prudence, hopin' to catch a glimpse of a nicely shaped ankle. These men were as wild as the wind and just about as hard to handle, but they could be as protective as a mamma bear with her cubs.

Preacher took the cup of coffee handed him. "Word from the Injuns we've talked to is you've raised unholy hell with them ol' boys a-huntin' you, Preacher," a man known as De Quille said.

"Yeah? Well, I'm a-fixed to raise me some more hell with them."

"You want a couple of us to ride along with you?"

Preacher shook his head. "Naw. There ain't but about thirty or forty of 'em."

De Quille smiled. "Seems to me there was two bunches of about forty each started out after you, Preacher."

"I been whittlin' 'em down some."

"Do tell? I got news, Preacher. Them warrants on you has been lifted. There ain't no charges against you. It's all personal on both sides now, ain't it?"

Preacher looked at him and his eyes told the whole story. De Quille nodded his head. "That's what I figured," he said.

Eleven

The next morning, Patience and Prudence held a short service before they pulled out. It was a strange, yet wonderful and moving scene. The rough and wild-looking mountain men standing with heads uncovered and bowed while the ladies sang sweetly and Otto said a short prayer. Fifteen minutes later, after the goodbyes, the wagons were rolling eastward.

Preacher sat by the fire, deep in thought, and finished the pot of coffee. He was trying to figure out a way to tell the men with Bones and those silly foreigners that all warrants against him had been lifted and if they killed him now, it would be murder. Then he wondered if that news would make any difference? Probably not, but he was going to try. Providing he could do so without getting his head shot off. One way or the other, he was going to end this man-hunt. If he could do it without spilling another drop that would be wonderful. But he had strong doubts. Like De Quille had said, and no matter how many excuses Preacher made, this was personal now.

Preacher made certain the fire was out, then he packed up and swung into the saddle. Might as well get this over with.

* * *

Bones and party had no knowledge of any trading post any closer than Bent's Fort, so they were riding straight south while Preacher was heading straight north. All of them heading straight toward canyon country. The only difference was, Bones and his bunch got lost in the maze of twists and turns and blind canyons. Preacher did not.

Preacher looped around the tortured maze of canyons, thinking even Bones would have more sense than to get all tangled up in there. He had stopped north of the canyons to rest and water his horse when the smell of death touched his nostrils . . . that sickly stench that he knew so well.

Preacher made no immediate move. Whatever it was out there was dead, and hurryin' wouldn't bring it—or them—back to life. And Preacher had him a hunch it was dead human bodies. Or what was left of them after the buzzards had feasted.

Preacher led Thunder, following the stink of death until he came to the scene. He ran around the scattered and torn-apart bodies, knockin' buzzards away until they finally got it into their pea-brains they were not welcome. It was something they were accustomed to, so they waddled off and waited with the patience of millions of years bred into them.

Preacher steeled himself and began trying to put body parts to the right body. What the buzzards hadn't worked on during the day, the critters had dined on at night. It was not a pretty sight; but one the mountain man had seen many times before. Buzzards will usually go for the belly, pullin' all the guts and soft organs out, the kidneys, and the eyes and mouth—diggin' for the tongue—first. Then they attack the rest of the body.

After a time, during which Preacher had to finally puke and get it over with, he finally concluded it had been a party of ten to twelve men, maybe as many as fifteen. And from the tracks, they'd each had them a pack horse or two.

There was no sign of arrow or tomahawk, the men had not been scalped, so Preacher ruled out Indians. This was white man's work, and he had him a pretty good idea who'd done it. Bones and the scum with him. The men had been trappers, judging from what was left of their clothing. Their weapons and powder had been taken, along with their horses and all the supplies.

Preacher picketed Thunder and went prowling on foot until he found some sign. He recognized some of the hoof-prints as horses being rode by Bones's bunch. He smiled. The fools was headin' straight into the maze. Odds were good they'd get lost, finally figure things out, and head right back this way. He would be waiting.

The bodies were, best as he could figure, 'bout two or three days old. He dragged the bodies and body parts into a natural ditch and worked the rest of the day covering them with rocks. Then he found a pointy rock and scratched into a huge boulder:

A PARTY OF ABOUT TWELVE MEN. AMBUSSHED AND KILT BY BONES GIBSON AND THE CRAP AND CRUD THAT RODE WITH HIM. 1840. I THINK.

Preacher mounted up and rode for a couple of miles, then picketed Thunder on grass and took himself a long bath in a cold creek, usin' some soap that Hanna had given him. The soap was so strong it stung like the devil when he got it in his eyes, but it washed away the stink of the dead and got rid of a few fleas too, he was sure.

Dressed out in clothes that Frank and Paul had given him—he was airin' out his buckskins—Preacher put water on to boil and then tried to relax. He just didn't have an appetite at all for food—not yet anyways. The longer he sat and drank the hot, black, strong coffee and thought and brooded about the men he'd pieced together and then buried, the madder he got. He'd make a bet that he'd known some of those fellers. But the bodies had been so tore up there had been no way to tell. Those men had been ambushed, murdered, and then robbed of everything they had, right down to their britches and boots and jackets. They even took rings and amulets and such. Several of the men were missing fingers that had been hacked off.

Then, all of a sudden, it got real personal for Preacher. That body back yonder with no thumb on his left hand. Preacher had been with him when a Pawnee tomahawk had taken it off. Jon LeDoux was his name. And Jon had saved Preacher's bacon one time, too. Preacher's face tightened. Yeah. Up on Crow Crick, it had been. If it hadn't been for Jon, Preacher's bones would be rottin' under the ground. And Jon was never far from Ol' Burley Movant. Yeah. Bodies began to take shape now as Preacher could put missing fingers and scars and hair to faces. One of them back yonder had been Bill Swain, he was sure of it. And Bobby Gaudet had been a friend of Bill Swain. They'd all been down to the post to resupply and were headin' back into the Lonesome for the autumn season. Sure. That's why the wooden castoreum bottles had been left behind. Them ambushin' filth hadn't known what it was. Probably one of them uncorked a jug and seen how bad it smelled and left it. The grisly picture was beginning to take shape in Preacher's mind, and it was not a pretty one.

Now Preacher could, with almost dead accuracy, name every one of the men who'd been ambushed. He dug out a scrap of paper and a pencil and began writing down the names. Most of the men back yonder had kin, and they'd have to be notified. John Day had an Injun for a wife, but Preacher didn't have any idea where they'd chose to cabin in for the winter. Sam Curtis, on the other hand, didn't have anybody. He'd been an orphan when he ran off from the home and come west. Same with Onie. Preacher didn't even know Onie's last name or even if he had one. The others in the ambushed party would just have to lie in peace unknown, for Preacher couldn't put names to them.

But he could avenge them. And to hell with giving them murderin' ambushers any more chances.

"I found a way out," Jackson said, stepping down from the saddle and gratefully taking the offered canteen and drinking deeply. He wiped his mouth with the back of his hand. "But when we leave, stay bunched up; don't wander off. It's a twisted mess."

Actually, it wasn't that bad. It was just that these eastern men had never seen anything like the tortured and rocky canyons and it panicked them.

"Good work, Jackson," Bones said. "Get some rest. We'll pull out at first light."

"Preacher?" Van Eaton asked.

"God only knows where he is and what he's doing."

Preacher was waiting and watching about five miles inside the entrance to the canyons. He could see Jackson winding his way through the maze, lost as a goose and had been amused by the man's uncertain actions. Preacher had always found his part of the country rather pleasing; but it could be a mite hard on a man if he didn't know his way around.

While Bones and his party were resting that late afternoon, Preacher dislodged a few good-sized boulders and blocked the trail that Jackson had so carefully marked out with loads of rocks and dirt. He returned to his camp and fixed his supper, working with a cold and savage smile on his lips. Tomorrow should turn out to be right interesting, Preacher thought to himself.

"I thought you said this way was clear?" Lige asked Jackson, a surly expression on his unshaven face.

"It was, yesterday," Jackson replied. "Rock slides happen."

"Now what?" Bones asked.

"We either dig through all that piled up crap or take that other way through I told you about," Jackson said.

Those were the last words he ever spoke. Preacher's rifle boomed and the ball struck Jackson squarely in the center of his chest. He toppled off his horse and landed heavily on the sand.

Panic erupted on the canyon floor. Dozens of hooves churned up so much dust it blanketed the area like a thick, dirty fog. None of the man-hunters gave even a second thought to Jackson; not pausing long enough to see if he was dead or wounded. They just spurred their horses and ran for cover.

Preacher knew a dozen other ways out of the canyons, easier ways, for the area in which Bones thought he was trapped was really not that large. It just seemed that way to a man who was lost.

Preacher knew he was safe on the rim of the canyon. The sides were high and straight up. From where he sat, several hundred feet up, he could see two ways to leave this particular series of canyons. But he doubted those below would ever find them in time. He waited until the dust settled and the canyons were as silent as Jackson, sprawled on the sands.

"Bones," Preacher called. "I found them trappers you and your scum killed back yonder." He waited for denial. None came. "Some of them boys was friends of mine. And the worst one of them was worth more than the whole bunch of you. I been fightin' with my mind for days, tryin' to figure out if I should just go on and lose you crappy bunch of fools. Them you ambushed back yonder made up my mind. I can't let you people get back to civilization and kill more decent folks. I can't have nothin' like that on

253

my conscience for the rest of my life. So y'all know what that means."

Preacher didn't expect any reply, and none came. "I just thought I'd let you know where you all stood," he called, then he began shifting locations, working his way around the edge of the rim, coming up, he hoped, behind Bones and his bunch.

"I warned you all repeatedly that we should have given those men a proper burial," Steinwinder chided all within the sound of his voice.

"Aw, shut up!" Sutton told him. "I'm tared of you and that flappin' mouth of yourn. Hell's far, boy. You was the one who wanted to scalp some of 'em."

He never got to say another word. Preacher's rifle boomed and Sutton took the ball through his head. He slumped against the now blood splattered, gray wall of the canyon.

"What a disgusting sight!" Steinwinder said, as he quickly moved to a more secure position, away from Sutton.

Preacher fired his second rifle and the big ball just missed Steinwinder's head, throwing sand in the man's eyes, and blinding him momentarily.

"I've been gravely wounded!" the Austrian hollered, stumbling to his feet. "Help me. I've been blinded."

Jon Jouviere jerked him down and bathed his eyes with water.

Preacher was moving quickly, again angling for a better position. But the men had moved into the shadows of the canyon walls, and they were very difficult to spot. Preacher was all through playing games with the manhunters. He wasn't interested in shots that only wounded. He wanted an end to this. And he hadn't been joking with Bones this time. Preacher was mad to the bone.

"We're trapped in here, Bones," Evans said. "Preacher'll just lay up yonder and pick us off one at a time."

"Maybe not. Jackson told me he'd found two ways out and marked both of them. Horace, you snake outta here and find that other pass."

"I'm gone," the man said, and began crawling out, staying in the shadows.

Up on the rim, Preacher passed up several shots that would have broken a leg or ankle or arm. He looked up at the sun. Nine o'clock, he guessed accurately. He had plenty of time.

Horace Haywood found the other exit, but it was narrow and dark and twisting and he didn't like the looks of it. But he liked it better than facing Preacher's shooting. He edged his way back to Bones.

"It's there, all right. But it ain't gonna be easy."

"Nothing has been on this trip," Bones said wearily. "Water the horses several times today. All that we can spare. Keep them fresh and in that pocket back yonder. Strip the saddles from them and rub them down good. Then tie down anything that'll rattle or make any kind of noise. That'll keep the boys busy for a time. And stay in the shadows and out of sight. Come full dark, we'll slip outta here."

Some of them wouldn't.

Flores mistook a round rock for Preacher's head. He slipped out of the shadows and lifted his rifle to his shoulder. Preacher's rifle sang its hot, smoky song and Flores was slammed back against the side of the canyon wall. "Mother of God," he whispered. "I am truly going to die in this horrible place."

"One place is as good as another," Prince Juan Zapata said, the Spanish penchant for fatalism surfacing at last in the man. "You are Catholic?"

"Sí."

"I will pray for you."

"Gracias, amigo."

Zapata's dark, cold, and cruel eyes looked at the man.

"Amigo?" He chuckled at the familiar usage from a man far beneath his royal class. "Well, why not? You know, Flores, up there on that rim is a better man than all of us."

"I know," Flores whispered, both hands holding his bloody stomach. "But we found out too late. Que hombre."

"Yes, he is. What a grand adventure this was going to be. Some adventure, right, Flores?"

Flores couldn't answer. He was dead. Zapata gently closed the man's eyes and lowered him full length to the sand.

"What were you discussing with that peasant, Juan?" Sir Elmore asked.

Zapata smiled. "You would never understand, Elmore. Not in a million years. I'm not sure I do."

Twelve

Preacher had spotted the second way out of this series of canyons and left the rim above the man-hunters just after high noon. He'd seen Haywood crawling away and guessed correctly he was looking for another way out. Preacher had watched him return. From his vantage point, high above the group, Preacher could also see where the horses were being held and shortly after the man's return, had spotted unusual activity there. He figured accurately that Haywood had found the way out and the trapped men would try to slip away just after dark. That would be just fine and dandy. He would be waiting.

Preacher fired no more shots the remainder of that day. Just as the day began to cool and shadows were covering the entire canyon floor, Preacher heard several horses whining. Rifles loaded, he waited.

As the pass widened near where Preacher waited, the escaping men would be outlined faintly. Preacher would choose his targets with care, for he did not want to kill a horse. He also knew that if he got two this time, he would be lucky, for at the sound of the first shot, the man-hunters would put the spurs to their horses and leave the pass at a full gallop.

When the lead rider was faintly outlined, Preacher sighted in and squeezed the trigger. The man tumbled from the saddle. Just as he'd predicted, the men behind the fallen man-hunter shouted and spurred their horses. Preacher grabbed up his second rifle and snapped off a shot. He saw the man jerk as the ball hit him, but the rider managed to stay in the saddle. Then the canyon was filled with dust and Preacher could see nothing. He reloaded his rifles and listened to the pound of hooves gradually fade into the early night. He wasn't worried; that many men would leave a trail anybody could follow. He'd pick it up come the morning. He made his way down to the canyon floor and stripped the saddle and bridle from the horse, turning the animal loose.

Preacher had been lucky, for the second man had been leading a packhorse. When the ball struck him, he lost the lead rope. Preacher smashed the weapons, rendering them useless, left the dead man where he was and took the pack-horse back to his camp. The man probably had gold on him, but Preacher didn't want it. He relieved the animal of his burden and sat down to fix supper. He'd go through the newly found supplies at first light.

Over coffee, Preacher tried to put himself in the boots of the man-hunters. Where would they go? They were all eastern men, and most would want to get back to familiar territory. They did not know this country, and would probably elect to go back the same way they came. That was only a guess on Preacher's part, but he felt it was a good one.

Or was it? By now, the news of all those warrants against him being lifted would be common knowledge at Bent's Fort. Bones might not want to take the chance of running into any of Preacher's friends at the fort and risk gunplay. So the group might decide to head north and then cut east. Well, he'd know come the morning.

* * *

It was a silent bunch of men who finally reined in their weary horses and made camp. They had escaped the canyon but they all knew they had not escaped Preacher. The mountain man would be after them like fleas to a dog.

They'd lost one packhorse, but still had supplies a-plenty to get them back to civilization. And to a man, that's where they wanted to go. They all agreed they wanted no more of the mountains and the mountain man called Preacher. Even the gentry agreed with that, albeit reluctantly.

"Preacher's gonna follow us if it takes him to hell," Van Eaton spoke softly to Bones. "We ain't never gonna be rid of that mountain man."

"I know," Bones said, weariness in his voice. Like the others, Bones was dirty and could smell the rancid stink from his body. His clothing was stiff with dirt and days-old sweat. "But I'm out of ideas."

"I got one," Van Eaton said. "We run like the devil hisself is after us."

"He is," Bones whispered. "He is."

Preacher had inspected the supplies, took what he needed, and turned the packhorse loose. Then he was on the trail of the man-hunters. He followed their tracks and found their now deserted camp. A dead man lay stiffening on the ground. Preacher figured it was the man he'd shot coming out of the canyon. Some of those with Bones had taken everything of value from the man, even taking his pants, jacket, and boots.

"You shore teamed up with a pack of lousy no-counts," Preacher said to the dead man. "But I reckon you wasn't no better than them so I ain't gonna waste my time plantin' you." He left the dead man and headed out, following the easy to see trail.

Bones was leading the men straight north. "You won't

go north long, Bones," Preacher said. "You'll have to cut east in about three or four days. And I know where that'll be." He knew that Bones had some sort of a crude map, for one of the men who chose to remain with the missionaries had told him so.

"So I 'spect you'll be cuttin' some east today. Just about noon. I'll be a-waiting' for you, Bones. I'm gonna drive you back into the mountains, ol' son. You ain't gettin' out on the plains. Not if I can help it. And I can help it." He lifted the reins. "Come on, Thunder. We got some hard travelin' to do."

"This ain't like Preacher," Bones said. "I don't believe for a second he's given up. So where is he?"

The nobility had been strangely silent for the past two days. They had finally begun to grasp the seriousness of it all. They had finally got it through their aristocratic noggins that there was a very good chance they were going to die. Juan Zapata had sensed it first, back in the canyon. Robert Tassin had been next in line to understand the gravity of it all, and that feeling of doom had quickly spread to the others. They understood now that out here in the wilderness, their wealth and station in life meant nothing. They were in a situation where their money could not buy them out of it. And that knowledge was beginning to show on them. For the past two nights they had huddled together, speaking in low tones.

Bones knew the gentry was up to something. What, he didn't know. And he didn't care. He personally hoped they would break off and go it alone.

And that's exactly what they did.

The group had been traveling through a rough and dense part of the country, with each man having to concentrate on his own business. No one seemed to notice as the nobility began lagging behind . . . along with several other men. When Bones halted the group for food and rest at about noon, the gentry were gone, along with Dutch, Percy, Falcon, Hunter, and Bates.

"Hell with them," Van Eaton said. "I'm glad to be shut of the whole bunch."

"Yeah," Haywood said. "We got our money so who cares. Maybe Preacher will spent his time chasin' after them and leave us alone."

"But they took two of the mules and a lot of supplies," Lige pointed out.

Bones shrugged his shoulders. "I'm just glad they're gone. Good riddance."

Preacher studied the ground carefully. The bunch had separated here. Bones and his people were still headin' for the plains, and twelve or thirteen others had continued on to the north. "Intertestin'," Preacher muttered.

He had miscalculated where Bones would cut due east, and lost time in backtracking. But Bones had made a bad choice and had to travel through mighty rough country. Preacher figured he was only hours behind Bones. So he'd come up behind them. That was fine. He knew a short cut around this brushy tangle that Bones knew nothing about. And that might put him ahead of Bones. But it would be close. Real close.

"You seem to be the most capable among us, Mister, ah, Dutch," Sir Elmore Jerrold-Taylor said to the burly man. "So we have voted and you shall lead."

"Fine. First thing we got to do is get hid from Preacher. And I mean, hid good. When we get done restin' here, we'll take to that crick over yonder and stay in it long as we can. We'll leave it several times, but always come back to it. That'll cause Preacher to waste a lot of time huntin' for our tracks. We'll find us a place to hole up. Bet on it."

"Excellent thinking!" the duke exclaimed. "You get us through, and you shall receive a bonus."

Dutch nodded his head. "I want me a shot at Preacher. I owe that no-good. I really do."

"Perhaps you might think up a fine plan for an ambush, Dutch?" Baron Wilhelm Zaunbelcher suggested.

"I been thinkin' on one. I surely have."

Preacher beat Bones and his bunch by only a few minutes. But it was time enough for him to load up all his rifles and get into position. He would be shooting downhill, but the grade was a gentle one. And they had to come through, or try to come through, this pass, or else go miles out of their way. But Preacher wasn't going to allow them through . . . if he could help it.

Preacher let the first few riders enter the pass and then he emptied a saddle. Will Herdman was slammed out of his saddle, dead before he bounced on the rocky trail. Preacher grabbed up another rifle, but he was too late. Bones and crew were learning fast. Those who had entered the pass had left their horses and taken cover behind the huge boulders that littered the gap. Preacher reloaded and settled down for a long wait.

"Preacher!" Bones shouted from the mouth of the pass. "Listen to me, Preacher. The gentry is gone. They left us. We ain't got no more quarrel with you. This was a job of work, Preacher. That's all. You takin' this personal."

"You mighty right, I am," Preacher muttered. "You kilt Eddie, Wind Chaser, and his whole family and band. Then you kilt a dozen friends of mine. It's personal, all right."

"Preacher!" Bones shouted. "We're just a bunch of ol' boys tryin' to make a livin', that's all. And we didn't have nothing to do with killin' that boy or them trappers. That was all the work of the gentry."

"Sure," Preacher whispered. "Wonder how come it was that the supplies I took the other day still had a few traps amongst the other gear?"

"Look here, Preacher," Van Eaton shouted. "We made a mistake in comin' after you. But we're big enough men to admit it. Let's just call it quits and call it even. No hard feelin's, all right?"

Preacher had a idea. "I'll think on that for a minute," he shouted. He found a stick and put his battered old hat on one end. "All right, Bones. I'm comin' down and you and me, we can talk some. How 'bout it?"

"Get set to blow his head off," Bones told Van Eaton. "That's a good deal, Preacher," he shouted. "Ain't no reason at all why you and me can't be pards, now, is there?"

"Right," shouted back.

Preacher crawled on his belly for a few yards, and then slowly lifted the hat until the brim was even with the top of a large rock. A rifle cracked and the hat flew off. Preacher screamed as if in terrible pain and then fell silent. He quickly crawled back to his loaded rifles and waited. "You sorry . . ." He bit back the oath.

Preacher kicked at a rotting log and the log broke free and rolled a few yards, thudding against a rock. It sounded, he hoped, like a body falling.

"I believe we got him!" Lige shouted.

"I think we did," Van Eaton said, his words carrying up to Preacher.

"Good shootin', Van Eaton!" Evans said. "You finished the man for good this time."

"There's one I owe you, Van Eaton," Preacher muttered, sliding around into a better shooting position. "And you can bet I'll pay that debt."

Stan Law jumped up from his cover, a large knife in one

hand. "I get to cut off his head!" he shouted. "Somebody bring the picklin' jar."

"No! I get to cut off his head!" Cantry shouted.

"We'll race to see who gets the head!" a thug called Billy yelled.

Preacher let them come, all of them, including Bones and Van Eaton, running up the grade, knives in hand, laughing and yelling and shouting and joking and racing to see who would get to cut off Preacher's head.

"Sorry, boys," Preacher said, then stood up. Holding two rifles like pistols, he fired, dropped those rifles, picked up two more, and emptied those. Then he grabbed for his pistols and really began uncorking the lead.

Billy went down, shot through the head. Cantry took a ball in the center of his chest and stopped abruptly, falling back against Bones and knocking him down, unknowingly saving the bounty-hunter's life. Stan Law took a ball through his stomach. The heavy ball, fired at such close range, tore out his back. Bob Jones stopped his running and for a moment, and stared in horror at the growing carnage before him. He only had a moment to look before Preacher grabbed up his pistols. Bob took a double-shotted charge in the face and would have been unrecognizable even to his mother. Jose screamed in panic and turned around just as Preacher fired. The ball passed through his neck, just below the base of his skull. Paul Guy's bladder relaxed in fear and the last thing he would ever remember was that he had peed his pants.

Then the gang was running and rolling and falling and sliding down the grade, some of them losing rifles and knives and pistols in their haste to get away. When they reached the bottom, they didn't look back, just headed for their horses and galloped away.

Preacher glanced at the dead and dying sprawled grotesquely below him and without changing expression, began reloading.

"You a devil!" Stan gasped at him.

"I reckon I might have shook hands with him a time or two," Preacher acknowledged. "The difference between us is, I know when to turn loose."

Thirteen

The man-hunters ran their horses over rough country, straight west, for several miles before the exhausted animals could go no farther. Reason finally overcame fear and Bones halted the wild retreat before he and his men killed their horses.

Slumped on the ground, trembling from fear, exhaustion, and shame, Bones looked at what was left of his party of bounty-hunters. He'd come west with just over forty men. He was down to fifteen, counting himself. He looked over at Lige, sitting with what was left of his bunch. Counting himself, Lige had been reduced to six men.

Bones Gibson shook himself like a big dog and stood up, amazed that his legs would support him. He was ashamed of himself for running away like a scared cat from a pack of dogs. He looked at the discouraged and thoroughly filthy bunch of men. "All right, people, listen up. Look at me, damnit, you dirty pack of cowards!" That got their attention. They stared at him, some of them through fear-glazed eyes.

Bones said, "We're through runnin'. I mean it. This is the end of runnin' from that mountain man. We're gonna get out of this fix, in an orderly retreat. We're gonna operate like an army from now on. With captains and lieutenants and sergeants and the like. And I'm the captain of this company. Anybody don't like it, leave and do it right now."

No one moved. But new interest now took the place of hopelessness in many eyes.

"I'm fixin' to give you my first order. Here 'tis: We take shifts guardin' while the others take a bath in that creek over there. And I mean bathe. With soap. Then we shave close and give each other haircuts. And we wash our clothes and air out our blankets. When that's done, and we all look like human bein's again, instead of like a bunch of people who just crawled out of a cave, then we make our plans. Now move. Move!"

It was almost dark when Preacher hunkered down and watched the last one die. He rolled them all into a pile and tossed brush and limbs over them. He smashed their weapons and threw them aside. Then he went back to Thunder, saddled up, and rode out. He knew of a little spot that was ideal for a camp. He'd pick up the trail of the man-hunters come the morning. Right now, he wanted some hot food and a good night's sleep.

Miles to the north, Dutch had halted the men and made a very tight and secure camp. Dutch was under no illusions. He'd come to realize they were up against a first-class fighting man who possessed all the skills needed to not only survive in this God-forsaken country, but to prosper in it. Dutch was going to call on all of his eastern woodsman skills to avoid Preacher. He did not want a fight with the man until the odds were all on his side. And he felt sure that would come, sooner or later. But for now, they had to stay alive.

The royalty had stopped their foolish antics, all of them finally realizing this was not a game, not a sporting event.

This was a life or death struggle against a very skilled and very determined fighter. And to a man, they had silently admitted they were out-classed by Preacher. And they had suddenly turned into the hunted.

It was not a feeling that any of them savored. Just the thought of it left their mouths experiencing the copper-like taste of fear.

Sound carries in the high country, and they had all heard the very faint sounds of gunfire to the south of them. They all wondered how many more men Preacher had killed.

"Canada," Sir Elmore said aloud.

"Beg pardon?" Dutch lifted his head and looked at the man.

"Canada," Elmore repeated. "We'll try for Canada. We'll be safe there."

"That's hundreds of miles away," Falcon said. "Up through the unknown. Winter's gonna be on us in a few weeks. We got to get out of these mountains."

"I concur," Zaunbelcher said. "I do not think any of us would live through a winter trapped in here."

Rudi Kuhlmann looked at the six men who had chosen to accompany the royalty. "Get us out of this alive, gentlemen, and none of you will ever have to worry about money again. And that is a promise."

"You got a deal," Dutch told him.

"We'll cut north in the morning," Bones told his group. "Head straight for Canada."

"Canada!" Lige blurted.

The men at least looked more or less human now that they had bathed and shaved and trimmed their hair. But their thoughts were still dark and savage when it came to Preacher. They had panicked back at the pass, and were ashamed of it. And each had silently promised nothing like that would ever happen again.

"That ain't a bad idea," Evans said. "I got some friends up there and they're doin' all right. They been up there for 'bout three years now. Huntin', fishin', trappin'. They're gettin' by, so's I hear."

"All right," Van Eaton said. "Canada it is. We'll pull out at first light."

"Now this is mighty interestin'," Preacher muttered, squatting down and studying the tracks. He had been following the tracks of Bones's bunch for two days. They had passed right by an easy way out of the Rockies and kept right on heading north. "Canada," Preacher whispered. "Canada? Now why did I think of that?" He didn't know, but the thought would not leave him. "Well, I ain't runnin' them ol' boys clear to Canada." He swung back into the saddle, curious now, and once more began his following the trail. He took his time, trying to figure out what in the world Bones had in mind this time.

Unbeknownst to either of the two groups, they were only about ten miles apart, and since Bones and his bunch were traveling faster, almost parallel to one another.

Preacher shared his supper with an old Indian and his wife who had stumbled onto his camp, and after eating, the men smoked and talked. The old man and his wife were of the Northern Ute, and both were not well. They were going back south to where they had first met, long ago, to build a lodge and die together.

The old Ute told him that there were two parties of white men, about eight or ten miles apart, both of them traveling north. He said he sensed evil in these men, and he and his woman had hidden both times. He said the men were not happy people; sullen and grim-faced. And they used bad language . . . at least it sounded bad to him.

The old man had heard of Ghost Walker, and was honored to be in the presence of such a fine and brave warrior.

When preacher awakened the next morning, he knew the old man and woman would be gone, and they were. Lying next to Preacher's blankets was a gift from the old Indian, one of the finest-made tomahawks Preacher had ever laid eyes on. Preacher hefted it and knew it was made to throw, and that was something he was a pretty fair hand at. He stowed it behind his sash.

As he rode, he smiled at the old Indian's news. So the gentry and the trash with them were only a few miles to the west of Bones's pack of hyenas. That was interesting.

"I believe we've shook him off," Fred Lasalle said, on the evening of the third day after the ambush in the pass.

"Maybe," Bones replied.

"I think we've lost Preacher," Percy said, at approximately the same time and sitting about six miles away from Bones's bunch.

"Maybe," Dutch said.

At that moment, Preacher was about four miles behind of both groups. He had cooked and eaten his supper, boiled his coffee, and then let his small fire burn down to only coals, just enough to keep his coffee hot. He sat with a blanket over his shoulders, drinking coffee and mentally fighting with himself.

He figured he'd more than avenged Eddie, Wind Chaser, and the trappers the man-hunters had killed and robbed. He ought to just give up this hunt and go on about his business.

Preacher had been fighting this mental battle for several days, and was no closer to a decision now than when he began. Even if there were some sort of law out here, he couldn't prove that Bones and his party had done anything. It would be his word against theirs. And if it came to that, Preacher might well be the one who ended up on the wrong end of the rope. Patience and Prudence and the others hadn't actually seen any of the man-hunters break any laws—and since everything had happened in so-called 'disputed territories,' he wasn't sure what country's laws applied where. Or even if there were any laws out here, was more like it. Preacher, like so many mountain men, was pretty much in contempt of the so-called laws of so-called 'civilized people.' Preacher felt that most of them were downright stupid.

Just before Preacher snuggled deeper into his blankets, for the nights were turning colder, he made up his mind to make no further contact with the man-hunters, other than continuing to push and follow them north. Well ... he might accidentally hassle them a little bit. If the man-hunters started trouble, then he'd fight. But they would have to start it. He'd let Canada handle the man-hunters.

The weather grew colder, the days shorter, and the nights longer the farther north the men rode. Even though the two groups were only a few miles apart, neither group was aware of the other. But both knew that Preacher was still behind them, staying well back, but coming on.

Preacher had begun trailing one group for a day or so, and then swinging over and trailing the other. Both groups were aware of him. And the hunt became a game with the Indians. Word was passed from tribe to tribe and the Indians were amused by it all. If so many men were running away from just one man—even if that man was Ghost Walker—the fleeing men must surely be cowards and therefore not worth bothering with. They would not be brave under torture.

"What the hell is he doing?" Van Eaton threw out the question to anybody who might have an answer, although he knew no one in the group did.

"Following us," Bones said. "Driving us north. He's got something up his sleeve, for sure. And I think I know what it is."

"What?" Titus asked.

"I ain't got it all worked out yet in my mind. But I figure I'm close."

"Well, I'm gettin' right jumpy about him bein' back there," Tatman said. "It's gettin' hard to sleep at night, worryin' 'bout him slippin' into camp and cuttin' a throat or two. I say we ambush him."

"Maybe," Bones said. "Yeah, I been givin' that some thought, too."

Van Eaton said, "You don't reckon he's somehow got in touch with the Canadians and they're waitin' for us at the border?"

Bones smiled. "You always could read my mind, Van Eaton. Yeah. That's what I think he's done."

"How?" George Winters asked.

Bones shook his head. "I don't know."

"Preacher had the missionaries inform the Canadian authorities about us," Sir Elmore said, about the same time Bones's group was discussing what Preacher was doing.

What neither group knew was that there were no Canadian authorities within five hundred miles of where they planned on crossing the still ill-defined border. And what neither group knew was that they had crossed out of Ute country and were now in the territory of the Northern Cheyenne and Arapaho. Furthermore, neither the man-hunters nor Preacher was aware that they were all being carefully trailed by a band of Ute, who had some ideas of their own. For the moment, a rare event was happening: representatives of the Utes had met with chiefs of the Northern Cheyenne and Arapaho and agreed to a temporary peace. The Cheyenne and the Arapaho could fully sympathize with and understand what the Utes wanted, and they agreed to it, for the time being.

"I say we ambush Preacher," Zaunbelcher said. "If we plan it carefully, we can succeed. I am certain of that."

"Maybe," Dutch said. "And that's a big maybe. Preacher is a wily ol' curly wolf. The problem is, we don't never know just where he is. He disappears for days at a time."

"Wonder where Bones and them got off to?" Percy pondered.

"Who cares?" Dutch replied.

Preacher had felt eyes on him for the past two days. But it wasn't the kind of eyes that make the hair on the back of his neck stand up. It was more a curious feeling he felt. He circled and back-tracked, but he could not spot a soul.

It was Indians, he was sure, and probably Cheyenne or Arapaho, tribes that he got along well with. He was known to them, so why were they spying on him and not coming near his camp?

Preacher rode Thunder down into a creek, stayed with it for about a mile, and then exited on gravel. He tore up an old shirt and covered Thunder's hooves and walked him for about a mile. He picketed Thunder, climbed up on a bluff, and with his pirate glass at hand, bellied down, extended the glass, and began scanning the territory all around him.

It took him awhile, but his patience finally paid off. He smiled and put the glass away. "Well, I'll be damned," Preacher muttered. He knew the Ute riding in the lead. He was one of the big chiefs, Black Hawk. Then Preacher remembered something that caused his throat to tighten. He slowly shook his head. "You boys would have been far better off if you'd let me kill you back down south."

Then he noticed two Indians not five hundred yards

away, below him. They were riding slow, studying the ground, trying to pick up Preacher's trail, and they looked frustrated because they had lost the trail and could not find it again.

Preacher watched them until they were out of sight. He made his way back to Thunder and then decided he'd just make his camp right where he was. There was water close-by, and plenty of dry wood. Besides, things were going to get real exciting in a very short time. Preacher decided he'd just stay out of sight.

After all, deep down, he was a peaceful sort of person.

Fourteen

"White Wolf has discovered us," Black Hawk was informed the next morning. "My scouts have found where he hid his trail and then watched through the long glass as we followed the two groups of men."

Black Hawk nodded his head solemnly. "And Ghost Walker did what?"

"Nothing. Returned to his camp, prepared his evening meal, and went to sleep."

Black Hawk smiled. "By doing so he has told us that whatever else happens to the evil men is in our hands. He will do nothing to interfere."

"How do you know that?" the man dared to ask.

Black hawk shifted his obsidian eyes to the man, but did not take offense. "How I know is but one of the reasons I am chief of this tribe and you are not."

The man wisely nodded his head and backed away, knowing he had come dangerously close to overstepping that invisible line.

One of Black Hawk's closest friends and advisors chuckled in the misty morning air. "Good reply."

Black Hawk waggled one hand from side to side. "Not too bad for so early in the morning."

The two men laughed softly.

Black Hawk said, "We have gone far enough north. Today we begin taking a life for a life."

"Look!" Tom Evans cried, jumping to his feet and pointing to the east.

About a quarter of a mile away, on the crest of a hill, Preacher sat his horse and was staring at the camp of the man-hunters.

"What's he doing?" Derby Peel asked.

"He ain't doin' nothin'," Van Eaton said. "He's just starin' at us."

"There's a reason for it," Bones said, looking at Preacher. "Preacher don't do nothin' without thinkin' it through. But damned if I can figure out what it is."

The man-hunters turned at the sound of a thud. For a moment they were frozen where they stood, staring at the sight. Benny Atkins swayed on his feet, his eyes looking in horror at the arrow protruding from his belly. Then he screamed as the first waves of pain hit him. He sat down heavily on the ground, both hands holding onto the shaft of the arrow.

Clift Wright jumped for his rifle. He managed to bring the weapon to his shoulder just as an arrow entered the right side of his neck, the arrowhead ripping out the left side. His eyes widened in horror as blood filled his mouth.

Joe Moss, using a stick for a crutch, hobbled for his guns. He didn't make it. Two arrows tore their way into his flesh, one in his back and the other in his chest.

Preacher sat his horse and watched the scene without expression.

Ray Wood began yelling as mounted Indians charged the camp, seeming to come out of nowhere. Ray's yelling stopped abruptly as an Ute lance ran him through, pinning his flopping body on the cold ground.

Bones, Van Eaton, Lige Watson, and several more who

had already saddled their horses, left their supplies behind and fled the scene, riding hard. The other men were slaughtered. Some were taken alive . . . they were the less fortunate ones. Utes could be quite inventive with torture.

Ed Crowe died cursing Preacher. One of the attacking Utes, who spoke English, would wonder at that for the rest of his life. White men certainly did many strange things.

Alan James, Derby Peel, Fred Lasalle, Evans, Haywood, and Winters died in the camp. Tatman, Price, and Titus were taken alive.

With the blood lust running hot and high, one of the younger Utes galloped his horse toward Preacher, his lance-point level with Preacher's chest. A sharp shout from Black Hawk brought the brave to a halt just a few yards from Preacher. The young Ute stared hard at Preacher, then his eyes touched upon that terrible-looking pistol in Preacher's right hand.

"Back off," Preacher said in the Ute's own tongue. "I am not your enemy."

The young Ute lowered his lance and turned his pony's head. He rode back to the camp and jumped down, a scalping knife in his hand.

Preacher holstered his pistol and rode away.

Willie and Lucas, Lige Watson, Pierre, Homer, Calhoun, Van Eaton, and Bones made it out alive. The only supplies they had were what they had carried in their saddle bags.

"I cain't believe no white man would just sit back and watch whilst red savages attacked other white men," Lige panted the words.

"What tribe was that?" Calhoun asked.

"Who knows?" Bones said. "They all look alike to me."

Homer fell to his knees and vomited up his fear, while Willie and the giant, Lucas, clung to each other, both of them trembling in fright.

"Now we know why Preacher was layin' back," Pierre said. "He fixed it up with them savages to do us in. Damn his eyes!"

"Take anything we got and wrap them horses' hooves," Van Eaton said. "We got to hide our trail and find a place to hole up. It's the only chance we got. I'll make a wager them Injuns was from the same tribe as them we kilt in that valley. They ain't never gonna give up looking for us."

He turned and grunted as an arrow tore into his chest and penetrated his heart. Van Eaton had hunted his last man.

Lige Watson lost control of his senses and ran screaming from the shady glen. He ran right into the Ute lance. The Ute left him pinned to the ground. Lige would be a long time dying.

Pierre died on his knees, praying.

Homer was taken alive.

Calhoun ran blindly in panic, fighting the slashing branches and stumbling through the thick underbrush. He could not believe his eyes when he saw Preacher, sitting his horse about a hundred yards away.

"Help me!" Calhoun screamed, hearing the Utes coming up fast behind him.

"Man who needs help hadn't oughtta left home in the first place," Preacher told him.

"You'll burn in hell for this!" Calhoun screamed at the mountain man.

"I might," Preacher acknowledged. "But you'll be there afore me." He lifted the reins and rode away just as the avenging Utes reached the man.

Bones, Willie, and Lucas had lept into their saddles and whipped their near-exhausted horses into a run.

They didn't get far.

Bones and Lucas were taken alive, the Utes having known for days that Bones was the leader. His death would be most unpleasant. The Utes looked at the tiny Willie, trying to figure out exactly what sort of man he was. They'd never seen a dwarf. They finally decided it would be bad medicine to harm such a thing. They turned him loose.

Ignoring the screams, Black Hawk rode over to Preacher.

"Howdy," Preacher said.

Black Hawk studied the mountain man for a moment. "You know why we do this?"

"I know. All who are with you are family members of Wind Chaser's bunch."

In the Ute society, such offenses as stealing, adultery, and murder were private matters, the punishment left up to the family members.

"It ought to be that way in my society, too," Preacher added, knowing his words would please the chief.

"I have severely chastised the warrior who threatened you, Ghost Walker. But in battle the blood runs hot."

"I understand."

"Tell me about the other band of evil men."

Preacher hesitated, then said, "They are better mannered in the white man's way than the ones you just killed, but they are much worse in here." He pointed to his heart.

Black Hawk nodded his head at that. He understood perfectly. He turned his horse and rode back to the blood-splattered camp. Willie rode his horse over to Preacher. The little man was so scared he stank of it.

"What am I gonna do?" he asked.

"Stay just as far away from me as you can, Shorty. 'Cause I might take me a notion to kill you yet."

"You've got to help me. I can't survive alone out here!"

"That's your problem. You come a-huntin' me, to kill me. Now you want me to help you. No way. You'll survive. You know the way back. I got no sympathy for you

279

a-tall. Now get movin'. Get clear out of my sight and do it fast. Git!"

Willie got.

Dutch was jumpy. He was all knotted up inside and couldn't keep his food down. Something was wrong. He had chosen this place to hide with great care, and felt they would be safe. But he hadn't heard a bird sing or a squirrel chatter all morning. The woods were as still as a graveyard.

"Something's awfully wrong around here, Dutch," Percy said, lumbering up, his big gut leading the way.

"Yeah. I feel it, too."

"I heard screamin' last night."

"You, too?"

"Yeah. It was faint, but I heared it. Like to have made me puke."

"I been told that Preacher is hell in any kind of fight— and we shore known that for a pure-dee fact now—but he don't go in for torture."

"Somebody was shore dyin' hard last night."

"Anybody else hear it?"

"Not that I know of. I was on guard. Give me goose bumps all over."

"Yeah. Me, too."

Percy looked toward the clearing and his eyes widened as if he'd seen a ghost. About four hundred yards away, there sat Preacher, just sitting in his saddle as big as you please, looking right at the camp. "Dutch!" Percy gasped. "I ain't a-believin' my eyes."

"What are you talkin' 'bout?"

"Preacher!"

"Preacher? Where?"

"Right there!" he pointed.

Dutch turned and as he did, his belly exploded in pain.

280

He looked down at the shaft of the arrow that protruded from his gut. "Oh . . ." was all he managed to say before another arrow split his spinal cord and he dropped to the ground.

Percy shouted out the warning but it was too late, far too late. He took one step and went down with several arrows in his body.

The Utes were all over the camp a few silent seconds later and the fight was brutal and brief. The braves knew who to kill quickly, and who to take alive. They had been following the group for days, and after studying the men, Black Hawk had pointed out the gentry.

The royalty who had come to America to kill men for sport were no longer the haughty, sneering, arrogant bunch of several months back. They stood in a group, their hands bound cruelly behind them. They knew they were facing death, and they were not facing it well. They stank of fear and relaxed bladders and bowels. The sweat dripped from their faces and their legs shook so hard several had to be helped to stand as the stony-faced Utes stared at them, the contempt they felt for such fear showing only in their eyes. Preacher still sat on his horse out in the clearing, Black Hawk sitting on his horse beside Preacher.

"For the love of God, man!" Sir Elmore Jerrold-Taylor screamed at him. "Help us."

"For the love of God?" Preacher muttered. "For the love of *God?*"

"The white man calls upon his God to help him?" Black Hawk asked.

"Yes."

"Will this God of yours help them?"

"Well, now, I can't speak for God, but if I had to take a guess, I'd say no."

"Good. I would not like to fight a God."

Preacher held out a hand and the Ute solemnly took the

offering and shook it. "I'll be goin' now, Black Hawk. You're welcome in my camp any time."

"And you in mine, Brother To The Wolf."

Preacher swung his horse and rode away. He wanted to put some distance between the Utes, their prisoners, and himself. He knew this bunch was going to die slow, long, and hard. And he knew why.

Black Hawk rode his horse into the center of the camp, his pony gingerly stepping around a sprawled out body.

"We have gold!" Burton Sullivan shouted at the chief. "We have money and jewels and all sorts of things we can give you."

"I will have them soon," Black Hawk said. "You have no more use for them."

"Filthy savage!" Baron Zaunbelcher screamed at the chief.

"Savage?" Black Hawk questioned. "You call me a savage? You are a very amusing person."

"Why?" Robert Tassin screamed at Black Hawk. "Why are you doing this to us?"

"I have done nothing to you. Yet. But I will."

"Why, damn you? Why?" Sir Elmore shouted.

Black Hawk smiled sadly. "Because Wind Chaser was my younger brother. I helped in his upbringing after our mother died. That's why."

EPILOGUE

Days later, Preacher holed up in a cabin he'd built some years back. He'd cleaned out the place, for pack rats and birds had been busy there, and then began cutting firewood for the winter ahead. He found his old scythe where he'd left it, sharpened it up with a stone, and worked for a solid week, from can see to can't see, cutting forage for his horses. He worked himself hard so he would not have time to think about what happened to the royalty, even though he knew perfectly well there was nothing he could have done to prevent it.

The entire Indian nation had put a death sentence on the heads of the man-hunters as soon as they learned of the massacre of Wind Chaser and his band. There was no way any of them would have been able to leave the mountains. And Preacher doubted that any of the men he'd sent packing had made it very far out. He didn't have a guilty conscience about what had happened, he just didn't want to think about it.

When his domestic chores were done, Preacher went hunting and started jerking and smoking the meat. He set out fish traps and began smoking his catch. He picked berries to make pemmican and dug up tubers and wild onions for the cellar. When he had done all he could do in preparation for winter, he relaxed. He hoped he wouldn't see a single solitary soul 'til spring. The past summer had given him a bellyful of people, both good and bad, but mostly bad. He occasionally thought of Patience and Prudence and those folks with them and wondered how they were. He knew they'd made it out of the wilderness safely, for a trapper friend of his told him that.

Preacher knew that the area west of the Mississippi was going to run red with blood very soon. As pioneer families began moving onto the land, the Indians were going to fight to preserve their way of life. It was going to be a terrible time for many years to come. But Preacher didn't know how he could do anything to prevent the blood from being spilled.

One fall afternoon Preacher sat on the porch, smoking his pipe and watching the sun go down. A family of wolves who were denned not far away had begun coming around and Preacher recognized both the male and his mate from a year or so back. They came around this evening to check on him.

"Howdy," he said to them, and then was amused in watching the young in their rough and tumble play. "Life's pretty good, ain't it?"

The wolves sat in front of the porch, cocked their heads to one side and looked at him.

"Yeah," Preacher said. "Life is pretty darned good. If a man just knows how to live it and rolls with the flow."

William W. Johnstone
The *Mountain Man* Series

__The Last Mtn. Man #1	0-8217-6856-5	**$5.99**US/**$7.99**CAN
__Return of the Mtn. Man #2	0-7860-1296-X	**$5.99**US/**$7.99**CAN
__Trial of the Mtn. Man #3	0-7860-1297-8	**$5.99**US/**$7.99**CAN
__Revenge of the Mtn. Man #4	0-7860-1300-1	**$5.99**US/**$7.99**CAN
__Law of the Mtn. Man #5	0-7860-1301-X	**$5.99**US/**$7.99**CAN
__Journey of the Mtn. Man #6	0-7860-1302-8	**$5.99**US/**$7.99**CAN
__War of the Mtn. Man #7	0-7860-1303-6	**$5.99**US/**$7.99**CAN
__Code of the Mtn. Man #8	0-7860-1304-4	**$5.99**US/**$7.99**CAN
__Pursuit of the Mtn. Man #9	0-7860-1305-2	**$5.99**US/**$7.99**CAN
__Courage of the Mtn. Man #10	0-7860-1306-0	**$5.99**US/**$7.99**CAN
__Blood of the Mtn. Man #11	0-7860-1307-9	**$5.99**US/**$7.99**CAN
__Fury of the Mtn. Man #12	0-7860-1308-7	**$5.99**US/**$7.99**CAN

Call toll free **1-888-345-BOOK** to order by phone or use this coupon to order by mail.

Name_____

Address_____

City_____ State_____ Zip_____

Please send me the books that I checked above.

I am enclosing	$_____
Plus postage and handling*	$_____
Sales tax (in NY, TN, and DC)	$_____
Total amount enclosed	$_____

*Add $2.50 for the first book and $.50 for each additional book.
Send check or money order (no cash or CODs) to: **Kensington Publishing Corp., Dept. C.O., 850 Third Avenue, 16th Floor, New York, NY 10022**
Prices and numbers subject to change without notice.
All orders subject to availability.
Visit our website at **www.kensingtonbooks.com**.

Complete Your Collection
William W. Johnstone
The *Mountain Man* Series

William W. Johnstone
The *Last Gunfighter*
Series

William W. Johnstone
The *Ashes* Series

__Out of the Ashes #1	0-7860-0289-1	$4.99US/$5.99CAN
__Fire in the Ashes #2	0-7860-0335-9	$5.99US/$7.50CAN
__Anarchy in the Ashes #3	0-7860-0419-3	$5.99US/$7.50CAN
__Blood in the Ashes #4	0-7860-0446-0	$5.99US/$7.50CAN
__Alone in the Ashes #5	0-7860-0458-4	$5.99US/$7.50CAN
__Wind in the Ashes #6	0-7860-0478-9	$5.99US/$7.50CAN
__Danger in the Ashes #7	0-7860-0516-5	$5.99US/$7.50CAN
__Smoke from the Ashes #8	0-7860-0498-3	$5.99US/$7.50CAN
__Valor in the Ashes #9	0-7860-0526-2	$5.99US/$7.50CAN
__Trapped in the Ashes #10	0-7860-0562-9	$5.99US/$7.50CAN
__Death in the Ashes #11	0-7860-0587-4	$5.99US/$7.99CAN
__Survival in the Ashes #12	0-7860-0613-7	$5.99US/$7.50CAN
__Fury in the Ashes #13	0-7860-0635-8	$5.99US/$7.50CAN
__Courage in the Ashes #14	0-7860-0651-X	$5.99US/$7.50CAN
__Terror in the Ashes #15	0-7860-0661-7	$5.99US/$7.50CAN
__Vengeance in the Ashes #16	0-7860-1013-4	$5.99US/$7.50CAN

Call toll free **1-888-345-BOOK** to order by phone or use this coupon to order by mail.

Name_____

Address_____

City_____ State_____ Zip_____

Please send me the books that I checked above.

I am enclosing	$_____
Plus postage and handling*	$_____
Sales tax (in NY, TN, and DC)	$_____
Total amount enclosed	$_____

*Add $2.50 for the first book and $.50 for each additional book.
Send check or money order (no cash or CODs) to: **Kensington Publishing Corp., Dept. C.O., 850 Third Avenue, 16th Floor, New York, NY 10022**
Prices and numbers subject to change without notice.
All orders subject to availability.
Visit our website at **www.kensingtonbooks.com**.